Amara's Rose

The Chronicles of the Key

Book One

By:

Brianna Goux

Dedication:

For my parents- whose unwavering encouragement and perfect love made me the person I am today.

For my Grandmother- who planted a love of books and adventure within my soul.

For my loved ones- who have never doubted me.

Thank you.

Prologue

David Sanders fled the battle scene, even though it went against every warrior instinct he possessed. But he had to warn his wife, and she had to get their girls out of the village. Alethia was no longer safe.

This shouldn't have been happening; it was too soon. They should've had another decade. The books had never mentioned this, so he had always assumed she would be older when It finally found her. And despite his wife's recent dreams to the contrary, he hadn't quite believed it. He had stuck his head in the sand, like one of those ostriches on Earth.

He had finally become suspicious when the giants suddenly mounted an attack. Not the smartest of species, they were rather cowardly when it came to battles. Yet they were attacking seemingly on their own. In the midst of fighting he had seen it—the Darkness—up on the looming cliffs, looking down on the valley below. Her blue form, crackling with energy, was eagerly taking in Its handiwork. That's when David had left.

David's stride lengthened when he hit the road out of the valley, but a new noise registered in his brain. He was being followed. He spared a glance over his shoulder and saw the Darkness. She crackled as she closed in on him. He was fast, but he knew she was faster. He could feel the hum of electricity charging the Darkness' body; one touch from her would be fatal. She could fry his entire village. He wouldn't be able to warn his wife, to get the girls out safely.

The Darkness was nearly upon him—her vile smell nearly suffocating him, her vibrations bringing him to his knees.

This is the end—

A bright blue-and-brown light absorbed his body, leaving only a scorch mark on the ground. David Sanders no longer existed.

He had left Planet Amara forever.

Chapter 1 – Rose

The greenish-blue light of the portal to Amara cast shadows through the trees as I ran. Usually the portal appears on the bridge near here, but tonight it decided to appear elsewhere, forcing me to run across the bridge and through one of Chicago's city parks in order to jump through the portal and return home to Amara. Why it decided to change location, I will never know. The universe has a perverse sense of humor.

I nearly fall as I hurtle over a low stone fence and trample a bunch of flowers. Whoops.

I probably have only a minute—tops—to reach that portal in time. If I don't, I'll be stuck on Earth for another year until the portal opens again. Normally I have my key with me so I can open a portal any time I want, but I forgot to bring it today. This was supposed to be a quick trip to Earth to pick up one item, so it wasn't a big deal that I'd forgotten the key.

My memory isn't always that great. My friends tease me it's because I'm blonde. Or maybe I somehow inherited the forgetfulness trait. My parents aren't exactly around to ask, so I guess I'll stick with the hair-color theory.

A stitch has formed in my side, and I can hear my own harsh breathing as I race across a stretch of grass. I hate running. I always have. Maybe it's because I don't have long legs—I'm only five foot one.

The bright blue-green light of the portal hasn't yet dimmed. It stands out like a lighthouse, guiding and, hopefully, taking me home.

Rose Sanders, Gatekeeper extraordinaire, I scoff at myself, *can't even remember her own Key and yet it's her job to carry it with her at all times. Protecting the key, traveling to planets, and making sure intruders don't get through the portals to Amara.*

1

I look around, making sure no humans have seen the portal. There aren't any, so at least I don't have to keep them away from where they shouldn't be, which is a miracle. The stupid species is *so* curious and nosy.

The portal's light dims when I'm about twenty feet from it.

Great. It's closing. While it's usually about eight feet tall, now I'll be lucky to fit through it upright. It's going to be a close call.

I will my legs to pump faster than they already are. But the closer I get, the faster the portal shrinks—as if it's mocking me.

After a few more strides, the blue-green light has nearly faded and the center of the portal is almost transparent. The entire thing is about to disappear.

It's all or nothing. I dive in headfirst.

Electricity charges the air as I travel through the portal for a split second before I'm launched out the other side with all the force of my momentum.

With a quick, neat tuck born of habit, I roll right onto my feet—

Smack dab into a tree. My usual grace has abandoned me, and my momentum only makes the problem worse. The tree wins the battle as my face rebounds off of it, and I fall back down onto the hard, unforgiving ground in defeat.

The tree branches overhead eventually come into focus. Slightly stunned, I lie there and catch my breath. When I can, I stagger to my feet and grunt as I feel a small bump forming on my forehead.

"Stupid tree, stupid portal, stupid woods with more stupid trees," I mumble while glaring at the tree I hit. It looks so innocent, with its magnificent array of small leaves in shades ranging from light to deep green. And very tough black bark.

"Ouch," I mutter as I rub my head again and check for blood. "Stupid head, for hurting."

"Talking to yourself?"

I whirl around, automatically reaching for my knife but quickly recognize my best friend, Phoenix. *Frick!* Just when I thought I was only *privately* embarrassing myself. A smirk crosses her face and I quickly change the subject.

"Not much in the traps," I nonchalantly nod at the three squirrels she's holding by the tails.

"Nope. They seem to be getting smarter," she says, looking sadly at them.

Poor Phoenix. She hates to harm any living thing, even the noisy and rather pesky squirrels. Phoenix is a kind, gentle person, but she sometimes has to resort to trapping squirrels for trade. Money is tight in her household. It's just her and her older brother.

"So what were you chatting about with yourself?" she asks, raising her eyebrows, whose color matches her silky brown braid and long bangs.

"Forgot the portal Key," I admit offhandedly, "so I had to dive through the portal. Ran into a tree."

"Again?" she laughs, her brown eyes twinkling. "How many times do you have to run into that tree before you remember its existence?"

I shrug and try not to grimace.

Phoenix laughs, "Today is just not your day, is it?"

Thank you, Captain Obvious. "Well, Phoenix, when you see someone talking to nothing, I think it's safe to assume that the person speaking is not having the best of days."

"Or someone might think you are mental, and then they *will* take your Key away," she jokes, then nods toward the trail leading to our village, Alethia.

3

I fall in beside her as we head down the path. "Yeah, and who else could do the job? It's supposed to be passed down through families, and I'm the only one left in mine, remember?"

"Okay, so maybe they would just take your Key away and not let anyone be the Gatekeeper."

But there has to be a Gatekeeper. If not for me having the only Key on Amara, we'd have to wait for certain portals to pop up so we could get the stuff we regularly use from the other worlds. I mean, we could live without those things, I guess, but why give up intergalactic travel? Besides, the stuff from other planets is cool.

As we approach a fork in the trail, Phoenix sighs and holds up the squirrels. "I have to sell these to the butcher now," she says. "So I will be at your house after that, by six o'clock for our Three Musketeers party. Is that okay?"

I laugh. "When you think about it, it's pretty funny that your brother named you, me, and Sylvia after a group of warrior humans." Phoenix chuckles and nods.

"Anyway, just don't come early. I have to clean, and that means cranking up the music and dancing as I tidy up, so I prefer not to have people watching me."

She looks at me sternly, her disapproval evident of me stealing things from humans. "I assume you just came from Earth?"

"Maybe..." I trail off with a cheesy grin, then add, "Actually, why don't you come over earlier. I know you love it when I sing along to Earth music."

She shakes her head and fakes a horrified look. "Maybe six-thirty then. I have errands to run anyway. "I'll see you later!"

Tonight I'm having a party. More specifically, a party for Sylvia, our other best friend. Sure we have more friends, but this is going to be a small party with just us Three Musketeers. We acquired that nickname after an incident with some minor explosives during a festival when we were kids. No one got hurt; we just scared them a bit.

As Phoenix disappears I take the right fork and head toward the village.

I pat my pocket, confirming my much-sought-after object from Earth is still with me.

Looking around at the woods of my home planet, everything seems comfortably familiar: the crisp smell of fresh air, the trees that tower hundreds of feet above me. The river that's nearby roars loudly down to a lake that's just to the south. I enjoy the noises as I walk—the birds singing in the trees, the squirrels squabbling about building up their food stores for the winter.

I've taken the well-worn path that we use to travel between Alethia and the town a few miles east of here. Reveling that my usual speed is back in action, I rapidly increase my pace. My full-out sprint on Earth was equivalent to my jogging speed on Amara. I hate that interplanetary travel often reduces my normal abilities.

The village is around the next bend, and suddenly I am surrounded by buildings. I slow to a relaxed stroll. The village may not be very big, but it's home, and even though I was gone only a few hours, I am engrossed in its rural, picturesque beauty.

Alethia is composed of a variety of quaint wooden buildings, and its old dirt streets have been tamped down by thousands of footsteps. The shops haven't changed since I was a child. They're all different from each other but no matter how they're built or decorated, they're familiar and bring me a warm, comfortable feeling of home.

A heavenly smell wafts into my nose—baked goods! I could go into the bakery just to look around, or say hi to Neva, or—

Wait a minute! I haven't gotten a cake for the party. *Whoops.*

"Hey, Rose!" Neva says from behind the counter when I enter. "What can I do ya for?"

It always bugs me when she says that: *What can I do ya for?* What about, *What can I do for you?* People's grammar is horrible. Mine is too, but I enjoy casting stones in my glass house; it creates a nice breeze.

It makes sense, though, why people have such poor grammar. We only have one school in our village, and attendance is mandatory up until age eleven. After that, if you fancy, you can have an apprenticeship. Phoenix did that for a couple years with a local painter and now she creates her own paintings in her spare time. She's even sold some to the King and Queen for the castle.

Neva clears her throat and looks inquiringly at me.

Oh, yes, I am supposed to be responding. "Not sure yet," I shrug with a smile.

Then I take a second look at Neva. Something is different . . . Oh! Her pale blonde hair has crazy colored streaks in it. I bet she used her icing as dye. It's odd, because not a single other person on Amara has artificially colored hair. I kinda like Neva's new look, though. Maybe I'll ask her how to do that sometime. But not today. No time.

"Neva, can I please have a custom-made sheet cake?"

"Sure. What type of cake would you like?" Neva's bright blue gaze shifts to the paper she's writing on.

An image of the perfect cake comes to mind. "Vanilla cake with chocolate frosting, and a simple, 'Happy Birthday, Sylvia' in the middle of it. Written in gold frosting, please."

"Yes, ma'am. I can do one vanilla cake with chocolate frosting and 'Happy Birthday, Princess Sylvia' piped in the middle in gold frosting," she says, writing down my order.

Everyone always insists on calling Sylvia *Princess*. Even if she *is* the princess, it doesn't mean she has to go by the title all the time. "No 'Princess,' Neva!"

"But—"

"Nope, nope, nope. Please put the exact words I said on the cake. Nothing more, thank you."

"Okay," she says in a hurt tone, her eyes downcast and shoulders slumped.

To keep things moving, I ask her, "Can I come pick the cake up in, say, an hour or so?" I mentally calculate the time. Ya, that'll work.

"Of course," she says. "It will be ready then."

Good. Unlike last year, we won't have to wait for the cake to be finished because I forgot to order it.

I set the right amount of coins on the counter. "Good, thanks." She doesn't reply because she is already in the back room— as if she'd rather be working in the kitchen than chatting with me.

As I walk out of town towards home, I glance around. This path through the woods is rarely, if ever, used by anyone but me, so it's deserted. Good. No one can see what I'm about to do.

I pull the item I went through the portal for out of my pocket and leaf through a few pages. It appears okay. Going through the portal didn't damage it.

But now is not the time to delve into its secrets. I have a party to get ready for. Besides, I'm not sure if I'm quite ready for the information it contains. Hopefully, its owner, Victoria Coulee, doesn't come looking for it. If my mom's old diary is anything to go by, the book in my hands has a lot of valuable information on Gatekeepers—it could change everything I thought I knew.

Chapter 2 – Phoenix

After Rose and I go our separate ways at the fork in the path, I stroll down the trail to the butcher's. The woods thin out as I turn off the main path onto a smaller one that leads to the western outskirts of Alethia.

The sunlight breaks through the canopy, warming my skin, and I smile.

A bothersome question works its way into my thoughts. Why did Rose go through the portal? And why did she not mention what she did there? Usually when she comes back from a planet, she's bursting to tell us about it, but today she was quiet. And when Rose is silent, it's usually not a good thing.

And why Earth? Besides pulling a prank or two sometimes, Rose isn't fond of going there, although she'll go when someone asks her to get something. My prank theory doesn't hold up because she didn't come back with that look of glee on her face and mischief dancing in her blue eyes. Well, at least no more than there usually is.

If it was anyone but Rose, I would think she'd gone there to visit friends, but she doesn't know anyone on Earth—

My step falters. She couldn't know about . . . about that *particular* subject, could she? I have made sure to never bring it up and to avoid any questions about it. There is no possible way she could know.

Switching the squirrels to my other hand as I approach the village, I briefly wonder what Lexi's army has been up to lately. Her army is the enemy of ours, and they've been awfully quiet lately. Maybe, for once, they are honoring the peace treaty. That would be a nice change from all the years of skirmishes and ambushes Lexi has instigated.

The butcher shop's door is open, and I gingerly step over the threshold. Seeing the meat from dead animals is unpleasant, but I still need to get Sylvia something for her birthday and the butcher pays good money for squirrels.

But it's not Mr. Metzger who is standing behind the counter. It's Collin, his son. Collin looks more like his mother than his father, with pitch-black hair that falls over his soft brown eyes.

My thoughts briefly turn to my own parents. I miss them. It's been years since I've seen them.

"What can I do for you, fair lady?" Collin jokes as he wipes his hands on a clean white towel.

I grin at his choice of words. I have never been called *fair lady* before.

"I'm actually looking for your father." I hold up the squirrels as explanation.

"I'm hurt. The pretty lady is not looking for me." He mock frowns and pretends to sniffle, and I giggle. He relents. "Well, how about I buy those squirrels from you?"

"Do you pay as much as your father?" I ask, arching an eyebrow.

"Well, considering I don't know what he pays you, I'll make you an offer." Collin tries to arch his eyebrow like mine, and unfortunately, he fails quite miserably.

I laugh again. "Name your price, and we will see if yours matches his."

Collin falls silent, scrunching his eyebrows as he thinks. While he does, I study him. He's gotten bulkier since the last time I saw him. He has always been over-average in muscle mass, fit from carrying giant slabs of meat back and forth from the freezer to the cases in the front of the store. But now he looks ripped, as Rose would say.

"Hmm. I could give you a great big hug in exchange for those three squirrels," he grins and winks. Collin's sense of humor

9

is almost exactly the same as my older brother's, so I know what he's up to.

I smile. "No, thank you. That does not sound like my kind of deal."

I have to look up to talk to him. Has he always been this tall or has he grown another inch practically overnight?

"Well, then, what is your kind of 'deal'?" He puts air quotes around the last part of his sentence.

"My kind of deal involves the exchange of my squirrels for your money, because I really do need some cash today." I like bantering with Collin. With people other than Rose, Sylvia, and my brother, I usually have very straight-forward conversations.

"I don't think my wallet likes that very much." He pats his pocket and I hear the jingle of coins.

"Then I guess I will have to take my business elsewhere...." I pretend to turn around and leave. I long ago learned the art of bargaining.

"Well, if you put it that way, I guess I will just have to give you this," he responds to my fake exit and digs in his pocket.

I retrace my steps. A moment later, he pulls out a bag of coins.

"How much is in there?" I ask, my interest piqued.

"Twenty-five coins. At least, I think that's what's in here." He quickly double-checks the amount.

That certainly beats what I usually get. "Your price is better than your father's, but you do not have to pay me that much. I'll just take his regular price of twenty coins for three squirrels," I tell him politely.

"No big deal," he shrugs. "Just think of it as something extra to go towards your present for Sylvia."

I'm surprised he knows what I'm planning to do with the money. On the other hand, I had told him about Sylvia's birthday

Chapter 3 – Rose

The trail home narrows as the woods thicken. The quiet almost stifling.

I pause and look around. Actually, it's much too quiet; a huge forest filled with animals should by no means be this silent. Silence means bad news.

The only threat I can think of is Lexi's army. After all, she's the only enemy we have on Amara. Lately, there's been talk around town about being attacked. Rumors run around like stray dogs, and people say she's going to try to destroy our village and that she's going to take another swing at us—an attack that only she and I know would be an act of revenge for what happened years ago. I wouldn't normally be worried, but rumors seem to have a grain of truth to them.

The only other enemy could be one from a different planet if there was another Key. Which there isn't.

Or . . . if mine was stolen.

Crap! That's possible. If my Key is gone, then I am in serious trouble.

I sprint down the winding path to the little log cabin in a clearing. It's what is considered fairytale-like; picturesque and quaint with ivy crawling up the single-story wooden sides.

Gasping, I finally reach my house, whip open the door, and bolt straight into the back room.

I yank an old jewelry box off the top of the wardrobe and open it. Removing the ballerina that theoretically should spin inside of the box—this one doesn't—I reach into the compartment where the motor once sat. A little brass Key sits in its place.

I grab it with relief.

The Key itself is nothing fancy, just plain brass. The sunlight streaming through the window dances off of the mass of charms and the silver and gold chains I haven't worn in forever that are now heaped in the jewelry box.

A sudden idea hits me. What if I put the Key on a necklace chain and wear it? People will simply think it's a pendant. Then I'll never forget or lose it again. I grab a thick brass chain out of the box and rip off its teddy bear charm. Putting the chain through the hole in the top of the Key, I slip the necklace over my head.

Now that I've verified the Key is where it's supposed to be, it's time for my other task: hiding the book I brought back from Earth. I stow it under the mass of chains. It's reasonably well concealed, so I shut the lid and set the box back on top of the wardrobe. I'm still not sure if I want to tell Sylvia and Phoenix about it yet. I'd rather read it first.

Going to my front door, I safely lock it and force my clenched hands to relax. Brushing off the lingering paranoia at the silence in the woods, I stride into the kitchen to do some cooking for the party . . . except the countertop needs cleaning first, so I take out my bucket of little-used cleaning supplies and I scrub the counter so there's a clean space to work.

Twenty minutes later and bored out of my mind, I crank up the only battery-powered CD player on Amara, otherwise known as The Land of No Electronics. We don't make or use machines here. I'm the only one who can get her hands on an electronic device, or anything, really, from another planet. Unless of course someone were to get a traveling permit, but that almost never happens. And I would know about it if they did because, after all, they would have to go through me to open the portal.

I spin around, loudly singing the lyrics to a human song about taking care of business, and accidentally knock several stalks of celery off the counter. Whoops, five second rule, I guess, so I pick them back up and continue to jam.

Thirty minutes later, a faint tapping noise from the direction of my entryway catches my attention, so I turn down my music.

"Rose! Open the door!" Phoenix is yelling, quite loudly, as it turns out.

When I pull open the door, Phoenix shoves a cake box in my hands as she juggles an armload of packages.

"Oh, hey, Phoenix. The cake! I almost forgot about that."

Phoenix follows me into the kitchen. "Thanks, and you *did* forget about the cake. I have been pounding on your door for about three minutes now," she says, sounding slightly annoyed.

My bad. "In retrospect I probably should've left the door unlocked."

"It's fine," she smiles. "Come on, we'd better decorate before Sylvia gets here."

She unloads the bags she brought and spreads the contents on the table. I set the cake on the counter, then join her in hanging up streamers.

An hour later, Sylvia still has not shown up, which is good because we aren't done cooking dinner, but her tardiness can only mean one thing.

"Do you think she's late because of her mother again?" Phoenix asks me.

"Probably. I mean, there's always an *important* meeting that the Princess *needs to attend* that is *life or death*."

"Remember that time you hid under a desk and had to sit through one of those long meetings?"

"I didn't know death by boredom was an actual occurrence until I had to listen to that. Poor Sylvia. I feel bad because she can't do anything. She has to attend, no matter what."

"How late do you think she will be this time?" Phoenix asks as she stirs the minestrone soup.

"I give her an hour at the most before she sneaks out her window again. That would make five times this year she's ditched some fancy-shmancy event her mother made her attend," I say with a laugh. "Seriously, how long can she stand those pompous government officials? They never speak with words of fewer than three syllables, and they always drink their tea with their pinkies in the air. I would go insane if I were her."

"That is true, but I think you're underestimating her. I give her forty-five minutes. She has more sense than that to stay any longer," Phoenix states as I pour the carrots I had just cut up into the soup.

"Wanna bet?" I ask, hoping she'll agree to it. This is a bet I know I will win.

"No, you know I do not make bets."

It's true. No matter how many times I try to gamble with her, she won't. She thinks it's a bad habit. She's probably right, but who said having only good habits is fun?

"Just one, small, harmless bet won't hurt you."

"Your last *harmless* bet ended up with that boy dancing through the main plaza, in a tutu, singing a human song about Wee Willie Winkie," she points out.

I laugh. "That was the funniest thing I have ever seen in my entire life."

She shakes her head in disappointment. "What did you guys even bet on?" she asks.

"Who would win if we arm wrestled." I smirk. I won, of course.

She changes the subject by looking around at the tidy, decorated house and the food simmering on the stove. "So, what do we do until Sylvia gets here?"

"How about a game of cards?" I ask, snagging a deck off the coffee table and sitting on the floor.

"Sounds good to me. Which game?" Phoenix sits across from me as I deal.

Phoenix takes a deep breath, "Rose, I want to ask you—"

A tapping sound at the window startles us.

A messenger pigeon perches on the window ledge. Rose opens the window and unties a letter from around the lovely white bird's leg. The pigeon immediately flies off, and Rose slams the window closed with one hand while holding the letter in the other.

She rips it open and quickly examines its contents.

"*Freak!*" Her jaw drops. The letter flutters to the floor as she rushes to the door and snatches her sheath of arrows, bow, and short sword off the wall peg. She slings the sheath and bow over her shoulder, then straps the sword around her waist, securing the end to her leg with a strip of leather.

"I've got to go," she tosses at us as she bolts out the door, a worried look on her face.

Phoenix looks about as shocked as I feel.

I close the door behind Rose, pick up the letter, and read it aloud:

Enemies spotted in the forest. Report for duty immediately. This is not a drill. Information upon arrival.

Turning it over, I see the seal of the Commanding Officer. I hand the paper to Phoenix so she can see the seal too. Her face is grave. I share her concern, because this can't be good.

"It must be Lexi, don't you think?" Phoenix asks as she rereads the terse note.

I breathe deeply. "It has to be. Do you think she's really going to attack us? Because if she does, Rose is bound to be in the thick of it."

"Why are they enemies?" Phoenix asks. "In all the time I've lived here, no one has told me why they hate each other so much."

"No one knows," I shrug. "Rose won't tell me. Every time I ask her, she changes the subject or refuses to answer." I think about it, then add, "It's really quite odd."

It *is* odd that no one knows the source of the hatred between Rose and Lexi. But what I *do* know is that Rose is going to use her rank to get as close to her enemy as possible.

Phoenix takes in a breath, "If only we knew why they hated each other so much. Or even who Lexi is, and why she hates Alethia and wants to attack us. She and her army have been very quiet lately though. I thought maybe she had given up."

Bitter laughter escapes my lips, "Lexi? Live with us in peace? I highly doubt that will *ever* happen. Either way, you and I aren't in the army and it's probably something small. Rose will be back sooner rather than later."

"But what if it's like the last big war, the one from eight years ago?"

I inhale sharply. "Then we're all going to be affected. The last war, it—it took lot of lives. So many brave men died in that war, so many were injured. The town was devastated."

"That's when Rose's dad . . .?" Phoenix falters.

"Ya, that's when. I was there for the memorial service, you know." My eyes begin to water. "The two Sanders girls were there, of course, with their mother. But there was no body to cremate. He just . . . disappeared. He was presumed dead because it was pretty much a joke that he would ever abandon his people. He was the best soldier our military has ever seen."

"But why? I mean, Lexi wasn't around then to mount an attack against Alethia. And Rose's mom . . . what happened to her?"

"No one knows why the war happened. It's as if the giants, for the first time ever, actually got a mind of their own. But no one led them into battle, so it was . . . odd." I clench my teeth in anger and manage to bite out the next words. "As for Mrs. Sanders, she abandoned the girls. I guess her husband's death was too much for her to handle. She just disappeared one night about a month afterwards and hasn't been seen since."

"Oh, poor Rose." Phoenix's eyes shine brightly with unshed tears. "I couldn't even imagine losing two parents so close together."

I look at my feet. "Ya, and her sister a month later, gone as well."

Phoenix falls silent, and doesn't say anymore. Rose's worried expression and sudden departure have unnerved me. I seriously hope this confrontation isn't as bad as the feeling I have says it is. "I should go back to the castle," I say reluctantly.

Phoenix nods. We both know I've got to go be a princess now.

I run all the way back to the palace, my hair streaming behind me as my legs quickly cover the ground. Dread settles in my gut.

Chapter 5 – Rose

I run as quickly as I can to the Valley of the Nomads. Something had felt wrong in the forest today; I should've listened to my instincts and investigated why it was quiet. Now I know at least partially why.

The threat to Alethia—to perhaps all of Amara—must be Lexi's army. No one came through the portal with me today, and no one else has been in possession of my Key. So the threat originated on this planet.

My thoughts race. I could face Lexi soon. Which would be good for me on the personal-vendetta-against-her level, but bad for my town on the possibility-of-a-war level.

I arrive at the valley more than a little out of breath. I count heads. Forty-four already. *Frick.* I'm the last one here.

"Join your rank," the General says sternly. Whew, no reprimand for being the last one here. I follow his order, my brain kicking into soldier mode.

The General holds up his hands to get everyone's attention. "We have spotted enemies across the valley. They are not encroaching on our territory yet, so the peace treaty is still in place. However, there is an entire army camping out on the border."

There's only one peace treaty on Amara, so we all immediately know that this is Lexi's army.

The General's voice breaks into my thoughts. "Nothing has happened yet, but we need scouts to get as close as possible and figure out what the enemy is doing. Her army is composed entirely of giants, and we believe her mission is to destroy our village. We do not know why she seeks to do this. . ."

She does it because she has a personal vendetta against everyone who lives in Alethia, I reply to him silently. She is full of rubbish, and none of them even know who she really is.

28

The General's next words grab my attention. "Gold Squad," he says, addressing the group I'm part of, "you are heading into the tree line. Sneak up on their headquarters. Listen for any plans they have. As you know, it is of the upmost importance that you are not caught because it would start a war if you were."

He turns to the group on my left. "Silver Squad, you are on the edge of the border, in the trees, as back up. It is also imperative that you are not seen or heard."

"Bronze Squad," he says to the remaining group, "you will be staying with me in case they try to send people across the valley. If it is peaceful, we will be acting as negotiators. If it is not, then we are the first line of defense." The General's face is deadly solemn.

Good. Gold Squad will go in and spy. I would jump with joy if I could, but that would get me yelled at. So I stay still, focusing on not smiling too widely.

"Sanders!"

Uh oh.

"You will be staying with the Bronze squad."

I try my best not to protest, and fail miserably. "That's not fair, sir," I huff. "I've earned my position on the Gold Squad. I should be allowed to go in."

Everyone stares at me. It takes guts to argue with the General. It also happens to be one of the stupidest things anyone can do. Stupid things are my specialty, though.

He shoots me a glare. "Sanders, stand down." He stalks over and gets right in my face. "Just because you were the youngest girl to enlist, and the first female to join Gold Squad, does not mean you are immune to the rules. You will listen to your orders and be happy that I am allowing you to stay on Gold Squad after that remark," he nearly spits, his voice radiating anger.

Everyone else is avoiding eye contact with the General and with me. I am just trying my hardest not to glare back at him. I do not appreciate public ridicule, even if by my superior.

"Thank you, sir," I say, trying not to sound like I want to choke him.

"Dismissed." He strides off with a final frown of warning.

All of my buddies on Gold Squad move away, giving me pitying looks that I despise. I glare at everyone on Silver Squad, and they all just look scared as they head toward their assignment.

I know why I was ordered to stay behind and I don't like it. The General knows that whenever I see Lexi, I tend to disobey orders, which risks my safety and that of everyone around me. So it's perfectly logical why he would order me to stay behind on a stealth mission. I still don't like it. Not one little bit.

Bronze Squad takes a position that overlooks the valley, and I find a spot with a good view but that's apart from everyone else. They're all talking quietly but doing nothing. Boring! They could be doing something productive, like making arrows, which I plan to do. There are a few straight sticks lying in the tall grass that will function—with a little work—just fine for arrows. The feathers and arrow tips at the bottom of my sheath, and probably everyone else's too, can be attached to the sticks. So I get to work.

I'm busily carving my arrows, convincing myself that the Gold Squad mission is probably boring anyway, when I feel eyes intently watching me.

I look up. A girl, about a year younger, than me is studying what I'm doing from her perch a few dozen yards away on the top edge of the steep hillside.

"Yes?" I ask. What's her deal, anyway?

She grabs the bow and sheath on the ground next to her and scampers over to me. "I was curious as to how you do that."

"How I do what? Make my arrows?" Finally, someone on this Squad decides to be productive.

She nods.

Seriously? How can she be an archer and not know how to make her own arrows? The army needs to raise its standards for Bronze. I might as well teach her. "Do you have a knife?"

She nods again and pulls one out.

I hand her a stick. "Hold your knife like this," I demonstrate, tilting my hands so she can see, and push it along the length of the stick.

She copies my actions.

Soon enough, we are carving arrows, and I actually enjoy the companionship. My stick is done, so I cut a slit in the top for the arrow tip and stick the sharpened rock in, tying it on with some brightly colored string I carry in my sheath for just this purpose. I do the same in the back with the feathers.

The girl mimics my movements with her own supplies.

I repeat the tasks with the rest of my sticks for the next hour, until the shadows lengthen. A dozen new arrows are lined up in front of me.

Tucking my knife back in my boot, I get up, stretch, and gather the arrows and my bow. It's time to see what this Bronze Squad girl has got. Walking over to a tree, I carve an X in it.

"What are we doing now?" She follows me like a puppy dog.

Usually I would find it annoying, but today I don't care. There are other, bigger things to be annoyed about, such as being left behind on a mission and having to babysit Bronze Squad instead.

"Target practice."

I walk twenty paces from the tree and draw back my bow. I'm able to see clearly despite the gathering darkness, and once again thank the stars that I am back on Amara with my usual powers.

The girl rushes to do the same. We both shoot. She's a good archer, but has room to learn more. I give her pointers as we shoot.

My shots hit the center of the X almost every time. The girl hits somewhere on the X about ninety percent of the time and only once misses the tree entirely, but her bow is angled up much too high for the distance we're shooting. She's aiming as if the target is much farther away.

"Do you shoot mostly long distance?" I ask her conversationally.

"Yes. I'm having some issues shooting short distance because I only do it every now and then." She looks frustrated.

I nod and continue to offer advice. After a few more minutes of intense practice, the girl is noticeably better. When we're both out of arrows, I put my hand up in the regulation gesture to tell her to stop so we can safely retrieve our arrows.

Once I've done that, I sit on the ground, fold my legs, and lean against the tree. With a rag from my sheath, I polish my bow and clear off the fingerprints. The girl mimics my actions yet again. If imitation is the sincerest form of flattery, then I must be the most flattered person on Amara.

"Your bow is really nice," she says.

"It is," I agree, hoping she won't push the subject.

"Where'd you get it?"

Dang it, why did she have to ask that? "It was a gift," I say tersely.

"From whom?"

Stupid people and their curiosity.

"My father," I say, barring my face of emotion.

"Wow, he must be really awesome," she says enthusiastically. This girl clearly knows nothing about my family history.

"He was." Whoops.

"Was?"

"He's dead."

Her eyes drop to the dirt, "I'm sorry to hear that."

"Ya, he made this himself and gave it to me just a few hours before he passed." *What the heck? Why am I telling her this?*

"He must've meant a lot to you."

I might as well tell her. I mean, the kid's a stranger, so who cares, right? "He was the closest person to me, and taught me all these great life lessons, like *words work better than fists*, and to *have patience*, an-" Faltering, I continue without thinking. "He was such a great warrior. I don't know how he, I don't-" I feel my throat start to tighten and I immediately stop talking. "Anyway, I don't ever talk about him."

She peers up at me, and I feel her trying to figure out how to react to my sudden gush of information. "I swear I won't tell anyone what you said. I mean, I'm the best at keeping secrets. This will be between just you and me, 'cause we're friends now . . . right? And friends keep secrets."

"I, uh . . ." The hopeful look on her face makes me halt what I had planned to say. "Of course, but you have to swear on your life not to tell anyone."

She lights up like a glowing stone fish in summer. "Oh my goodness, of course, on my life I swear to keep your secret and take it with me to the grave."

***

"Sanders, Hanaway," the General calls a short while later. The girl—Hanaway—and I jump to our feet and stand at attention. "There is a party of delegates coming across the valley to meet us under a white flag. Go find out what they want."

Finally, a little action! I think gleefully.

"Yes, sir," we respond and salute like the trained soldiers we are. Someone from Bronze Squad hands Hanaway a white flag. As is customary in these situations, we leave our bows and my short sword at the base of the tree—but I discreetly check that my knife is still in my boot.

Hanaway's eyes widen as she notices what I did. "I thought this is supposed to be peaceful?" she whispers.

"You never know what tricks they have up their sleeves. Having a weapon could make a big difference in the end. Never underestimate the importance of a knife."

Hanaway nods and tucks her own knife down the side of her right boot.

At a nod from the General, we scramble down the steep hillside. After several dusty minutes, we reach the valley floor.

The opposing delegates have halted halfway across the valley plain. A few trees dot the tall grass, with many more on the surrounding hillsides. Hanaway and I are exposed to everyone's view. But then, so are the enemy's representatives.

"We need to look formidable," I instruct Hanaway as we cross the plain to meet them. "Let's have an air that says we mean business, but don't appear like you won't negotiate. Just copy me and hope for the best."

Within a couple of minutes, we are close enough to distinguish the features of their faces. Giants, ugh. And three of them. At least these are smaller giants, only six feet tall; they must be younger. Maybe they were chosen to show that this really is a peaceful delegation. Or maybe not. We'll just have to find out.

We stop a few yards away from them, a bubble of safety between us.

"What is the business that requires this meeting?" I say, trying to sound professional and authoritative.

"We wish to discuss negotiations about a new peace treaty," one of them grunts. "We require an audience with your Queen."

I'm debating if I should take them seriously or not, but then I notice a familiar light flashing from behind the giants. My Gold Squad buddies, on the hillside near the enemy's camp, sending me a coded message with the handy laser pointer I brought from Earth: *This is a trick. Pull back.*

I roll my eyes. Gold Squad really should know better than to tell me to pull back. I'm just not the type of girl to go home without a little fun first.

"I would be honored to take you to her," I step toward the three giants. "It's a pleasure to work with you." *Ugly, ugly creatures.* I hope my disgust doesn't show on my face.

I stick out my hand for the leader of the delegation to shake. He clasps my hand, and I jerk him forward, right into my other fist.

BAM!

Good thing they sent small giants I can push around, and even better that I've got my full strength back after that little trip to Earth earlier today.

The giant groans and holds his face with both hands. The air thickens as the other two realize that this meeting is not going to be the slightest bit peaceful.

A giant launches himself at Hanaway and she jumps to the side. He misses her and tumbles end over end for a few yards. With the flagpole still in hand, she stabs the third giant in the eye, an expression of malice on her face I didn't think she was capable of. He falls to the ground, screaming in pain.

The giant I punched roars as he lunges for me, blood dripping down his face from a broken nose. The giant Hanaway sidestepped is also on his feet and looking murderous—probably from hurt pride.

All right, *now* we pull back, as instructed. I turn tail and sprint with Hanaway right behind me. As we race across the valley floor, I grin with a bit of pride at Hanaway's sharp wits and bravery. I'm glad I earned her trust, and her mine.

With my heart pounding and adrenaline rushing through my veins, I listen to the sounds of pursuit, trying to gauge if they're gaining on us. Something behind us makes a whizzing noise, and I tug sharply on Hanaway's arm, causing her to stumble towards me.

A sharpened metal disc flies by her head with incredible speed. That was close! Since when did the giants get metal weapons?

Zig-zagging our way towards the cliffs while dodging the projectiles aimed at us, I realize the two giants in pursuit are gaining on us.

We're not going to outrun them. "It's going to come to a fight," I gasp at Hanaway.

Maybe instigating wasn't the brightest idea.

With lungs heaving, we stop and pull our knives out of our boots, then turn swiftly and prepare to face our attackers head on. "Told you . . . we'd need these," I can't help but remind her in between panted breaths.

The giants stop, eye the knives, and we have a stare down. The air is thick with tension as the four of us calculate what we should each do, and as we watch for the others to attack. My eyes dare the giants to make a move, to throw the first punch.

Various defensive and offensive patterns come to mind. I won't be the first to attack, I decide. The space between us is too large to guarantee a hit. Okay, okay, I need a plan. *Aha!* I'll distract them.

I point to the cliffs behind the giants. "Look, there are our archers!" I say excitedly to Hanaway.

The giants quickly spin around and look, so I launch myself at the bigger one. Okay, maybe I lied about not being the first to attack, but we had to do something to end the standoff. Besides, it's not my fault giants are so stupid.

"Made you look!" I chortle gleefully as I kick the feet out from under the giant I'm fighting, then stomp on his solar plexus.

I hold my knife to the giant's throat. He gets the message and remains still, a menacing look on his face.

Out of the corner of my eye, I catch sight of Hanaway.

She has just landed a blow to the face of the other giant, and I hear the crack of its nose breaking.

The giant doesn't go down, though, and Hanaway fights intensely. She darts in and out of her opponent's range, slicing at him with her knife. The giants may have brute strength, but they're not very agile.

After a couple of tries, he grabs her wrist and forces her to drop the knife. *Frick!* I can't help Hanaway because I'm too preoccupied with making sure my guy doesn't get up.

Hanaway yelps in pain, then swings a kick at her attacker's knee that has him hunched over in pain. *Yes!* She's a better fighter than I anticipated.

I hear our backup scrambling down the cliffs and racing toward us. "We'll take it from here," one of the taller boys on Bronze Squad calls out.

"Bye, then," I say to the giant on the ground. "It was nice having this lovely chat with you."

I walk backwards, keeping my eyes on the enemy. Hanaway runs backwards to a safe distance. I join her and we watch two of the boys use rope to tie up the enemy I felled while a third holds his knife on him. The giant that Hanaway fought and brought to his knees will be easy for the Bronze soldiers circling him to subdue. But there's still one giant left, so three more Bronze Squad members set off to find the one Hanaway stabbed in the eye. He can't have gone far.

I roll my shoulders, glad that the confrontation didn't turn out too badly.

Tucking my knife in my boot, I head up the cliffs toward our basecamp, with Hanaway trailing a few feet behind me. We're both too out of breath to talk yet.

At the top, I flop down in the grass. "Well, that was mildly exciting."

"Mildly!" Hanaway exclaims. "That was the most exciting thing I've ever done!" She jabbers on about the confrontation while I sit up, lean against a tree, and verify our bows and my short sword are within arm's reach. If it comes to a battle, I'll need my armor, which is with the rest of Gold Squad's in our armory tent.

Fatigue overwhelms me and I'm glad I'm sitting down. I figure someone else will report what happened down in the valley to the General—Hanaway, or one of the Bronze Squad boys who came to our aid. The General probably saw it all anyway. I wonder if he'll get any information from the three giants. Prisoners don't usually talk, though. Not even giants.

The way it's looking, there'll be a battle very soon, and I need to be well rested to take on Lexi.

Closing my eyes, I drift off to sleep.

Chapter 6 – Hanaway

That has to have been the most exciting thing I've done in my entire life! I have no idea how Rose—er, Sanders can sleep right now. I can't believe that just happened.

From here, I can see where we fought down in the valley. Wow, it doesn't even look like anything happened there. Even though it was just, like, thirty minutes ago... Oh my gosh, I can't even believe it! I can't wait to tell my parents.

Footsteps catch my attention and I see the General walking toward us. Oh no! We never reported in to him.

I hustle to my feet, an apology on my lips. "Sir, I'm—"

"It is fine, Hanaway." He looks down at Rose. "Sanders here—who appears unconscious—should have known to report in to me. One of the Bronze boys already told me what they saw, and what happened after they got there. And why we have prisoners." He frowns.

I attempt an apology again. "Sir, please, just let me—"

"Hanaway, if you apologize to me, I will take away your rank."

I bite my tongue.

"Now, get some rest. Tomorrow, when the horns sound, we will be off into battle."

"Yes, sir, right away."

I gather my gear from camp and return to the tree where Sanders remains asleep. I'm way too excited to sleep right now. We're going into battle tomorrow, which is going to be the new most exciting thing I've ever done.

The only issue is that I might get hurt, or die, or something like that. That's only a minor detail, though, because I get to go into battle with none other than the legendary Rose Sanders, the first girl to ever make it onto the Gold Squad! I get to work with my idol, who is now my friend, and tells me her secrets and ohmygoodness, I cannot even . . . !

How in the world am I going to sleep?

***

Battle horns blare and I immediately open my eyes. The night sky is fading and there's a glimmer of pink on the horizon. How could I have fallen asleep and slept until nearly dawn?

I try to jump up but fall over because of my still-asleep legs. I succeed on the second try, and grab my bow. I'm ready!

Rose is calmly stretching and murmuring something about how "there should be a law that battles can't take place this early in the day."

How can she not be excited to go into battle? Best day ever!

The General rushes over to Sanders, who's now on her feet, and speaks in hurried undertones with her, no doubt giving her an update before rushing off to do the same with other people. Gold Squad must also have new information, because they're spreading it around to Silver and Bronze Squad members. Someone passes by and throws a bundle of armor at Rose. She quickly puts it on with the ease of having done it hundreds of times.

"Bronze Squad, over here!" Sanders yells in a demanding voice while strapping on her sword, and slinging her bow and sheath of arrows over her shoulder. No one listens but me. When she lets out an ear-piercing whistle, everyone stops. "Bronze Squad, I suggest you listen to your new leader and assemble *right now*." She bites out the last two words in a nasty tone. I guess she's not a morning person.

My squad scrambles into place around me.

In a firm voice, she orders, "All hand-to-hand fighters, such as swordsmen, go report to Silver. All archers stay with me."

The squad members hustle to follow her orders. Soon just the archers—about twenty—surround Sanders and me.

My eyes are riveted on the battle between Sanders and our arch enemy.

Both women are exceptionally good fighters, and I'm mesmerized by the way they move. They're dueling with short swords. I can tell Lexi is a better swordsman from the way she flawlessly performs maneuvers while Sanders looks sloppy in comparison. She also looks tired, but unharmed—so far.

Lexi's sword dances around Sanders like a snake, lunging towards her head. Sanders ducks, and the metal barely clears her.

But Sanders is quicker than Lexi, and she can dart in and around the attacks that she isn't capable of blocking. Lexi lacks the grace to follow my idol's movements with her body, but her sword follows closely behind. What Sanders lacks in sword skills, she makes up for in agility. The result is a very dangerous and even duel.

***

The battle has been going on for what seems like hours, but in reality, it can only be a few minutes. The sun has barely cleared the horizon.

I don't know what to do and find myself frantically pacing. When she put me in charge, Sanders didn't relay the General's instructions to me. I don't know if we should climb down the hillside and try to help, or if we should stay and wait to see what happens— to see if the armies separate enough for us to get in some clean shots. I am in way over my head.

All the combatants in the valley fight fiercely but more are falling as time goes on. I don't know if it's from injury, or worse.

I wrap my arms around myself and rock back and forth. I can't believe that living beings can do this to each other. Sanders and I fighting the three giants last evening was fun because even the guy I poked in the eye didn't get hurt all that badly. Our little battle was exciting, and cool.

This is not cool. Not one bit.

I can't stop shaking.

Hopelessness radiates off of the archers around me. This battle is not going as well as we thought it would. And, actually, most people—including the soldiers—had hoped the battle wouldn't happen at all.

The sweat pours down my back, and I feel the eyes of my archers looking to me for instructions.

Suddenly a blinding light flashes in the center of the valley. The flare is brighter than the sun. I close my eyes and turn away. I can feel its heat on my skin.

What is going on? I fall to my knees, my eyes tightly shut. My urge to vomit has never been greater. Bile rises in my throat, and it's all I can do to swallow it down.

But the light disappears within seconds, so I shakily rise to my feet and look down into the valley.

The battle has stopped. The two armies are slowly backing away from each other.

Something big has just happened, and the weight of it is heavy in the air. Not a sound can be heard. Silence rings in my ears. What is going on?

My archers and I gaze in horror at the battlefield.

Where are Sanders and Lexi?

I can't see them. They should be right there, in the center of everything. But they're not.

The two armies suddenly turn and run toward their respective sides of the valley, looking fearfully over their shoulders and fleeing as quickly as possible.

Now that the sun is fully up and the dust is settling, I see that the grass in the center area is scorched black—right where the blinding flash of light originated. There's a good-sized depression in the ground there, too, where Rose and Lexi had been battling . . . but there is no one there.

Nor are Sanders or Lexi in the fleeing forces. They're just . . . gone.

"Back to camp!" I order, and everyone instantly obeys. We need answers, we need to hear what happened.

Panting from running at full speed, I go straight to the crowd that has gathered in camp and push my way to the front. Everyone quiets when the General raises his hand.

"What has happened to Sanders is classified," he announces. "That is all." He turns on his heel and walks away, his face devoid of emotion.

I follow him beyond the edge of the group until we're alone. "General, wait, I—"

"Why could she not listen to orders for once?" he mutters to himself as he stalks away. "If her father saw what I let happen, he would kill me . . ."

I freeze. So Sanders really hadn't listened to orders! She wasn't supposed to be down there in the battle, just as I'd suspected. I bet she was supposed to stay with the archers. Oh no, oh no! This is bad, bad news.

My father, who had been high up in the army once upon a time, had told me that *classified* means that the army either doesn't have an answer or they have something worth keeping a secret. In any case, the word classified is never good news. So whatever happened to Rose is bad.

Her body hasn't been found, so I can only assume she's alive. And yet no one saw her leave.

She simply vanished into thin air.

Chapter 7 – Phoenix

Standing in Rose's house after she ran out, and Sylvia returned to the castle, I debate if the carrier pigeon's message signals a peaceful negotiation or a full-blown battle. Either way, I would rather wait here for Rose to return and tell me, than at home. My brother is in Silver Squad and he would have already left to report for duty. Being alone in our house while he's gone would be too unsettling.

I will not be called out to battle—or to negotiate—because I am not in the army. I would not be able to do what they asked of me.

After pacing and worrying for who knows how long, I plop down on the couch. My mind roams everywhere, and my imagination conjures all sorts of horrors.

Hours pass. Night falls and the sky grows pitch black. The crackling fire dies, and I barely move, waiting on pins and needles for Rose to return. But she doesn't, which makes me think it's not simply peaceful negotiations she was called to attend.

I realize I'm pacing the floor again and have no idea when I stood up and started doing that. I make myself a cup of tea in the kitchen, and my thoughts return to that long-ago battle and its effect on Rose's life.

Rose does not like to talk about all the bad things that happened, and nobody in the village ever does. Sometimes I suspect that everyone forgets—or chooses to forget, for Rose's sake—that Rose had a sister, that her father died, and that her mother apparently abandoned them.

It is sad, really.

***

Eventually, I lie back on the couch, exhausted. I fall into a deep sleep.

A loud knocking on the door wakes me up the next morning and I rush to answer it. A royal messenger is standing outside, holding his horse's reins in his hand.

"Ahh!" he intones in the voice of someone who basks in his own importance. "You *are* here, Miss Phoenix. I have been sent by the Princess to fetch you and bring you to the castle." He sticks out his uniformed chest with pride and resumes his slow, measured speech. "She has told me to let you ride back on my steed, Miss Phoenix. And that you must make great haste. It is," he clears his throat pompously, "an emergency."

An emergency! I grab the reins out of his hand, and swing up into the saddle.

I spare him a glance. "Thank you for delivering that message and letting me use your horse." It wouldn't do to forget my manners.

I urge the magnificent creamy-white beast into a gallop, thrilling in his powerful gait. Everyone in our village knows how to ride, seeing as how the only transportation is by horse or on foot.

I guide the horse down the trail, whipping past trees and taking the path that skirts the town so I won't be slowed by anyone. Colors blur together as I focus on the path in front of me and my mind races. Sylvia has never sent a horse for me before; she would only do this if it truly was an emergency. And I know in my gut this summons has something to do with Rose and that whatever it is, it most certainly isn't good news.

I click to the horse to go faster, and hope for the best.

Chapter 8 – Rose

I'm getting goosebumps on my arms. Opening my eyes, I see nothing. Pitch black. My heart races.

Where am I? I have no idea how long I've been here, or even where here is.

Finally, what feels like hours later, I'm pulled from the bone-chilling darkness. Warmth envelopes me. I awaken to a serene blue sky overhead and hard ground beneath me.

Blinking rapidly to help my eyes adjust to the sudden brightness, I sit up and take in my surroundings: black, charred structures, eaten by a flame long gone, stretch out of sight. The buildings' metal frames are warped and crumbling, and scorched debris litters the ground and even the sidewalk beneath me.

There's not a person in sight. I shiver, despite how warm it is.

I wrap my arms around myself. My *bare* arms. "What the—?" There's no armor over my clothes; it's disappeared. So has my sword. At least I'm still wearing the clothes I had on yesterday when I dashed out of my cottage and reported for duty—jeans and a T-shirt and my boots.

So. . . what in the worlds happened?! Where am I and how did I get here?

I was battling Lexi in the Valley of the Nomads, and then a bright light blinded me, followed by too long in that cold darkness. And then I ended up here.

Oh, frick! This isn't my world; it's not Amara. There is pavement—although it's pockmarked—and the multi-level structures are much too big. And the air stinks. Amara isn't polluted like this.

I'm on Earth! But how can that be?

I got away from here yesterday and made it safely back to Amara in time to celebrate Sylvia's birthday. So what am I doing back here again?

I leap to my feet. In the distance, normal, Earth-like, urban buildings appear completely intact. Why am I in this burned-out section of what's obviously a large city?

So how did I get here? Only portals can transport people from one planet to another. So it must have been a portal of some sort that brought me here—it's the only way. But the portal to Earth drops off and picks up on the bridge, which is nowhere to be seen. Although two nights ago it was in that park—

Which reminds me . . . as a precaution, I reach up and touch the Key suspended on the chain around my neck. *Thank goodness, it's still there.* I yank it off the chain. Oh, but it's twisted and burnt. How did this happen? But more importantly, does it still work?

I clutch the Key and picture my home, the valley, and the woods, and I put all my heart into every detail.

No portal appears, even though it should have with that much effort from me.

I try again, this time picturing my village and everything about Amara I can think of.

Still no portal. Nothing, nada, zip, zilch. Not an inkling of that beautiful blue and green portal I love. Panic steals my breath and my eyes tear up.

I swallow hard and my sorrow quickly turns into anger. *Damn Key!* It's of no use to me now. I fling it as far as I can and am quite proud that I manage to throw it across what I assume used to be a street and almost to the next building.

Then my foolish pride evaporates. I should have tried to fix it somehow, so now I need to go look for it.

Otherwise, I'll have to find another way home. Or wait for someone to figure out where I am and come get me. Or somehow get another Key. Or, or, or—there are too many *or*s! I need an answer, and, even more than that, I need to go home. My Amarians need me in the battle against Lexi and the giants.

Stepping over blackened timbers that have fallen onto the cracked sidewalk, I trudge over to where the Key landed.

A noise nearby catches my attention. What the? I dash to an archway which probably once held a door and hide on the other side of it.

Peering out, I see a person walking through the rubble, staring at the ground as if he's looking for something.

The human is male and appears to be somewhere around my age. Taller, though, but that's about all I can tell.

He glances my way and I try to squeeze myself behind the metal beam. Not a great tactic, but it's all I can think of.

The boy studies me with a curious look on his face, probably wondering why a girl is attempting to hide behind a beam that's only half as wide as she is.

What is he even doing here, anyway? Who hangs out in the burned-down part of a city? And what is he looking for?

He slowly takes a few steps toward me, and my brain quickly does the whole fight-or-flight thing. He has about a foot on me, and his legs are a lot longer, so I decide *flight* would just turn into *fight* anyway. If I really am on Earth, my Amarian speed has left me. I don't think I could outrun this idiot. He looks built to run—tall and lanky.

I step out from behind my beam and lean against it, attempting a menacing look as I study him. The stranger is lean, although he definitely has muscle. His short brown hair is the same color as his eyes.

When he's still on the opposite side of the street, he pauses to pick up something from the ground and pockets it before continuing toward me.

I narrow my gaze and glare even harder at him.

He stops when he's about thirty or forty feet away and studies me with a puzzled expression.

"Hi," he says, sounding slightly awkward.

"Hello," I reply in a cool voice, trying to scare him.

"Who are you and what are you doing here?" he asks, his voice now just as icy as mine.

"Who I am is not important, nor are my reasons for being here," I say. I need information first, before I can form a plausible story he'll believe. I seize on the obvious. "When did this fire happen?" I gesture around us.

"Five years ago. No one's put the money into cleaning it up." He shoots me a suspicious look, which is followed by a small, triumphant smile. "What are you doing here if you didn't know that?"

"You wouldn't believe me if I told you."

"Try me," he challenges, raising both eyebrows.

"Fine," I say childishly, quickly thinking of a lie. "I'm here because I had relatives who died in this fire. I'm just mourning their deaths. No reason for you to be all up in my business."

"You're lying," he says in a know-it-all tone. "No one died in this fire." He takes a step closer to me and it's all I can do to hold my ground. "Now, I want to know why you're here." He pulls a small pocket knife from his pocket and flicks it open like it's a big deal.

I scoff. Is that all he's got? Pathetic humans and their small knives. Nothing to worry about from him.

"Now listen here," I say, grabbing my hunting knife out of my boot, smirking as terror quickly flashes through his eyes. "Why I'm here is not important to you or anyone else, for that matter."

I take several threatening steps towards him. He tenses.

Aha! I've got him now. "All that's important is you telling me where I am and what the date is, and then quickly leaving before I decide to put this knife to use."

A few more steps and I'm within arm's reach of him.

The brief flash of terror I saw across his face is long gone. Now he just looks as if he can't believe I'm serious.

I am.

"Fine," he replies airily, not budging an inch. "But I have this." He holds up my Key. "You threw it, but I'm thinking you want it back."

"Give it to me," I command.

"I'll give it to you, but only if you tell me why you're here," he says, smirking and relaxing. He knows he has the upper hand.

"Don't make me use this on you," I say, holding my knife in a ready position while trying to figure out how to retrieve the Key. Even though I clearly have the bigger weapon, his eyes tell me he won't back down. You gotta hand it to him; he's got courage.

"You wouldn't use that on me," he sniggers.

My gut tells me he is right. I can't use my knife on this guy; he's too intriguing to stab right now. And I need information he can provide. Besides, I don't normally go around stabbing innocent people. Not to mention the fact that he seems to know that the Key is important to me, and therefore he might actually know something about it. From past mistakes, I've discovered it's best if I listen to my gut.

Obeying my wiser inner voice, I scowl and put my knife away and prepare to be civil.

As soon as my knife is gone, he shuts his and returns it to his pocket.

I let out a deep breath. "Fine, here's the deal: I got here somehow, and I don't remember how, so stop asking. I don't know how much time has passed, but I do know that I need to get back home quickly. So, if you would kindly tell me the date and give me back my beloved bit of burnt metal, which I'm not telling you about, I'll be on my way."

When I finish speaking, I grab for the Key, but he holds it high and out of my reach. Tall people ruin everything. Now it's my turn to look at him questioningly.

"Fine, I'll help you," he relents, as if he's doing me a big favor.

"I never asked for your help!" I cross my arms over my chest.

"You know you need my help," he states, and when I protest, he just talks over me. "But you have to be honest with me. Where are you from?" He gives me a look that suggests he knows more than he is letting on, which really infuriates me. I'm used to having the upper hand and knowing more than others do.

"I'm from a completely different world that's under attack right now. I need to get back before everyone dies," I say, hoping the statement shocks him enough that I can pull his arm down and get the Key.

He smirks again. "Funny how things work, huh? I just happen to be the Gatekeeper here," he says while pulling out a Key from his jacket pocket and waggling it in front of me.

My mom's journal was right! This changes everything. There's a Gatekeeper on Earth. So does that mean he knows Victoria Coulee? No, he can't. Keys are supposed to be passed down to one of the girls in the family. Boys never have them, so he must've gotten it from somewhere else. But where?

Most importantly, though, is that here is finally someone who can understand what I go through—and can help me get home!

But how likely is that? This human giraffe—good grief, they grow them tall here—hasn't been generous so far.

Before I can stop myself, I demand, "Exactly who in the worlds would make *you* Gatekeeper?"

"World*s*?" he questions.

I wave him off with a flick of my wrist. "Yes, like multiple, plural? Come on, keep up with me."

"Whatever," he shrugs as if my insult doesn't bother him.

"Yeah, whatever. But you have a Key. So I can go home now!" I take another swipe at his Key and he holds it even higher than mine. Now he has a Key in each hand.

He grins. "Let me tell you a funny story . . ."

My heart sinks. Those words never end well. I know, since I use them all the time.

He continues, "My Key stopped working a month ago. It's usually always warm to the touch, but since then it's been dead cold."

So what does that have to do with me? "Give me your Key."

"What?"

I stick out my hand, palm up. "Hand it over. Clearly you haven't used it. You're saying it just 'felt' different," I reason. "So it might still work, thus you should give it to someone who actually knows how to use it."

Apparently I got through to him because he hesitantly drops it in my hand. I clench my fist around it, close my eyes, and imagine home, every single detail I can think of. This should definitely work.

Nothing happens. *Frick!*

I try again, picturing everything as if it were right in front of me. I open my eyes and I'm still in the burned-down building. *What the heck?*

I shove the Key in his chest. "Take the damn thing back. Your stupid Key doesn't work."

He slides it into his pocket. "I told you it stopped working a month ago."

A month ago . . . a premonition snakes up my back. How long was I in that cold, dark place? Before I woke up here on Earth? "Tell me the date isn't *June* 24, 2017?"

"Yes, it is. How'd you know? You said you didn't know the date," he frowns.

His words knock the breath out of me. It's *June* twenty-fourth here. When I left Amara, it would have been *May* twenty-fourth on Earth. It's been a month. I've been teleported into the future!

But what has happened on Amara during that month? My people could still be fighting, or the battle could be over. Did we win? Are Sylvia and Phoenix okay? Is my village still standing? A month is a long time and anything could have happened. I need to get home.

But first I have to decide if this guy can help me or not.

"Okay, here's the deal, Mr. Earthling. I blacked out for a month, and your Key stopped working a month ago," I state confidently. I doubt I was actually lying unconscious in the rubble for a month, so I assume the portals are messing with time.

He frowns at me. "The two are *obviously* connected. I agree. We need to find a way to fix our Keys and get you home."

Didn't I just point that out? What a moron.

The idiot grabs my arm and starts pulling me with him down the sidewalk.

"Where are we going?" I demand.

No response.

"Wait!" I dig my heels into the wreckage beneath my feet, refusing to move.

"What?" he complains, turning to face me. "We have to get moving. We can't stay in any one place for too long." He gives me a look that tells me not to question him.

I don't even bother because I have bigger fish to fry. "What's your name?" I ask as I pick my way around the debris on the sidewalk.

"Derek. Yours?"

"Rose."

Shock registers on his face, but quickly passes. "Seems like such a pretty name for a girl with such a big knife," he says with a slight chuckle.

"Roses have thorns, you know," I reply smugly. He almost stumbles. Klutz.

I'd rather figure out how to get home on my own but I need to work with him, since his knowledge of this planet will come in handy.

Speaking of his knowledge . . . "By the way, where on Earth are we?"

"Downtown Chicago."

I nod. Just as I thought. I've been here before. It's not my preferred location at the moment, though, because I know I can get help from an Amarian who currently lives on Earth—not by her choice—and not in Chicago. "Would Chicago be close to Oregon, by any chance?"

"Nope. Not even close. That's a different state on the other side of the country."

"Any chance of us getting to Oregon?"

"Not unless you have a lot of money sitting around somewhere."

"Could I borrow money from you and return it later after I get home? I need to get to Oregon."

"I don't have enough money . . . why do you want to go to Oregon so badly anyway?"

"I know someone there who might be able to get me home. Are you absolutely positive there is no way to get me to Oregon?" I ask, trying to keep desperation out of my voice.

"Unless you hitchhike across the country, which is extremely dangerous, no, there is no way for you to get there," he replies.

"Then I'll hitchhike, whatever that means. I *have* to get home."

"Are you serious?" He must have decided I was, because he stopped. "I can't let you do that. It's too risky." He thinks for a moment. "I'll stick with you and help you find a way home or another way to Oregon."

I mull over my choices. "Fine, but if we don't have a plan soon, I'm hitchhiking to Oregon."

Derek smiles slightly. "I'm sure we'll think of something."

We're still walking by burned-out buildings, although now I can faintly hear the sounds of cars in the distance. The sunset behind us turns the sky a violent shade of red and casts an eerie glow across the charred landscape. A shiver runs up my spine. This is not a good omen.

Out of the corner of my eye, I notice someone following us. I haven't seen anyone else except Derek. I wonder what this guy's deal is. He's probably some crazy human. A lunatic.

Whatever. He's keeping his distance.

I glance at Derek. He doesn't *look* too bad, I guess. I could be traveling with worse.

I sigh as I trip over a piece of metal I didn't see.

All I know is that this unexpected trip to Earth has shot off in a fantastic fashion. And by fantastic, I mean it sucks.

Chapter 9 – Derek

Well, my day has certainly been out of the ordinary, but then again, they usually are lately.

First, I was on a bus heading to the west side of town to try to sneak into my parents' house to get some more of my stuff. When someone wearing a hoodie abruptly sat down next to me. I could only assume it was a girl by her figure, because she kept her hood pulled up over her face the entire time and didn't let me see who she was. She was silent for a moment, until the bus picked up speed again.

"Derek Coulee. Huh. So I have to come help you out *again*. This is really too much effort." She sounded sarcastic, definitely female, and vaguely familiar.

Where do I recognize her voice from?

"In about two minutes you're going to see a bright flash out this window. You should go investigate it. It will be to your benefit to discover what lies there and to keep it close."

What is she gibbering on about? "Who *are* you?"

She laughed slightly. "All in good time. Meanwhile, I have other business to attend. Just remember—roses have thorns."

Before I could ask her another question, the bus stopped and she flitted away. I stood up to try to get a glimpse of where she was going and follow her, but a bright flash on the horizon caught my attention. I figured it would be worth my time to investigate. After all she has apparently helped me before. I wish I could remember when.

And so I did investigate the flash of light. I met a Rose, who told me the same thing the girl did—roses have thorns. Which is more than peculiar because, judging by Rose's confused state when I met her a few minutes ago, she and that other girl don't know each other. Not that anything in my life is ordinary anymore—not since I became the Gatekeeper—whatever that means—and was forced to keep track of the Key.

A car horn blares loudly a few streets away, and Rose flinches.

I wonder if she has to keep the Key away from others like I do, people who want it in order to wreak havoc. When I first got it, I had to learn—fast—what kind of people I could trust just by looking at them.

Like when I saw Rose for the first time. I knew I could trust her. It's in the way people hold themselves, and the look in their eyes. Rose's green-blue eyes just seem trustworthy—maybe a little mischievous—but trustworthy, nonetheless. Besides, there's something intriguing about her. I mean, a Gatekeeper who knows what she's doing—that's freakin' awesome. Plus, there's the weird but good feeling in my gut I have from being with her right now. Well, and the weird chick on the bus who told me to keep something close; I assume she meant Rose, as I haven't found anything else.

I've also learned that having friends is not a good idea because I can't tell them about me being a Gatekeeper. Not even my own mother, because when I did that, I got kicked out of the house.

However, since Rose is a Gatekeeper, that shouldn't be a problem. My spirits lift.

"Someone's following us." Rose nods over her left shoulder.

Darn it! I was so preoccupied with my thoughts that I didn't even notice him. I glance over my shoulder nonchalantly.

Uh oh.

Short, bulky, very scary looking. Why is he following us? Is it a coincidence, or does he know about me—us—being Gatekeepers? Is he going to try to steal my Key?

This is bad news and the kind of mistake that I can't afford to make. *Crap.* How long has he been following us?

More bad news: the street we're on dead-ends up ahead. "We need a plan," I say quietly, trying to hide my panic, when what I really want to do is grab Rose and run. "*Right now.*"

"Just follow my lead," Rose replies calmly.

"I thought you didn't have a plan?" I remind her archly.

She replies as if the answer is obvious. "We don't. I'm making this up as we go. Just try and keep up, Princess."

"Excuse me?" I retort, shocked. Did she seriously just call me a *Princess*? What is her deal?

She flashes me a grin. "You're excused."

Rose suddenly darts across the street, heading in the direction we just came from. I follow, still not sure about her improvising.

We're getting closer to the man who is following us. He's wearing a black hoodie pulled up over his head, hiding his face, with dark-washed jeans and black running shoes. He's so muscular that he looks as if he's stuffed into his clothes, like he'll bust out of them if he moves wrong. If Rose is planning a direct confrontation, she's going to have trouble. He's a whole lot bigger than her—than both of us together.

"Do you have a cell phone?" Rose says under her breath.

"Yeah. Why?" It's not like we can call anyone for help. We'd be toast by the time the cops got here.

"Take it out, and turn on the little device that captures images."

A camera? Who doesn't know what a camera is? But I do what she asks. We're about ten feet away from the man now, who is still walking toward us although he's keeping his head bent to hide his face. Rose has yet to do anything.

"You!" Rose says loudly to him. He ignores her.

"That's your plan?" I whisper-yell at her.

"Shut up," she whisper-yells back.

"Hey, you there!" she says again. "The person currently ignoring me? Yes, you."

The man finally looks up and we're able to see his face.

"Now!" she orders me in a loud whisper.

I quickly hold up my phone and take a picture, praying it isn't blurry.

So now what? Is Rose actually going to fight this guy? She's going to get flattened, and since she has information I need about the Key, I would prefer for that not to happen.

"Would you like to keep your face the way it is?" Rose asks him in a pleasant, friendly voice. That's what serial killers sound like, I bet. I study her out of the corner of my eye. Maybe she secretly *is* a serial killer. I'm suddenly not so sure I should be befriending this chick.

The man grunts, and my attention shifts back to him. He's staring at Rose with a look of disbelief. "You've got to be kidding me, right?"

At five feet away from him, Rose and I stop at the same time. How odd.

"I don't listen to threats from little girls," he snarls, pulling his hood away from his face and clenching his fists. Rose's face darkens, and her features contort into a snarl. Note to self: calling Rose a little girl makes her mad.

I sneak another picture. This one clearly shows the guy's black crew cut, menacing jawline, and beady little eyes.

Rose recovers quickly. "I don't listen to threats from people who don't even have two brain cells to form a coherent thought."

Mystery Man grinds out, "You don't know who you're messing with."

"I know exactly who I'm messing with." She crosses her arms, and stands up straighter. "A big dunderhead who's going to fight with brute strength. He has little to no agility, and he thinks he can scare anyone into doing what he wants. And by the way? *You're* the one who has absolutely no clue what you're getting yourself into." Rose has such a nasty expression that I'm slightly scared for the man picking a fight with her; he looks a bit taken aback too.

Cue Rose's triumphant smirk. "Now who knows more than who?"

His eyes narrow again and he takes a half-step forward. "I'm fighting a little girl who's all bark and no bite, and she will run away screaming"—he flicks his wrist and a knife appears—"or have her boyfriend fight for her after the first punch."

"Oh, good," Rose says in a syrupy voice. "You do have enough brain cells to put together a metaphor." She pulls the long hunting knife out of her boot for the second time today. Its blade gleams wickedly in the day's fading light. "I know 'metaphor' is a big word with more than two syllables, but don't worry. I gave you a compliment. Sorry, that was another big word. A 'compliment' is a nice thing for me to say to you."

The man lunges at Rose. She dances sideways, and he slashes at thin air. A wicked smile forms on her face. She sidles up next to me and puts her hands behind her back, seemingly relaxed, with the knife dangling carelessly from her fingers.

Realizing he missed, the man snarls. Rose's expression brightens. The man adjusts his grip on his knife and tries to stab her. Again, he fails miserably. Rose just slides to the side really fast, and he blows right past her. Man, she's quick.

I relax a little bit and enjoy Rose's performance. And carefully stay out of their way.

The jerk's frustration grows as he misses her again and again.

Rose shakes her head. "Dude, I can see your foot move before your arm. You should lead with your weapon. It gives me less time to react."

He gets angrier with every word she says and continues to viciously lunge at her.

On his next attempt, Rose grabs his outstretched arm, twists it behind his back, contorting it into a shape I thought impossible for a human arm to bend, and forces him to his knees. He drops his knife with a yelp. Ouch.

What just happened? He's twice her size, and she took him down like it was no big deal. I'm dumbfounded.

"'Nighty night," Rose says before putting him in a choke hold. Two seconds later, his body slumps onto the dirty pavement.

This girl is very skilled. And violent.

Yawning, she says to me, "Sorry, I got bored."

I stare after her as she walks—more like swaggers—down the street, her long, blonde ponytail swishing from side-to-side with each step. "You coming?" she calls back.

I close my gaping mouth and catch up with her—which isn't hard because she has to take two steps for every one of mine. "How did you manage to get a giant guy like that to his knees?"

"Fighting isn't always about strength; it's about leverage," she shrugs. "If you can put the biggest guy in the world in an arm lock or hit a pressure point, you will always have the upper hand. That arm lock I put him in hurts really badly, so when I pushed my foot into the back of his knee, he went down easily."

She looks me up and down and slows to a halt. "Considering you have strength on your side, you've probably never learned that, but for smaller people, however, it's quite important. Leverage and agility are the only tools we have to win a fight."

She takes off down the street again. I don't know why she chose to lead; she has no clue where she's going. I smother a chuckle. It'll be fun to watch her mess up, though.

Of course, when she reaches the street corner, she doesn't stop and wait for my directions. She keeps going around the block, in the wrong direction.

Ha! I knew it. "Do you even know where we're heading?" I yell from the corner.

"I'm sure I'll figure it out." She waves me off.

I roll my eyes. Time for the real leader to take charge. Besides, it's getting late, and we don't have enough daylight left for Rose to walk us all over kingdom come.

I jog around the corner and catch up with her, grabbing her arm and turning her around so we're going the right way. Rose comes along so smoothly, almost as though it was her idea, although she pulls away from me again.

"So, you have some fighting experience?" I ask casually.

"A little bit," she says nonchalantly.

That tells me nothing, and certainly not why she's so quick on her feet. "Since you're so fast, and I know you're not from Earth, what exactly are you?"

"A twelve-foot-tall purple giraffe," she replies in a snarky tone.

"You know what I mean. Are you some special-fighter type of person?"

"No. I just know what to look for that indicates a person is about to attack. And, when I'm on Earth, I use that to my advantage."

"Then what are you off of Earth?"

"My normal self, who is much faster and stronger than you humans are," she states, bragging.

I'm never going to get a straight answer out of her. I sigh. "Nice to know there's a superior species to humans. Makes me feel all warm and fuzzy inside."

"Don't worry. Once we come over here, we lose nearly all of our powers. It keeps the playing field level. Like, if you brought guns to Amara, they wouldn't work, and don't ask me why. I don't know. This happens everywhere, as far as I know. You can't bring anything to another planet that would enable you to take it over, but you can bring insignificant things." She grows more animated as she talked. "The biggest thing I've got through successfully is a CD player."

"What if I came to Amara?"

"You would have the same powers I do there. Anytime you go to another planet, you will be elevated to the standard of the planet, if necessary, so you blend in and don't get killed."

"So you're not really a superior species," I say, mostly to needle her.

"No, we are. Trust me."

"Hold on a second." I pause and so does she. "You didn't kill that guy, did you?" I don't want a murder on my hands.

"No. I just put him to sleep for a while."

wonder if all her people are as trained as she is. "So *were* you specially trained to be a fighter?" I ask.

"Nope."

She has to be lying. No one is this good at fighting unless they've been working on it since they were a kid. I mean, she's younger and a lot shorter than me, and she can take down opponents that I would have some difficulty beating.

I give up on the subject. If I learned one thing from that fight, it's that I'm glad Rose is on my side.

Chapter 10 – Rose

That confrontation with Mr. Follower turned out well, and I can tell I gained some respect in Derek's eyes. Respected people get places in the world. In any world.

Speaking of getting places, I used up all my brain power in that confrontation because, sadly, I only have that hitchhiking-to-Oregon plan to get home, which even Derek thinks is stupid and dangerous.

"Do you have any idea what we're going to do next?" Derek asks, as though he's reading my thoughts.

"Nope," I say, popping the *p* at the end, and staring at the ground in front of me. I'm really hoping he has an idea. I need to get back to the battle and help my people, even though I'm exhausted.

We turn a corner and now the buildings look more normal. Maybe a little run down, but not burnt to a crisp. The shadows are lengthening as the sun finishes setting.

"No plan? That's reassuring," he scoffs, sarcasm oozing from every syllable.

In a tone of mock hurt, I reply, "Your words wound me," and place my hand over my heart for dramatic effect.

He shakes his head. "Since you're lacking any great plans, I think we should go to a diner, get a cup of coffee, find somewhere to sleep, and figure all this out in the morning. I have a connection that will let us stay at his place tonight."

"By a connection, you mean a friend, right?" I ask, really hoping that he says *connection* for everyone he associates with. Connections equal people you don't completely know or trust, I've always believed, but you go to them anyway to get stuff (or because you owe them). Staying at a connection's house never turns out well.

Derek interrupts my thoughts. "No, I mean a connection, not a friend. It's not the greatest situation, but I'm out of money, and he'll loan me some."

Sounds suspicious. "Why would this guy give you money? And why in the worlds are we not just going to your house?" No one—especially a connection—just gives away money to a homeless guy, which I'm assuming Derek is since he didn't mention going to his own place, and he's carrying a backpack that's stuffed pretty full.

He avoids eye contact. "Let's just say my father is a rather imposing figure," he says vaguely. "And we're not going to my house because I said so, and I don't want to talk about that anymore."

But I think he should. "Care to elaborate?"

"Nope." He mocks me by popping the *p*.

It was worth a shot. "So where is this diner we're going to?"

A window with bars on it catches my attention as we walk past an old building. At least we are passing people now, even though they're freaky looking. Black clothes, bad posture, those skin-stamp things humans decide to cover themselves with. Sketchy part of town, not cool. How do I always manage to end up in these kinds of places?

Derek grabs my elbow and pulls me into the street. "The diner's just down a few blocks."

I quickly pull out of his grasp. I'm not really into people invading my space bubble.

Besides, something else is bothering me. "So if you know the area we're in, then why in the worlds did we end up hitting a dead end back there?" The confrontation with that burly jerk really could've been avoided.

"I was preoccupied," is Derek's extremely simple, really annoying, and totally unhelpful reply.

Hmm. "So how much do you know about the portals?" I ask, to keep him talking.

"Pretty much nothing, actually. So if we're going to come up with a plan, I'll need to combine your knowledge of the portals with what I know about Earth."

I sigh, then reluctantly agree. "When we get to the diner, I will teach you all you need to know about the portals."

A flashing sign down the street proclaims we're approaching a diner. Probably the one Derek is heading toward. "One question, though, before we get there. Did you ever use your Key before it broke last month?"

He blushes. "I didn't because I'm not entirely sure how, and I'm afraid that if I leave this planet, I'll be stuck somewhere else where the inhabitants might think I'd make a nice entrée."

Well, at least he's honest. "Most planets don't have inhabitants that will eat you. Well, actually, that's a lie. Most do," I say, thinking about it. "Except for a handful of special safe planets, but they're generally fairly boring."

"Like Earth," he says smartly.

"No, Earth has things that will eat you. Sharks, for example," I shudder. I'm not a fan of them.

Just as we reach the diner, he takes my hand in his and I about jump out of my skin. I throw him a pointed look, my face on fire and my hand tingling. I'm not exactly up to date on the whole relationship thing because I never really cared for having one, but I am pretty sure only couples hold hands. Besides, he's walking too close to me, and this is not okay.

I start to tug away but change my mind. Maybe it's an Earth thing I don't know about, but should.

"What are you doing?" I say under my breath.

He opens the door with his other hand and holds it for me. "If we pretend to be a couple, they'll give us the booth in the back where we can talk privately and not have people bugging us."

So . . . ? I'm confused.

He says quickly, "I'll explain when we're seated. Just try and look like you're happy."

Easier said than done. He pulls me inside. I do not like Derek's plan at all. Humans are weird.

"Table for two, please," Derek tells the server at the front.

Just as Derek said would happen, she smiles when she sees our clasped hands, and leads us to a back corner booth where no one is sitting.

"Perhaps you two would like some privacy?" she asks, making it seem more like a statement than anything else.

Derek looks at me warmly, and I try to smile back. I'm a good liar, but I don't know anything about being an actress, especially when I have to pretend to be happy with the invasion of my personal space.

Derek nods at her. "That would be lovely," he says warmly.

She leaves and we sit down across from each other. I quickly let go of his hand, as if it burns me.

"Explanation?" I ask, trying to calm my erratically beating heart and get my face to cool down. I am probably an awkward shade of red by now.

"You're blushing."

I glare, flushing harder and silently swearing revenge. Apparently public displays of affection are more than just an Amarian thing. "I don't exactly do PDA, especially with boys I've just met," I state, attempting to regain my dignity. Well, whatever is left of it.

"That wasn't exactly PDA in American terms," Derek eyes dance, and his lips turn up mischievously.

If that didn't count, what does? "Then what classifies?"

71

"I can show you." He leans across the table toward me.

I'm puzzled for a moment, but then I blush yet again when I realize what he means as his face gets closer to mine. Revenge, stone cold revenge, will certainly be in store. "I'll pass, thanks." I shove my palm in his face.

The idiot laughs and sits back in his seat.

"So why couldn't we just *ask* for a back booth?"

He grins. "Because this was so much more fun."

Oh, joy. This guy has a messed-up idea of fun. Cliff jumping is fun, holding hands is not. Playing pranks is fun. Holding hands is not. "Maybe for you, but for the rest of us, that was anything but fun."

"Liar."

A subject change would be great right about now. "So you really don't know anything at all about the Keys, or what they do, or about the portals?" I ask, switching gears to a more important—and comfortable—topic.

"Subject changer," he accuses before answering my question. "Well, I know the Key takes you to other planets that actually contain and sustain life. I also know that other people want the Key from me, like that creepy stalker guy from earlier today, I think. I don't know why else he would be following us. But, that's about it—that's all I know."

That reminds me. "You did get a picture of that guy, right?" Bad guys hate having their picture taken; I learned that in a movie I saw here on Earth one time. He had to be following us for a reason. There's no way he was randomly there in that deserted part of town. And Derek had said that some humans wanted the Key for bad reasons. I'm beginning to wonder if Mr. Follower knows something about the portals malfunctioning. If I can figure out who he is and follow him, maybe I can find out something about what happened.

It's a long shot, but it's the only one I have. Well, that and hitchhiking to Oregon.

"Ya, it's on my phone. Remind me to show you later. But please, help me out here with this whole Key business." He fiddles with the cup on the table.

"I have a lot to teach you," I sigh.

Footsteps approach and Derek grabs my hand from across the table. My stupid blush comes back, and I try to smile like a normal, happy person would. Too bad I'm not normal, and I am most certainly not happy.

Our waitress smiles, pen and pad in hand. "Hi! My name is Jessica, and I'll be your server today. What would you like to drink?" she says in an all-too-happy voice.

"I'll have a coffee." Derek smoothly flashes her a smile. For a guy who is supposedly in a relationship with me, he sure is grinning warmly.

Not that I care what he does; I just met him.

She turns to me. "And you, sweetheart?"

Who in the worlds says *sweetheart* anymore? "I'll have the same thing," I reply, then gaze at Derek again. My smile may be saying I'm happy, but I bet my eyes are shooting daggers at him for coming up with such a stupid plan when we could've just asked for a back booth.

"I'll be right back with that," Jessica says and walks off with a spring in her step.

"What does coffee taste like?" I ask him. I realize we're still holding hands, and I jerk mine away.

He laughs at me. "You'll see."

I hope I didn't just order poison.

Chapter 11 – Sylvia

"Why can't anyone figure out what happened?" I suppress a scream that would be inappropriate for a princess and settle for slamming my armoire door shut instead.

The poor maid looks scared so I remind myself that I shouldn't shoot the messenger. It's only been a few hours since Rose disappeared this morning during the battle with Lexi. I shouldn't be surprised that no one knows what happened yet.

No one knows where Lexi disappeared to, either. All we've heard is that the two of them were fighting, then everyone saw a blinding flash of light that gave off intense heat, and then they both left or vanished—no one really knows which. There is no evidence as to where or how they left—no footprints, no blood, nothing. All the army can find is an indentation in the scorched ground a few yards in diameter where Rose and Lexi were fighting. They are simply gone.

But that is impossible unless Rose used the Key, and she wouldn't have, not during a battle. It's interesting that after they disappeared, the enemy retreated. Although, for that matter, we did too. Everyone was too terrified.

Something makes me wonder if Lexi planned it, if she somehow caused that explosion and Rose's disappearance. Lexi could be out there, hiding, plotting her next move. After such a shock, our village is vulnerable and it would be very easy to attack us.

But the worst part is that Rose hasn't returned, nor have we heard anything from her. Without a Key, spontaneous and totally random interplanetary travel has never happened that I know of. So she's got to be here on Amara . . . but if she were, she should be back by now. Amara isn't a very big planet, and it would only take a couple of hours for her to send a messenger pigeon our way. She would have done so by now if she was able to.

So, considering she isn't back, and we don't have a message from her, she's either seriously injured—or worse.

But that's not a possibility I'm willing to accept.

My thoughts race and collide with each other. I'm sick of the turmoil. I can't just sit here in the castle, doing nothing. Phoenix and I have to do something to find her.

Earlier I sent a maid to ask a messenger to get Phoenix from her house or, more likely, from Rose's. The two of us will brainstorm and discover exactly what in the worlds has happened. If we put our minds together, we can figure something out.

Another half hour passes. I stay in my room, waiting for Phoenix, staring blankly at my wall.

Crap! What the heck am I doing? I'm wasting valuable time. I should gather all the information we have and put it together. The pieces of the puzzle are bound to fit if I can just find them all.

I need information . . . and the best place to get information is the castle library. We certainly have enough books, and there's bound to be something pertaining to Rose's unusual departure.

I set out with determination for the library. When I pass a maid in the hallway, I'm reminded that Phoenix will need to know where to find me. "When Phoenix arrives shortly," I ask the maid, "can you please tell her to meet me in the library? I will be searching for any information that might help us solve Rose's disappearance."

"Of course, Princess." She curtsies and rushes down the hall.

When I reach the library's grand mahogany doors and quietly enter, there's not a soul in sight. Good. No one to interrupt me. I run my gaze around the large room and settle on the bookshelf on the far wall. I may as well start there. At least some of those books should contain information about missing warriors. After a couple of trips between the bookshelf and a large reading table, I realize there are a lot of tomes in the rather sizeable pile I have gathered.

Hmm. Phoenix and I are only two people, so how are we going to accomplish this research?

Something my mother says all the time echoes in my head: *In order to finish, you have to start.* I sigh and sit down at the table, opening the book on the top of the stack. I am in for a very long day.

But soon Phoenix arrives and silently sits down to my left, picking up a book. She nods at me. The maid must've passed along my message.

Sometime later, my father sits in the chair to my right.

What—?

Without a word, he grabs a book out of my stack and opens it.

I'm speechless. What is he doing here? I stare at him, probably looking at him as if he's grown another head. My father is a very impersonal man, and he won't usually take time out of his busy day—he's making sure the kingdom is prospering, he says— to help me with something. I was mostly raised by my mother. But don't get me wrong. I love my father, and I understand why he does what he does.

He notices my stare and calmly looks at me as though nothing is out of the ordinary. "I lost one of my best warriors today," he says in a quiet undertone.

Oh. I look back at the book in my hands. Of course he isn't here because I lost my friend. He's here because it will affect his military, having someone like Rose gone. My father likes to keep his Gold Squad functioning like the well-oiled machine it is.

I return my attention to the thick book in front of me.

A few minutes later, one of the maids comes in. My father moves out of earshot to talk to her in hushed tones. What are they discussing? It's probably not anything about Rose; otherwise, he would come tell me right away.

I shrug and get back to reading. My stack of read books is growing at a frustratingly slow pace.

Over the next few hours, people trickle into the library, go to the shelves, and pull out their own books to read. I don't pay them much attention. People come in all the time to read from our vast library.

But the flow of people doesn't stop; it only increases. And no one leaves. Some people are jotting down notes as they pour through the books, I notice. Not that that's out of the ordinary for children and young teenagers to do, but for older teenagers and adults who are no longer in school? Strange.

The next time I look up and glance around, it seems like a quarter of the population of Alethia is in the library. Then it hits me. They're here to help!

I didn't tell very many people about my research idea. "How did they know . . . ?" I say under my breath to my father.

"I commanded one of the maids to send a message throughout town. Your idea is a marvelous one," he nodded in approval, "fit for a future queen, my dear, and I was obligated to ensure that the town knew of your plan. I have already deployed Gold and Silver Squads to do a physical search for Rose."

Hearing that makes me proud I have pleased him. He isn't the kind of person to give out unnecessary compliments. Besides, it's good that they're out there searching for Rose; although I have the strangest feeling they won't find her.

I smile proudly at the industrious and caring Amarians. Although it's a bit weird, because I've never seen so many people so quiet. If Rose were here, she'd run through the room pretending to be a dragon or something childish to disrupt the general peace and to cause mayhem. I swear Rose feeds off of chaos. Mostly though, she just doesn't like it when it is quiet.

The silence emphasizes her absence. The emptiness rings in my ears and makes my stomach sink.

I finish the brown leather book I'd started, and move on to a smaller one bound in a deep-red leather. Unfortunately, my inner voice distracts me from the text. What will happen if Rose never comes back? Who will be the person who makes the quiet moments interesting? What will we do without her?

If I were in Rose's place, and missing, what would other people ask themselves? Would they wonder who will rule the kingdom next? Would they say I was never fit to run the kingdom anyway?

I glance over at Phoenix, who frowns as she reads a dusty old book. What would happen if she disappeared? Who would create beautiful artwork to decorate the history books and our buildings? Who would replace Phoenix's logical contributions to Rose's barely-thought-out plans?

My eyelids get heavy, and I shake my head to dispel the fatigue. I can't allow myself to be tired now. But the lack of sound lulls me to sleep. My eyelids droop again.

Okay, maybe just a quick rest for a few seconds, then I'll go back to reading. I slowly rest my head in my arms. Guilt floods me as soon as I close my eyes. I need to keep reading so I can find Rose and bring her back home.

But I am so worn out, and I can't even lift my head.

Stay awake and continue reading!

My internal battle lasts only a couple of seconds. I feel sleep creeping up on me. Before I succumb, I have only one thought.

Where are you, Rose?

Chapter 12 – Derek

The waitress sets our coffee down in front of us, and I wait for Rose to take a sip. She's either gonna love it or—

"Aargh! This stuff is vile," Rose exclaims, her cute little nose wrinkling in disgust. She viciously stirs her coffee with a spoon as if it would improve the taste.

"*I* think it tastes brilliant," I reply and take a giant swig of my own.

Rose makes gagging noises to emphasize her point. I ignore her. We need to get back on track to getting her home. "So, tell me all you can about your Key and how it works."

She looks at her coffee disdainfully and stirs it faster, creating a whirlpool. Smiling at it, she counters, "Fine, I'll tell you, as long as you get me something less poison-esque."

Her eyes sparkle when she looks up at me.

I nod. "Deal." That was relatively easy. "Now, bore me to tears with all the information you have." I clasp my hands together on the tabletop and get comfortable for a long lecture.

Rose returns to stirring her coffee like a normal person would. "First, I should probably cover the basics, so I don't confuse you with the more complicated stuff."

I notice her jab, but choose not to comment.

She takes a deep breath and begins. "To use the Key, you hold it in your hand and think of the place you want to go, which means you need to know what the other planets look like. We have a book of drawings back home that I use to go to places I've never been before. I'll assume you don't have a similar book because you don't appear to have a book on you at the moment and you would have to, since you're homeless," she says, her blue eyes glancing at my leather jacket and its standard-sized pockets. "Unless it's in your backpack?"

I narrow my gaze. "How'd you know I was homeless?" That's the second time she's said that, and it's not information I give out.

"Earlier, you didn't suggest we go to your house for the night. Instead we're going to a *connection's* place. Not to mention you seem to lack something called a job. People with houses have jobs, and people without houses lack jobs."

I slump in my seat and stare off into the distance. I'm not homeless by choice.

Rose's words break through my misery. "Getting back to using the Key, Derek, you have to picture the world you want to go to, and a portal will open up. I assume you know what a portal looks like . . . ?"

"No." I haven't got a clue.

"Oh, good grief!" Rose sighs loudly. I marvel at her impatience. She is worse than a five-year-old waiting to go to Disneyland.

"Well, basically, a portal is a bright ball of spinning light that kind of looks like it's on fire. Its color depends on where you're going. Amara's portal color is blue with random swirls of green. The portal to get to Earth is blue with random swirls of brown. So, to get to another world, you have to jump through said colorful ball of light."

She wants me to jump through a ball of fire? Is she freakin' serious?

She must see the expression on my face because she holds up her hand. "But don't worry. You won't get burned or anything. Portals are mostly harmless. Very weird at first. It's as if you're in the middle of a lightning storm—electricity everywhere. But you get used to it."

I nod. Okay, I guess I can handle it so far. Besides, if she can do it, I can too.

"Then you land where the portal takes you on that planet. It could be anywhere, but it shows up in the same place almost every time. If you go there once, you should know where you're going to end up each time after that. Amara, my home planet, for example, has a tree on the other side of Earth's portal so I always crash into it when I am coming back from Earth."

I laugh at the image of Rose hitting a tree.

"Not funny," she glowers. "It hurts. It's not my fault. The portal throws you out with the same amount of momentum you have going in, and I tend to take a running leap through."

I smother a grin and try to look sympathetic.

Her expression turns serious. "Occasionally, though, the portal's location is somewhere you don't want to be on a planet. You could be dropped off in the middle of an ocean, or a desert or, quite possibly, somewhere worse, but that's rare. That only happened to me once. I landed in the middle of the river and I got soaked from head to toe. It sucked. Anyway, there are a billion different worlds. I mean, the book I look through is huge."

"How big, exactly?" I ask. Why didn't I receive a book when I got the Key?

"Bigger than the biggest picture book you've ever seen," she replies, her eyes sparkling with mischief.

"So, naturally, as a teenager, you read picture books?" I match.

"Who told you I am still a teenager?" she quirks an eyebrow.

Aha. Now I'll find out if she is older or younger than me. "Well, you look about fourteen or fifteen. How old are you, actually?"

"I'm fourteen."

So she's a year younger than me. Hmm.

"Now, back to the portals. Anyone can go through them, so you have to be really careful about where you use your Key to open them and how quickly you shut them behind you. Trust me; it's not fun discovering a wide-eyed, frightened stowaway and having to return that person or creature to wherever it came from. Why anyone would decide to jump into a mysterious ball of light, I don't know, but it happens," she shrugs.

Crazy people. I wouldn't choose to jump through a mysterious ball of fire unless I knew a heck of a lot more about it first.

"Another difficulty," she continued, "is that if you incorrectly imagine the world you're going to—you mix up two of them, or get some big detail wrong—you get sent to the wrong world." Despite the fact that Rose is not drinking her coffee, she dumps a sugar packet into it. "I'm not really sure how that works, to be honest, because I've never done it myself, but as a safety precaution, don't go anywhere you're not sure about. I've heard stories about past Gatekeepers who have gotten stuck in this in-between place, almost like a void, but those are just myths as far as I know. Either way, it sounds like a not-so-fun thing."

Well, no duh. Clearly everyone wants to slowly rot away in limbo.

She holds up a cautionary finger. "One more thing: The Key can be used by anyone, but I don't generally lend mine out. Most people don't want it anyway, and everyone—except me—needs a traveling permit to leave Amara, so the Key is just not that big of a deal to people."

I'm shocked. "Really? People here who know a Key exists—and not a lot of people do—try to steal it from me. Does everyone where you live know about it?"

"Yes, everyone knows about it, but Amarians don't generally cause too much trouble. Not a lot of my people use sarcasm, either, like I do or go around stirring things up and creating mayhem. Basically, they can be very boring at parties."

She's got it easy! "Well, that would be a welcome change to what I'm dealing with. I wish I didn't have to change where I sleep every night just so people can't find me and steal the Key."

Surprise flashes across Rose's face, but it's gone as soon as it comes. "Hmm. Well, that's basically everything about portals. If I think of any other important details, I'll tell you."

Our discussion reminds me to be more vigilant. I glance around for anything that's out of whack or suspicious. The coffee is nice, but I don't like staying in the same place for any stretch of time.

Everything appears normal, but we should leave anyway. "Come on. I'll pay, and we'll go." I stand up and reach for my wallet.

"Wait, you never got me my less-vile drink," Rose protests.

I put money down on the table, but when I grab her arm to pull her to her feet so we can leave, she grabs onto the table.

"I'm not leaving yet."

The hair on the back of my neck tingles, and a sense of urgency suddenly overwhelms me. I try to pull her up, but she's stronger than I thought, and I don't want to hurt her. Of course Rose won't make this easy. How could I have thought otherwise?

"Are you really going to act like a two-year-old?" I ask impatiently, risking another look around the diner.

"If that's what it takes to get me a better tasting beverage, then yes. Something like that fizzy drink I had when I was here one time. The man who sold it to me called it 'zoda' or something like that."

Zoda? Oh, *soda,* probably. "Come on. That guy who followed us might come in here looking for coffee after he wakes up. We aren't that far from where he passed out."

"What about my fizzy drink?" Rose demands.

She's impossible! "You mean a *soda,* right? Because *zoda* isn't even a word."

"Soda! That's what it's called. I remember now."

"I'll buy you a soda at the counter as we're leaving."

I offer her my hand. She looks at it warily.

"We have to keep up appearances until we're out of here." I remind her. "We're a couple, remember?"

Rose takes my hand reluctantly. Her hand feels so small in mine.

She mutters under her breath, "Fine. As long as I get my soda, I couldn't care less."

At the counter, we wait for the cashier to come out of the kitchen, and I lean over to whisper in Rose's ear, "Liar."

I receive a look that would probably liquefy my kidneys if given the chance. I give her a cheesy smile in response.

The cashier appears. "So, should I ring you up now?" she asks me.

"We left some money for the bill on the table,   but—"

"I'd like some soda to take with me," Rose finishes my sentence sweetly. Gone is the ferocious look that said she wanted to punch me. What a good little actress, to switch from hate to love in a millisecond.

"What kind of soda?" The cashier taps keys on the register.

Expecting Rose not to have an answer, I reply for her. "Sprite, please."

The cashier nods and pushes a few more buttons. "A dollar fifty. Cash or credit?"

"Cash." I pull my hand free of Rose's and fish two dollars out of my pocket and hand them over to the cashier. I casually put my arm around Rose's shoulder. She stiffens slightly and shoots me a warning look out of the corner of her eye. This is really too much fun.

The cashier hands me back two quarters and a chilled Sprite from a little refrigerator under the counter. "Thanks. Have a nice day and please come again." Her smile is too big. Waitresses are always too happy.

"We will. You too," I reply.

Rose smiles at her, and then we both turn to leave, my arm still around her shoulder.

"I wanted a Mountain Dew," Rose complains as we walk out the door and onto the sidewalk.

"You don't need that much sugar," I tell her. I'm surprised she knows the brand names of soda but not what soda is called.

"Fine. I'll take Sprite," she says tersely. I hand her the can. She fumbles for a moment as she opens the can, then guzzles about half the drink.

The sugar must be helping because she looks up at me a lot more calmly. "Where to now?"

"We're going to see that connection of mine, remember?" I say, pulling Rose closer to me and using my arm to guide her down the darkening street. She gives my arm a very pointed look.

As soon as we're out of the sight of the diner she yanks my arm off her shoulder rather aggressively.

Ouch! "Geez, get violent much?" I question her, rolling my shoulder around. I think something cracked.

"No more plans like that, to have us be a couple. I've got a personal-space bubble I like to keep," she tells me sternly.

I get her point, but that doesn't mean I'm going to listen to it in the future. Rose's reaction is too entertaining for me to pass up any opportunities. Despite my aching shoulder.

"Oh, and I want my Key back," she adds.

"One of your wishes, at least, is my command, Princess. You can be in charge of the plans from now on, but I keep the Keys." She'll *think* she's in charge, at least, so that should solve some problems.

She flips her ponytail over her shoulder and looks away. "Whatever."

I'm too busy laughing inside to care. Taunting this girl is really too much fun.

Chapter 13 – Rose

I ignore Derek's cheap "Princess" taunt because I'd rather focus on the dimly lit street we're on. Anytime I'm away from Amara, I've developed this habit: I take in all my surroundings so I know exactly where to go if trouble arises (which happens quite a lot).

So far I've spotted a ladder up ahead, leaning against the wall of a large store selling food. The buildings are so close together that if I can just get to a roof, I can cross the city quickly.

"What if we took a car?" I ask, looking at the automobiles parked on the street.

"That's illegal."

"So that's a no?"

He gives me a pointed look.

"Okay then. I don't really keep track of laws on other worlds. I mean, when you have planets like Futdon where you can't walk on your feet, which is weird when the first half of your planet's name sounds like foot, it all gets a bit tedious to keep track of."

"Well, on Earth I'm keeping track and you're not stealing a car."

Sassy.

We walk without saying a word for the longest time. The diner's been out of sight for a good ten minutes now. Silence makes me uneasy. It's boring, slightly unnerving, and awkward. Needless to say, I think silence should be illegal, although I'm not sure how to enforce that rule.

Good grief, when are we going to get where we're going? "Exactly how far away does your friend live?"

"About twenty minutes from here on foot."

I heave a big, dramatic sigh that does me no good.

Bored again, I scope out escape routes: A bicycle that's been left unlocked outside a gas station. A bus that comes by every twenty minutes. A fire escape on an apartment building, and on the opposite side of the street, a skinny alley that leads who knows where—

Whoa, there are some scary-looking people leaning against the entrance to that alley . . . scary people with threatening looks on their faces and who are now walking across the street toward us, like they're going to assault us.

"You might want to walk faster," I whisper to Derek. "Four o'clock."

I catch him looking over his shoulder. "They won't bother us," he says confidently.

"How can you possibly know that?" I'm not sure he's in his right mind. He must have a few, or maybe a dozen, screws loose.

"That lead guy, Joey, that's the guy I told you about. My connection. I'm not sure what he's doing in this part of town, but he'll probably follow us all the way to his house just to try to scare you."

It's working. "Well, it's not working," I say with my arms stiffly shoved in my pockets. Who cares if I'm lying just a bit?

"It is too," he says, glancing at me out of the corner of his eye.

"Is not," I deny.

"Whatever." He gives up and shrugs.

Keeping an eye on the motley crew behind us, I continue to look for escape routes. I'll be ready just in case Derek is wrong about what his connection is up to. No one creepily follows people down the street at night just for kicks and giggles.

"Exactly where will we be staying?" I ask, to break the silence.

"We'll be staying above a car workshop."

I look at him blankly. A what?

"A car-repair shop is a place where the vroom-vrooms go to get fixed," he says facetiously.

The nerve! Why, out of all the people on this planet, am I stuck working with him? Couldn't I have gotten someone nice, and not sarcastic?

"I'm not five," I retort. "I know what a car is. You could've just said a place where cars are fixed."

"Just making sure. You don't seem to know a lot about Earth. Do you even have cars, or cell phones, or TVs? Anything that runs on electricity, by chance? You don't even have a watch on, although that doesn't surprise me."

I sniff and explain proudly, "Amara doesn't have electricity, and so we cannot run electronics for that reason. Besides, we don't want to destroy our world with global warming like you did with yours. We do have some things from the human world, like jeans and T-shirts. I introduced those on Amara because we needed a fashion upgrade," I rattle on. "We also have laser pointers—"

"Oh wow, that's *really* advanced."

I continue as if he hadn't interrupted me. "We got those because the old Gatekeeper thought they'd be useful for flashing signals to people far away, like during a battle."

Which reminds me of the warning Gold Squad flashed me when Hanaway and I met the giants. My worries resurface, and I can't help but think about my people, my planet. Is everyone okay? Did we win the war? Is it still going on a month later?

"So you got sucked here, a month into the future, during a war on your planet," he says, looking sympathetic.

"Pretty much. I was about to defeat my worst enemy too."

"Double bummer," he says, but his sympathetic look suddenly disappears. "But you can't possibly hate a person so much that you want to kill them." He looks irritated. "Why would you do that?"

I don't understand why this bugs him, so I turn away from his judgmental gaze and resume walking.

Maybe he's one of those World Peace people who try to make everyone get along and what not. The more I think about it, the angrier I get. "It's easy for you to say that. You don't know anything about my life. Judgment comes so easily to you humans with your close-minded brains."

Tears of sadness and frustration come to my eyes as I recall all the misery Lexi has caused me over the years. Not to mention that she could be ruining Alethia and all of Amara at this very moment, and there is nothing I can do to stop her.

My tears threaten to run down my face. But I can't let them show the weakness I've tried so hard to hide since I lost my parents. I take a deep breath. The last time I cried in public was my father's funeral, and I am not about to now.

Besides, I have more important things to be doing. And not just the battle. I have Victoria Coulee's book about Gatekeepers to read too. I can't afford to waste time here on Earth. First though, I need to get along with Derek if we have any hope of working together to get me home.

I silently promise myself that I will try harder to get along with him. Well, maybe not *get along with him*, but not bug him too horribly—at least, not to the point of him leaving me. As hugely as it pains me to admit, I really need his help. He's right—I don't know much about Earth. I need Derek to get me through everything until I figure out how to get home—or at least to Oregon.

Derek's voice finally penetrates my thoughts, but his actual words didn't sink in.

"What did you just say?" I look up at him.

Chapter 14 – Derek

I'm thrown off by the tears glistening in her eyes. Rose seems like someone who doesn't cry often, or at all. Besides, I have no clue how to deal with a crying girl.

Hmm. It's intriguing that Rose teared up when she mentioned her enemy. Clearly there's a good story here. Maybe she'll tell it to me and I can get to know more about what makes Rose tick.

She seems to be holding it together, so I prod her. "Why do you hate this person so much?"

She's quiet for a moment. "Um, what did you say?" she looks up at me, blinking rapidly, with a confused look on her face.

"What makes you hate your enemy so much?" I move a little bit to my left and away from her. Hopefully she won't beat up on me for asking that question, and if she tries, I'll be out of arms' reach.

"It's a long story," she says wearily.

"I've got time," I say, deliberately walking slower.

She slows down with me. "Fine. She stole my pet turtle and set him free," she tosses out.

Seriously? The spark of mischief has come back into her eyes. How does anyone change moods that fast? And how will I ever get a straight answer from her?

"Liar," I accuse.

"I'm not kidding. His name was Larry. I caught him at the pond near my house and convinced my parents to let me keep him. She stole him and set him free. I never forgave her."

Right. Clearly turtles cause wars. Between two females. Does she really think I believe that? "No one would steal a turtle named Larry."

"She was jealous that she couldn't catch a turtle, and Larry is a fine name for a turtle," Rose says haughtily. "Besides, I never lie."

"Okay, fine. But how can she *not* catch a turtle? They're insanely slow."

"Don't ask me. She clearly wasn't patient enough to wait for a turtle to show up in the first place."

"And you, of all people, were patient enough?" I ask, remembering her lack of it just a while ago.

"I'm patient for some things; like turtles, for instance. I'm just not patient with stupid people, or, really, with anyone from Earth. Not my favorite planet, to be honest," she says, shrugging her shoulders and avoiding my eye as I turn us left down a side street.

I glance back at the guys behind us. Yup, they turn as well.

"Tell me the real reason you hate her so much," I say, hoping I can wear her down into admitting the truth. And so I can distract her from the people following us.

"Would you believe me if I said she cut off half my hair while I was sleeping?"

"That's not something to go to war for," I scoff.

"When you're five, you go to war over anything you fancy. Don't you have siblings?"

"Nope."

"Great, no wonder you're so weird. You're a single child," Rose sniffs.

Is she insinuating there's something wrong with me? "What's wrong with single children?"

"Nothing," she says, trying to hide a smirk.

Now I'm annoyed. "Really, why do you hate this girl, whoever she is?"

"How about if I told you that she threw my pet rock in the lake?" Rose tries again.

Why am I yet again surprised at what she says? "You had a pet rock?" I ask, not bothering to accuse her of lying because, clearly, that's all she's been doing.

"Yes. His name was Bob."

"Your pets don't have very original names," I point out.

"I know. I name them the first thing that comes to mind: Larry, Bob."

I give up on the name issue. "Why would she throw your rock in the lake?" Can't that girl just get a pet of her own?

"She was jealous that I had gotten a pony for my birthday and that she hadn't. But she didn't even ask for a pony!" Rose groans. "I mean, really, that's just pure spite right there."

"How does a pony equal a rock for revenge?"

"Well, clearly she couldn't release my pony into the woods because then my father would be able to find him." Her condescending tone implies any idiot should've known that. Rose glances over her shoulder again.

"Right, so your rock got thrown in a lake," I laugh. "Well, that's a little unfair for your poor rock. Out of curiosity, what did you name your pony? Bill?" I ridicule her.

"No, I named my pony Flita," Rose says offhandedly. "Who would name their pony Bill? That's not a very good name for a pony."

"Like 'Flita' is any better?"

"Yup," she shoots back, popping her *p*. "It is."

She is infuriating. I'm getting peeved that she won't tell me. "Why do you really hate her?"

"I told you already."

"No, you didn't. You gave me a bunch of stories that aren't true, and that you thought I would believe."

"No, actually, I was under the impression you would *not* believe them. That's why I told you those stories," she says. Rose gets way too happy at other people's misery. "But everything I told you really is true."

"More lies are spewing from your mouth by the second," I accuse her. "Are you even capable of telling the truth?"

"I *am* capable of telling the truth, and I'm *not* lying. I would never lie; well, not *outright* lie. Just a little white lie maybe, every once in a while, and maybe I stretch the truth every now and then," Rose says.

Aargh! I decide to ignore her for the rest of the walk, and instead watch the gradual decline of the buildings around us. We've moved from the somewhat kept-up and borderline decent part of town to the truly run-down and shabby section. But I know my way around, and we're safe enough.

Rose doesn't realize this because she's worriedly looking at the neon lights and pothole-filled street.

"Are we there yet?" She seems to have forgotten about Joey and his buddies behind us. Maybe they will be able to scare her when we reach the car repair shop. At least I'd get a laugh out of that.

Serves her right.

Chapter 15 – Phoenix

I scan the top paragraph on the page and realize I have read the same passage multiple times. My mind drifts once again to the recent events here in Alethia.

When I arrived at the castle two days ago, a footman took the horse, and a servant walked me to the library and filled me in on what she knew. Rose had apparently been taken away via some sort of bright flash of light, and no one knew exactly where she was. Joining Sylvia's research efforts in the library was the best way to help Rose.

When Sylvia and I spoke later, we ruled out the possibilities of Rose being dead, or that she used the Key to disappear. If she had died, someone would have found her body, and if she had used the Key, she would be back by now.

The possibilities we are left with are that Rose is dead and there is simply no body to recover, or that the strange light transported her somewhere and she is not able to return home or contact us for whatever reason.

So now we are still stuck—miserably—at square one. No closer to square two than we were two days ago. No one has discovered any information on mysterious lights appearing during battle and spiriting away the combatants. We decided that if we had another Key, we could use it to go look for her. It might take a while, but it would be a place to start. So now everyone here in the library has added *Gatekeeper Key* to their list of things to look for.

"I found it!" a little voice shouts from the back of the cavernous room.

Everyone looks up, and I swivel in my chair toward the young girl who spoke. Her innocent brown eyes are full of surprise as she notices everyone staring at her. She quickly hides her face in her hands.

I grin. It is so easy to solve problems during childhood; if she can't see us, we can't see her. If only that kind of logic worked in real life.

The girl's mother puts a reassuring hand on her shoulder and strokes her plaited hair tied with a white bow at the end. How could such a young girl—maybe five years old—have found the answer to such a big problem?

"Sorry," the mother grimaces apologetically to the roomful of expectant faces. "She was looking for a lamb in a book."

A collective sigh goes up and everyone returns to reading.

The embarrassed mother grabs her daughter's hand and leads her out of the room. As they pass, I recognize the pair; it is one of the palace's maids, Maria, and her daughter, Mary. I can't help but overhear Mary ask her mother in that sweet voice children have, "Mommy, why don't we just make a new Key?"

I watch them retreat. The little girl probably does not understand exactly what is going on . . . but her question does give me an idea. Maybe, we *could* make another Key. At some point in time, someone, somehow, made the first one. If we were to figure out how they did that, and then make another one, we could use it to look for Rose.

That's it! *That's* what we should be looking for! Not *if* there's another Key, but how to *make* another one!

Information about the Key's origin should certainly be in these books. Which means that, instead of looking through every single book, we can narrow it down to just the history books or those written a long time ago. Why didn't we think of that before? It makes so much sense.

I rush to tell Sylvia.

She's at a separate table with the rest of the royal family and their servants—probably her mother's idea. And poor Sylvia. She's wearing formal princess attire—gown, tiara, everything—and looks completely out of place, but again, I'm sure this is her mother's doing.

Sylvia looks up at me, relief crossing her face.

Because her mother is here, I follow protocol for addressing a royal. "May I speak to you, Princess?" I say in my most polite tone and then curtsy to her.

It's all so weird for me, but I was raised to know that this is what I have to do. I usually act quite naturally around Sylvia, but today I'm forced to act like everyone else does in the presence of royalty.

She gives me a small, regal nod. "Yes, you may now speak." I can tell Sylvia feels uncomfortable being so formal with me, too.

I lean over and whisper in her ear, "I overhead that little girl asking her mother why can't we *make* a new Key, and it gave me an idea: Let's search the history books to find out how the first Key was created. And then we can replicate the process. Rose taught you how to use the Key when she first got hers, so if we can make one, we can look for her!"

Sylvia's face lights up and she leaps to her feet, then clears her throat. "May I have your attention, please?" she says, broadcasting her voice so it travels to the back of the room but doesn't sound like she's shouting.

Everyone looks up from what they are reading and gives her their attention.

"A friend of mine has just suggested that we look into the Key's origins to discover how it was made. Then, once we have that found out, we follow up by making a new one. So instead of trying to find a second Key that likely does not exist, we simply make a new one."

Most people look skeptical at her suggestion, and I can see the slight tension in her face that probably is not noticeable to anyone who does not know her well. She's not liking the way everyone is looking at her, as if she is making an impossible suggestion.

She speaks out again, her voice determined, "It is a long shot, I agree, but I am sure that with this many people looking, we can come up with information on the subject." She forces a smile. "I thank you for your assistance."

Some people murmur and nod in agreement now.

Encouraged, Sylvia continues, "Now is the time to attempt what we have never done before," she says firmly and with conviction. "This is the day we set out to make another Key. Not only to bring Rose home, but to be ready if this were to happen to someone else. I urge you all to join me. I am confident the information on the Key's origin is in one of these books, and if we just look hard enough, we *will* be able to find it."

The last part of her speech was said with such passion I think no one in this room doubts Sylvia's abilities to lead anymore. Sylvia's mother is smiling at her daughter. It's the kind of speech-giving that she has been teaching her daughter all these years: straight, to the point, and politely combating arguments before they come up.

Sylvia sits down, triumph and relief battling on her face. People talk quietly with each other and exchange notes and ideas with renewed energy, their heads nodding.

"Excellent job, sweetheart," the Queen says to Sylvia while smiling and putting a hand on her shoulder.

Sylvia glows under her mother's compliment. "Thank you, Mother."

Sylvia shoots me a look of gratitude, and I leave her with a curtsy to return to the bookshelves to gather historical texts.

I jump, startled, when someone walks up behind me. It's Collin, and he picks up the books I've taken off the shelves. Gratefulness flows through me.

He whispers, "I know that was your idea, Phoenix. It was very clever. Good job."

Smiling to myself, I continue searching the shelves. A book with a red cover, titled, *Great Discoveries and Creations of Our Time,* catches my attention, and I place it in Collin's arms. After gathering a rather sizable stack, Collin easily carries it back to my table and places it in between my chair and another one.

So, he's here to help, and he's choosing to sit next to me. I resist the urge to grin like an idiot. We each pick up a book, and I smile at him in thanks. He returns the look and we get down to work, studying in silence. His friendly and supportive presence reinforces my commitment to this project.

I am determined that the next twenty-four hours will be better than the last forty-eight have been, and that we will get closer to locating Rose. Most importantly, though, we will bring her home.

That's all that really matters right now.

Chapter 16 – Hanaway

I can't believe Rose Sanders is gone!

I mean, I was there, on the cliffside overlooking the battlefield, and I saw it, but wow. I didn't think something like that was possible.

When it first happened, I thought Lexi had made them both disappear. But when I arrived at the library two days ago, the general consensus was that a portal somehow caused Rose's disappearance.

I wanted to going the Gold and Silver Squads in looking for Rose, but the general wouldn't let me. I definitely could've helped, but he wouldn't even give me the chance. So, I had to settle for helping to find Rose another way.

As soon as I could gain access, I checked the Book of Portals in the War Room to see if an annual portal could have taken Rose, because we don't need Keys for those. But no portal was scheduled to show up in the valley or anywhere near it on that day.

I told Princess Sylvia and Phoenix what I found. They wrote it down in their notes and thanked me. I'm not sure if they've done anything with that information, but at least they have it.

But then last night, I decided to check the book again to see if any portals are due to appear soon. Because if one is, and it turns up as it normally does, then we would know the annual portals are working properly.

I found out that a portal was scheduled to appear near my house this morning, and it did, just as the book predicted. So I think the annual portals are still working. I didn't go through the portal, of course, because I didn't have a travel permit. It was odd, though. It wasn't pink and purple like it was supposed to be. Instead it was a mixture of every color imaginable.

That was hours ago. Since then, I've been in the library. I glance at the towering pile of scrolls on the table in front of me.

When I first arrived here the other day, it dawned on me—no one was keeping track of what books were being read. Everyone was simply reading, and no one was organizing. We needed a system so people wouldn't overlap each other's efforts.

Figuring out a system was easy. On the end of each bookshelf is a scroll that lists which books are on the shelf, and where exactly on the shelf they are. So with Princess Sylvia's permission, I gathered the scrolls, recruited help from my aunt, Ami Brant, and set up a check-in table of sorts. Aunt Ami and I made a master list from all the individual scrolls, so when someone is done with a book, they come to one of us and we cross that book off the master list. That way, we will be able to cover the most information as efficiently as possible.

I'm actually rather surprised no one thought of this before I did, and that the palace didn't already have a comprehensive list of the library's contents. But it's a time-consuming task that we're actually not done with yet, so maybe that's why.

But now that the Princess announced her new plan a few moments ago, everyone will search only the history books and those written a long time ago. So we can cross off a lot of items on the master scroll that don't need to be read. Which means a lot less work for my aunt and me.

I'm excited as I pick up the scrolls we no longer need. "Auntie, can you help me take back the scrolls that aren't for the history books?"

"Of course," she says, snatching up a big pile in her tanned arms. "Just the history ones stay here, right? And the books written a long time ago?"

"That's what the Princess says to do. I think it's a brilliant idea." I follow her to the closest set of bookshelves with my own armload.

My aunt returns the scrolls in their holders and tucks a strand of graying hair behind her ear. "I do too. Hopefully we'll be able to find Rose. She does bring a *certain* energy to a room."

I reply confidently, "I'm sure we'll find her, or she'll find us. Rose Sanders would try her hardest to get home, no matter what it takes. After all, she was the first girl to join Gold Squad, which certainly takes determination."

"Yes, it does, and I know you'll soon follow that same trail she blazed." My aunt smiles, the laugh lines in her face deepening.

My cheeks warm at the praise. If only I could follow in Rose Sanders's footsteps someday. That would be so cool!

But I immediately sober. We have to find her first, though. I'm not doing anything else until we do.

After we put away the unnecessary scrolls, there aren't many of them left. It certainly won't take two of us to manage this check-in task. "Auntie, I think I can handle the scrolls on my own if you'd rather do something else. Do you need to go home and work on your paintings?"

"It's okay, dear, I need to wait for the paint to thoroughly dry on my current painting anyway. Besides, I was never one for reading much, so I'll sit here and leave it to you to join in the search."

Excellent! Now I can do more to help.

I start to walk toward a bookshelf to gather my own stack of books, but it occurs to me that my aunt is also a source of information.

"How much do you know about portals?" I ask her as I sit back down at our table.

She looked pleasantly surprised that I would ask her. "I know quite a bit, Nolana. Why, everyone was popping in and out of portals back in my day. We didn't need permits to travel, nor were there any of the restrictions we have now, so it was in everyone's best interest to know as much about the portals as possible because we used them so often." She pats my hand and looks at me inquiringly. "Why do you ask, dear?"

"I want to make sure all my facts are right." If I'm going to help find creative solutions to our problem, I need to know every detail relating to the portals. I can't come up with solutions to a problem I don't fully understand, and it feels like we're overlooking something. Her disappearance has got to be related to a portal. If Gold and Silver Squads couldn't find her after a few days chances are she isn't even on Amara anymore.

I take a deep breath, "Can you listen to me while I go over what I know about portals, and you can tell me if I'm right or not?"

"Of course." My aunt settles back in her leather chair.

"Okay, so portals take us to other worlds, and Rose Sanders uses the Key to open them. But there are portals that show up at certain intervals that don't need the Key in order to appear." I pause.

My aunt nods her head encouragingly.

"And when we go through the portals—any portal—we are changed to match that planet's standard for what their people look like . . . right?"

"Only physically," she reminds me. "Mentally, we stay the same. We are still able to sense if our family members are nearby, for example, and to know if one of them is lying to us."

Right. I forgot that part. Mental stays, physical changes. Next question. "Each portal has a specific color, right? An indicator that helps someone figure out which planet it will take them to. And the portals will drop you off at the same spot each time on a particular planet?"

My aunt furrows her brow. "Well, on the rare occasion, portals have been known to move for—as far as we know—no particular reason."

What? This is the first I've heard about portals moving. "You mean *anywhere* on a planet? So you could die falling out of a portal because you landed somewhere dangerous?" What if that's what happened to Sanders?

My aunt leans forward reassuringly. "They are always close to the ground, Nolana, so we don't need to worry about falling. However, if it's an ocean or desert you land in, you can get in a bind quickly. But you won't die from the fall."

Okay, well, that's good. But something is nagging at me . . .

"Wait! You just said each portal has its own distinctive color? I didn't know that!"

"Yes. No two portals have the same exact color or blend of colors."

Oh, this is great news! I jump up excitedly. "That's it! We just need to figure out what color the portal was that took Rose, and we can figure out what planet she went to."

"Oh, very clever, my dear." My aunt beams proudly. "What color was the portal when you saw the flash of light?"

My happiness dies and my shoulders slump. "I looked away from the portal because it was so bright. I have no idea what color it was."

But maybe someone else remembers. There are plenty of warriors in the library. "Let me go ask around and see if anyone saw."

"I'll be here," she smiles encouragingly. "Let me know what you find."

I make a beeline toward the nearest table of warriors. They're Silver Squad, I think.

"Did anyone by chance see if the bright light that took Rose away had a color?" I ask them nervously, not sure if I should follow military protocol or not. We are all technically civilians right now, but they are all higher rank than me.

They look at each other, shaking their heads. Well, it was worth a shot.

Then a younger guy, Seth, who has brown hair and angular features, pipes up. "I saw it. It was blue with random swirls of brown in it. Really bright. I thought I was going blind."

One of the other boys chimes in, "Seth, looking at bright lights is yet another reason why you are a certified idiot."

"Ya, ya, save me the taunting," Seth retorts, then turns back to me. "Why do you ask?"

"Seth, you are my savior! Thank you so much! You may be an idiot according to these guys," I gesture at the others at his table, "but you may have just helped us figure out where Rose Sanders is." I dash away to find the Princess.

Behind me I can hear Seth's friends break out in excited conversation.

Chapter 17 – Sylvia

Phoenix's suggestion on how to get Rose back makes me hopeful, at least for the time being, and my successful speech leaves both my mother and I pleased. I know it wasn't the best speech ever given in the history of Amara, but my mother is elated because I actually did it, and in front of a sizeable crowd, too.

I open the cover of the first history book in my new pile, and then the second one. *Crap.* The older volumes don't have a table of contents. Without one, I'm going to have to skim every single page of every single book. I never liked school, especially since I had How-to-Be-a-Perfect-Princess lessons on top of regular classes.

I sigh loudly and close the book's cover harder than I should, then intercept a meaningful glance between my mother and Evelyn, the personal servant assigned to me by my mother to make sure I'm behaving properly in public. Evelyn quickly heads in my direction.

Double crap! From previous experience, I know this means I am about to be removed from the room before I embarrass myself or my mother. So much for basking in Mother's approval of my speech.

Evelyn curtsies respectfully. "Perhaps you need to get some rest, Princess? You have been up for quite a while now."

"I think I need to search for clues to help my best friend," I say curtly, trying to keep my voice down.

Out of the corner of my eye, I notice my mother staring sternly at Evelyn with a look that says she's not to back down.

The maid turns back to me reluctantly. "I must insist that you have at least a short nap, Princess. It is only in your best interest that I suggest it," she says softly, lightly placing her hand on my shoulder.

It's all I can do not to shrug off her touch. Instead, I silently weigh the pros and cons of arguing with her.

Triple crap. There's no use fighting this battle. The benefits of sleep clearly outweigh the cons, and add to that how angry my mother will be if I don't follow orders, so I capitulate. "I see what you mean now," I grind out through clenched teeth. "A nap will help me think clearly and come up with better solutions to our issue."

Evelyn removes her hand from my tense shoulder. I think she is just glad she doesn't have to keep choosing between my mother's orders and mine. Not that it should be a hard choice; obviously, listening to the Queen is best, but the maid is young, ever so polite, and doesn't like disagreeing with me.

Suddenly, Nolana Hanaway rushes up to me and curtsies, a look of unadulterated joy on her face. Her words tumble out. "Princess, permission to speak?"

This must be good news. My mood instantly soars, and a smile spreads across my face. "Permission granted."

"Princess, I have been talking to the other warriors, trying to discover what color the light was that took Sanders away." Her words tumble out. "I have just learned that portals have colors that correspond with their destination, and I was hoping to use that to help us discover where Rose went. A Silver Squad member, Seth, saw the light and said it was blue and brown. I do not know what planet that portal belongs to, but whichever planet it is, I believe that Rose is there."

My heart just about leaps out of my chest with joy—

But my mother suddenly appears next to me, cutting off my plan to figure out which portal it was. "Dear, it's time for you to go rest." She turns to Nolana. "Whatever you need to talk about with the Princess can wait until later in the day."

Nolana curtsies respectfully, and reluctantly leaves.

Should I tell my mother Hanaway's news? Again I weigh the pros and cons of returning to my room. No, I'll go, fake sleep for *maybe* an hour, and try to get a hold of Phoenix so we can figure out which portal it is. This is too important to leave to anyone else.

With my nose slightly in the air, I nod briefly to my mother and father as I pass them on my way out. Evelyn follows me down the hall, which is annoying. I was hoping she would give up once I left the library.

"Would you like me to get you anything, Princess?" she asks as she walks briskly behind me.

"I would like to be left to sleep." I pick the politest way to say what I'm really thinking—that I just want to be left alone—as I walk into my room and firmly shut and lock the door behind me.

Ha! That'll show her I don't need to be babied. Without even changing clothes or removing my shoes, I flop on my giant red bed in the middle of the room, sinking into its plushness. It really does feel good to lie down.

Trying to collect my racing thoughts and plan my next step, I realize my eyes are closing and there's nothing I can do about it.

I dream over and over of the death of Rose's father. Then Rose's disappearance enters my dream. Then I bounce back to the wailing and agony of Rose's mother as she's told her husband is missing and presumed dead. Then the shock and fear on the palace maid's face when she told me what happened during the battle a couple days ago. And, most hauntingly, what could be happening to Rose right now. Different scenarios play out of Rose on various planets, fighting for her life. Or worse, Rose lying on the ground, her eyes staring blankly into an unfamiliar sky.

Dreaming these scenes over and over is torture, but I can't wake myself up. Something is keeping me glued to these events. It's like my subconscious has a morbid fascination with watching the more distant past, and intertwining it with the possibilities I've tried to ignore about Rose's disappearance.

Thankfully, voices in the hallway outside my bedroom door halt the rerun of tragic events cycling through my head. Despite the quiet tones the two speakers use, I'm wide awake, so I sit up.

Evelyn tells someone, "I ask that you please leave the Princess alone." Oh my goodness! She hasn't left her post at my door? Does she have anything better to do than babysit me?

Phoenix's voice floats through the door. "It is very important that she is informed of this new development immediately."

"I must insist you leave," Evelyn's voice leaves no room for arguing, yet still maintains that polite tone necessary in her position.

There's a moment of quiet while I'm sure Phoenix decides what to do. "I'll leave then. Sorry to disturb you." Her footsteps fade down the hallway.

I punch the pillow. Phoenix gave in way too easily.

I get out of bed, trying to shake the aftereffects of the dream. A terrible feeling settles in my stomach, telling me I'm missing a very important point. What that point is, I have no idea.

I fix my hair in the mirror so it isn't all tangled and gently set my tiara back on my head. I can practically hear my mother's stern lecture: "Princesses are supposed to look and dress properly at all times. They are supposed to be setting an example, and not look like sloppy teenagers."

Never mind that that's exactly what I am, but it's another one of her innumerable rules. I can say all of them backwards and forwards if I want to.

Clink, clink, clink.

Something softly hits one of my windows. I throw the window open and a small pebble promptly hits me in the face.

"Ouch," I squeak before I realize I should be quieter.

"Sorry!" Phoenix's loud whisper reaches me from below. Okay, now I've identified my rock thrower. I should have known she'd not give up so easily.

"It's okay. What's going on?" I inquire, raising my voice enough so she can hear me but not enough that Evelyn can.

"We need to talk," Phoenix calls quietly as she emerges from her hiding place. "I just thought of something really important."

I quickly think of a plan. "Climb the tree up to the balcony below mine, and then I'll reach down and pull you up."

Without another word, she does as I suggest.

Once she's carefully balancing on the railing of the balcony below me, she reaches up. I lean down and our fingertips barely touch even though she's standing on her tiptoes. She looks like she might fall at any second.

Crap. This is not my best idea. Whenever I sneak back into the palace, I use the balcony below and then finish my journey by going through the inside of the castle.

"I think we underestimated the height between the two balconies," Phoenix gasps as she tries to stretch farther, even though she's swaying.

I wrap my legs around two of the railing's support posts and slide a little more over the edge. I can just grasp her hands in mine.

"One..." I say slowly.

"Two..." she replies. It's an old tradition of ours to count this way.

"Three," we say at the same time, and I heave up on her hands, and Phoenix tries her best to jump up from the railing.

Straining, I pull her up enough so she can grab onto the railing, then swing her legs up. Phoenix nimbly hops over the balcony railing to safety.

"Well, that was a workout," she pants as she stands and stretches her arms. "Why couldn't you just come down?"

I stare at her. How very like Phoenix to simply trust that I would come down if I could, and that therefore she had to come up.

I give her a quick hug and ignore my aching arms. "I'm supposed to be asleep," I reply after taking a deep breath and letting it out. "Oh, and remember to be quiet. Evelyn is still out there. I heard you talk to her earlier. What did you find? And I have something to tell you, too, that Hanaway figured out!"

"Come on, let's sit down. It's a long story if I want to fully explain my thoughts." She leads the way into my bedroom and pats a spot on the bed beside her.

My stomach is knotted in anticipation as I sit and fold my legs under me. I hope what she has to say will give me one of the missing pieces to the puzzle, and maybe help me to interpret my unsettling dreams.

"Here's what I think," she begins.

Chapter 18 – Rose

"*This* is where we're staying tonight?" I exclaim, looking at the dinky, dilapidated building in front of me.

Oops. I spin around and look at the guys following us. They're still several yards away. One of them is the owner—Joey, I think Derek said—of this decrepit building. They all look rough around the edges, like personal hygiene is very low on their priority list.

I turn back toward the building and study its filthy walls and the windows with bars on them. "People trust that dude not to steal their cars?" I ask Derek in an undertone.

"I heard that," a gruff voice says from right behind me. I jump slightly and Derek snickers, so I elbow him in the side as we turn around. The guy who spoke is tall, bulky, and has greasy brown hair. And sort of a stupid look on his face. But he's evidently faster on his feet than I gave him credit for.

He says out of the corner of his mouth, "How much longer you gonna stand there, Derek? Huh? I hope you have what you owe me. I could be out with my buddies at a party tonight if it weren't for you." His friends grunt goodbye to him and continue down the street.

"I don't have what I owe you, Joey, but I will pay you back." Derek puts his hands up and warns him, "If you push me, though, I will not hesitate to call my father. I have information about where you acquired the parts for your cars that he'll find interesting."

Oh, right, cue the imposing father figure who I know nothing about, I snort to myself. Apparently, I'm the only person in this city missing that tidbit of information.

Joey snarls, "If you don't pay me back soon, I guarantee something bad will happen, and your daddy won't be able to help you."

Derek's eyes widen, and he nods. I feel him withdraw, almost as if he took a step back. Why does that threat scare him? I'm surprised Derek would show any fear in front of this uncouth jerk.

The man brushes past us and pauses at the door of the building. "Well, come on in, then," he says grudgingly, his threatening tone gone now that he has apparently gotten his point across and Derek is suitably cowed.

I shoot a withering glance at Derek. Huh. I'm not impressed.

The man unlocks the door and Derek follows him inside. I slowly enter the building, unsure what to expect.

Harsh overhead lights blink on. My nose is hit with the horrible smell of human sweat and dirty machines.

"This place could use some air freshener," I mumble.

I look around. No one else is here. Three old cars are parked with the fronts open. Numerous tools lie around on the floor and others are strewn across the messy workbenches ringing the room.

But in the place where a fourth car could go, I spot the most wonderful human invention ever—in my opinion.

I wander over to it. "So, you play much poker?" I ask conversationally. Two decks of cards and a whole lot of scattered poker chips nearly cover the top of the poker table.

"Yeah. Some say I'm the best player in this city," the man boasts. He joins me at the round, felt-covered table.

Pride cometh before the fall. I smirk.

"Well, then, we'll have to play. I haven't played poker in a while," I say as I lightly pat the table.

Derek gives me a what-do-you-think-you-are-doing look. But I ignore him, sit down, pick up a deck of cards, and glance inquiringly at my opponent.

"Fine with me. I don't mind taking more of Derek's money," the man says, sitting across the table and rolling up the sleeves on his grimy shirt.

"So, you're Joey, right?"

"Yup." He looks me up and down, then glances questioningly at Derek. "You in?" He indicates the cards.

"I don't gamble," Derek says, his arms folded across his chest and his eyes blazing at me.

"That's okay. I'll gamble enough for the two of us. Besides, we need a dealer." I toss the cards towards Derek. "And, Joey, even though you didn't ask, my name is Rose. You're going to want to remember that for when people ask who beat you." I say it playfully, but I do mean it.

The guy grunts, then lights up a cigarette. Filthy things.

I make my first move before the game even begins. "Of course, Joey, we should back our chips with real money, don't you think? It will make it a little more interesting."

Joey pulls out his wallet. "Yup. Let's do it."

I smirk as I separate and stack the scattered chips in front of creepy Joey and me. "Derek, you want to give me the cash so I can play?" I ask him, holding out my hand.

"Derek, I'm shocked," Joey guffaws and I see how yellow his teeth are. Disgusting. "Your little girlfriend's a gold digger. I thought you had better taste than that," he adds amid gales of laughter.

Derek leans over to whisper in my ear. "What are you doing? Do you even know how to play poker? And may I remind you I don't have a lot of money?" he says with barely suppressed irritation.

"Trust me," I whisper back.

Derek sighs, straightens up, and pulls out his wallet. He hands me what I assume is his remaining cash, since his wallet is now empty.

I put the money next to my chips and smirk as Derek takes a seat and deals the cards.

After an hour of my well-placed verbal jabs and witty banter to distract my opponent, it's clear to all three of us that the city has a new best player.

I'm not at all surprised I won, but I was a little worried that my poker skills would be rusty. It's been a long time since I learned how to play the game as a way to learn about Earth money. It turned out to be easy. Pretty much all I have to do to beat most people is be an exceptionally good liar, which just so happens to be my specialty. Not to mention I learn valuable information on their ability—or inability—to lie.

Ol' pot-bellied Joey is sweating and angry right now, and I don't feel like pushing it. I lazily stretch my hands above my head and throw in my cards. "I think I'm done for the night," I say nonchalantly.

Joey grunts. I take that as agreement.

I count up my chips and play with them while grinning; okay, so maybe I am pushing it just a little.

Derek collects all the cards and puts them into a pile, then rises and tugs his backpack over one shoulder. I pick up all the money next to my chips and stand, stuffing the cash in my pocket.

I walk around the table. "I present to you the highest of fives," I say in a mock regal tone and stick up my hand, high-fiving Derek.

Derek shoots a worried look in Joey's direction, probably due to my blatant bragging, but nonetheless, he high-fives me back.

"Well, I'd love to stick around ..." I say to the glowering Joey. "But seeing as we now have enough money to get a hotel room for the night, we'll be taking our leave."

He leaps to his feet, his teeth clenched and his posture rigid. "I believe Derek still owes me money."

I glance between the two men and judge the distance to the door. Nope. Not possible to make a run for it—not with the need for Derek to be aware of the plan before I put it into action. For the moment, I don't question Derek as to why I need to hand over some of my well-earned money to this loser on Derek's behalf. That question will be directed at him later. That, and all the ones that are piling up in my mind about his father.

I pull the cash out of my pocket and hand it to Derek. Derek throws some of it on the table, keeping his eye on Joey the entire time.

"There you go. Now we don't have to call my father, and I no longer have to associate with you," Derek snarls. "Goodbye."

I walk toward the door, not even trying to squelch my laughter.

Joey jumps to his feet, shaking, and splutters as he tries to say something.

I call happily over my shoulder, "We'll have to play again another time." I can feel his eyes glaring at my back.

Derek opens the door for me and I walk out, when I remember something from the earlier conversation. Popping my head back inside, I yell, "And, by the way, I'm not his girlfriend, and I'm not a gold-digger!" I take off down the street—giggling. Sometimes I even surprise myself.

Derek lopes along beside me and chuckles at my behavior. "Was it necessary to make that point?"

Still giggling, I slow down to an excited skip. "Yes. Yes, it was. People should know not to make assumptions about other people. It comes back to bite them. Besides, that was really too much fun," I say merrily. The night isn't as cold as I thought it was going to be. It's actually rather warm.

"Well, I guess you're right. And that game *was* entertaining. I have never seen Joey at a loss for words, or really, at a loss for anything."

I snigger. Ruining stupid people's winning streaks is enjoyable.

"So what's the plan for spending this wonderful money that I have so amazingly acquired?" I ask, following Derek as he steps off the curb to cross the street.

"Well, Miss I'm-the-one-making-the-plans, I'm thinking that we should get you a change of clothes. I have clean clothes for myself in my backpack." He hitches the strap higher on his shoulder. "After that, we hit a pay-by-the-hour motel, because they're cheaper and fewer questions are asked. We sleep for a few hours and then figure out where to go from there," he says, not breaking stride.

His legs are so much longer that I have to take an extra step every so often in order to keep up. "Well, I wouldn't know what to do with the money, but I am still the plan-maker," I say, defending my title. "And I approve. Lead the way Mr. I-totally-know-where-I'm-going-and-won't-get-us-lost-in-the-first-thirty-seconds-of-our-adventure."

Across the street, a raucous group of men stumble out of a building marked *BAR* in bright, colorful lights. They're shouting to each other, and I quicken my pace, glad we're on the other side of the street.

Derek ignores them. "That was one time, Rose. One time. Besides, I told you, I was distracted earlier. I had just met some random, crazy alien girl from another planet. Not to mention that the insane girl had a knife the size of my forearm in her boot."

"I don't think that's crazy, and just because my knife is bigger than yours doesn't mean you have to panic and get lost," I retort.

"Well, you're weird enough that everything must seem normal to you."

"Now that insult was good, and I applaud you for your skill," I mock-clap at his jibe. "But I think if you were less of a scaredy-cat, your clueless self wouldn't have been as shocked and distracted by my awesome knife. Then we never would've taken that wrong turn. I blame you for all the extra effort I had to put into this day." I sidestep a crumpled newspaper and a few other pieces of disgusting trash.

"Lazy," he coughs.

Touché! "I would deny that, but it's not becoming of someone to lie," I explain. "So I won't deny it, and I will agree that, yes, Derek, I am lazy."

He laughs. "Well, hurry your lazy butt up. We shouldn't be out at this time of night," he says and walks faster, going towards several stores with more of the colorful, bright lights.

"Is the clothing store going to be open this late?" I ask. Don't the workers have to go home?

"I know of several stores around here that stay open late," he tells me, crossing the street towards the brightly lit shopping area. "Actually, they're open 24/7 for weird people like us who decide to go shopping in the middle of the night."

"That's good because I don't want to be stuck in these clothes for however long—and hopefully it isn't long—I'm stuck here. I need to get home, or at least to Oregon."

He nods and holds open the door of the store for me. "Clean clothes now—and in the morning, a plan."

Chapter 19 – Derek

Rose skips into the store, as happy as a child who just won a game of rock, paper, scissors. Just inside the door, she stops and turns around, her blue eyes shining with delight. "What can I buy here, anyway?"

It's weird seeing her happy for this long.

I shrug. "Just pick out some clothes." I'm not sure how much she needs.

"I proved my point back there with that creep, Joey, didn't I?" Rose says, beaming.

That's why Rose is so happy. Not because we're shopping for clothes. And not because she won all the money—I have a feeling she didn't really care about that—but because she'd proven to me that she could, in fact, play poker *very* well. I wonder how long Rose has spent trying to prove her point to people. From what I've seen, most petite hyperactive blondes aren't taken too seriously.

"Ya, you proved your point," I say. She turns away but not before I see her triumphant grin.

Rose's attention suddenly shifts as she makes a beeline for a display of shoes. "Hey, this is the store I stole—er, got my shoes from."

I don't even ask her why she stole a pair of shoes. Out of all the things I've learned today, this isn't even slightly shocking. "However you got them, yours look fine. Focus on clothes—and not spending all my money," I tell her. "We need it for other things."

"Whatever," she says flippantly. "What season is it here?"

"Summer," I reply. I wonder if her seasons are different on Amara.

Rose grabs a pair of jeans from the rack without even looking at the size; she does the same thing with a T-shirt, then stalks off to the closest dressing room.

A couple minutes later she comes out wearing a short-sleeved, dark-green shirt that fits better than the dark-washed jeans do. They're clearly too long. She's tucked the ends sloppily into her boots. I can see the glint of her hunting knife peeking out of the top—of course she wouldn't get rid of it or put it in her pocket. Boots are clearly the most logical places for knives. According to Rose.

Her long hair is no longer in a ponytail but is braided straight down her back.

Wait . . . are those the price tags in her hand? Why did she pull them off? "You have to pay for those clothes, you know."

"I know. Just watch," she replies and approaches the counter.

"I'd like to buy these clothes and wear them out," she tells the cashier and hands her the tags.

The cashier, who doesn't look like this is anything interesting or weird, scans the tags and tells Rose the price. Maybe it's some weird girl thing? Surprisingly, Rose manages to hand over the right amount of money. I guess bills are easy to understand because the numbers are printed on them. Rose shoves the change and receipt in the pocket of her new jeans.

"See, told you I knew what I was doing," she says flippantly as we walk out the door, never minding the fact she *didn't* tell me that.

But she's not quite as on top of things as she thinks she is. "By the way, you left your old clothes in the changing room," I say, curious what her reaction will be.

"I know I did," Rose says a little too fast.

"Liar," I cough as we head to our next destination. I have a feeling that that was not in Rose's plan, but I don't let on that I'm wise to her.

"So how far away is this motel, anyway?"

"Just around the corner and across the street," I tell her, adjusting the strap on my backpack. Which reminds me that I never

120

did accomplish my errand this morning, now that I think about it, thanks to meeting Miss Rose.

We walk in silence until we reach the motel I have in mind. It's a clear summer night, and I feel warm and kinda sticky because of the humidity. I open the cracked glass door for her and let her walk in ahead of me.

She instantly recoils, backing up into me, and makes a gagging noise. "Just when I thought Earth couldn't smell any worse. We are *not* staying here. We are taking that money, and going to the nearest, nicest hotel."

"Rose, the nicer the hotel, the more expensive it is."

"Well, I'm using *my* money and I'm staying somewhere nicer than this dump. Let's go." Rose turns on her heel and walks out.

I reluctantly follow her. After all, she did win us more than enough money. Splurging for one night won't hurt our funds too much. It'll be better than this dump, in any case.

Outside I turn left. I know just the hotel. "Come on, Rose. I'll take us to a nice hotel."

"Yay, you're the best!" Rose cheers, an adorable grin on her face.

***

Minutes later, Rose and I are walking up the steps to the Hotel Veatro.

"This is more like it," she says, taking in the luxurious entryway, crystal chandeliers, leather couches, and wide marble staircase.

I walk over to the counter. "A room for one night, please." I pull out my wallet.

The blond receptionist looks me up and down. "How old are you? You have to be eighteen in order to get a room for the night."

Nice hotels ask far too many questions. "Old enough." I slide a rather large bill across the counter to her, hoping it will work.

"Of course, sir." She takes the bill, and starts typing on her computer. "Cash or credit?"

"Cash," I reply, then cringe as she tells me the amount. Nonetheless, I hand it to her, glancing over my shoulder at Rose.

Rose . . . who is still in the middle of the lobby, spinning in a slow circle and taking in the luxury of the place.

"Here's two key cards for you. Room 10E," the receptionist tells me with a smile. "I hope you enjoy your stay."

"Thank you." I grab the cards, walk over to the elevator, and push the button. Immediately the doors spring open and Rose and I step inside.

"What does—" The elevator moves, and Rose grabs onto my arm for support. "What in the worlds is this thing?" she screams.

"It's an elevator. It takes us up faster than climbing the stairs." I resist the urge to laugh.

Rose peels herself off me and stands on her own. Within seconds the elevator stops, jostling her into clutching the handrail for dear life. I can't help but laugh at the look of terror on her face.

"This is *so* not funny. This thing is a death trap."

As soon as the doors open on the tenth floor, Rose leaps out and heads down the hallway towards room E. I slide the card through the door scanner, and in we go.

The hotel room is huge, and everything is very plush. Rose immediately flops down on the couch.

"Now this is more like it! By the way, I get the bed and you're sleeping on the couch."

I laugh. Of course she would waste no time calling the bed. But I don't mind. The couch is probably more comfortable than most of the places I've slept.

She abruptly changes the subject. "So, using the picture on your phone, is there any way to ID the man?" Rose asks. "Because I was thinking—you said some people follow you for the Key, so if that's the case with this guy, then maybe he knows something about the portals not working. He might have information we can use."

I'm impressed. "Actually, yes, there are several ways we can use that picture. Let me think about it, and tomorrow after breakfast I'll let you know and we'll work from there. But I gotta get a few hours' sleep first."

Rose's eyebrows scrunch together. I'm guessing she doesn't like waiting. "Okay, we'll do that and see if your idea works. If not, we're heading to Oregon."

An idea sparks in my head. "Can't you call the people in Oregon and ask them for help?"

"Uhhh, what? Like, on the phone thing?" she asks, looking confused.

"I assume you don't know the number then? I bet you don't even know their last name!" Well, there goes that plan.

"No, I don't, so let's stick with the plan we have now," she suggests as she gets up off the couch and heads to the bedroom. She throws open the double doors, and I glimpse a huge bed. "Talk to you in the morning," she says and shuts the doors behind her with a click.

That works for me. Now we have a plan and a nice place to sleep and shower. Everything is going decently well now, although it would be better if the Keys would magically come back to life.

I move to the couch, yet I don't fall asleep. Thoughts race through my mind as I lace my fingers behind my head and try to relax. Originally, all I wanted to do today was to retrieve a few of my things from home while my parents were at work. Instead I ended up befriending someone from another planet.

It's been a weird day.

I take the Keys out of my pocket and turn them over—one damaged almost beyond recognition, the other still shiny and unused.

I set the damaged one on the table, and take mine in my hand. Remembering Rose's instructions for using the Key, I close my eyes and think of her planet—Amara. She had said there was a tree in front of the portal, a large river with fish, and woods. I open my eyes. Nothing. Maybe I didn't imagine Amara well enough? But Rose said that even if I got details wrong, it's supposed to open and then take me to some limbo place. I sigh and put my Key on the table next to Rose's.

I wonder if either of the Keys will ever work again?

***

The next morning Rose and I sit across from each other. We're stuffed from raiding the mini-bar fridge for breakfast, and now we're both reluctant to check out of the hotel.

"So, are you ever going to tell me where you got your Key?" I ask her.

Rose leans back against a chair and squints at me, a line forming between her eyes. "I got it from the Gatekeeper before me. She didn't want it anymore, so I volunteered for the job, and the Queen granted me permission to take over." She stares at me, as if she's watching for my reaction.

I have the strangest feeling she's lying to me. Something in her eyes changed as she talked. "That's it? That's your story?"

"Yup. Did that not happen to you?" She looks shocked. Too shocked? Fake-shocked? I have a hard time telling with her.

"No." I decide not to question her on the lying. If she doesn't want to tell me, then I'm not going to push. I've got bigger hurdles to jump today.

"Then how did you get your Key?" she asks, resting her elbows on her knees and her chin in her hands.

I hesitate. "It's a long story." If she doesn't want to tell me the truth, why should I tell her about me?

Especially since this story is the one that changed my life and drove the final wedge between my family and me. Basically, my mom thought everything I told her about the Key was nonsense, and my dad refused to speak to me as long as I kept the Key. So I left—after yelling some regrettable things at my parents. But I'm not ready to spill my guts to Rose about all of this.

"That's fine if it's a long story. I've got time," she says and eases back into her chair, relaxing and kicking her feet up on the glass table.

She's wearing her boots, and I can see her knife sticking out of the top of one. I can't let her stay in possession of that weapon. The last thing I need is to try to explain to the cops that Rose can't be arrested for pulling her knife on someone because she technically isn't human.

"Give me your knife first," I tell her, holding out my hand.

"Why?" she asks, taking her boots off the table so her knife is farther away from me. Like I would try to take it from her by force; she'd probably kill me.

"Because I feel like you pull your knife on people a lot, and we don't need to get in that kind of trouble," I tell her, wiggling my fingers to indicate that she should put the knife in my hand.

She waits a few beats. "Fine, but I want it back after we figure out our plan," she says, crossing her arms. "And you have to tell me everything about how you got your Key. No secrets," she grins knowingly.

So that's her game. She wants the full story. But I want the knife. "Deal."

Looking pained, she very slowly places the knife in my hand and watches me safely stow it in my backpack. She kicks her feet back up on the table and gets comfortable, then looks at me expectantly.

I take a deep breath. Here goes nothing.

"About two years ago, I was downtown and had gotten lost as I tried to walk home from a new burger joint where I'd met a couple of friends."

She snickers, and I shrug. "Hey, it's a big city. And the burger place was way across town. I didn't know my way around as well as I do now. Anyway, the streetlights were coming on, and there weren't a lot of people out and about . . . and, well, back then, I didn't have the street smarts I do now. So when this big, tough-looking dude was coming down the sidewalk toward me, I stupidly stayed on the sidewalk too. There was plenty of room for both of us.

"When he passed me, his hand shot out and grabbed my arm. I couldn't think what to do. I thought I was going to die.

"He stared at me and just gripped my arm. His face had scars all over it, which made him look a mess, and I swear half his teeth were missing.

"I was petrified. I'm surprised I didn't piss myself." That confession earns me a quiet laugh from Rose.

"Anyway, he said in this scratchy, sinister voice, 'You are the new Gatekeeper. Good luck.' Then he shoved a Key into my hand and walked away, laughing hard, as if he'd just done something hilarious.

"It took me a minute to unfreeze, but by then the man was gone. I wrote him off as a crazy, so I shoved the Key in my pocket and eventually found my way home."

Rose is hanging on my every word. Her eyes are alert, and she's leaning forward.

"For some reason, I had this insane need to carry the Key around with me all the time. I told myself it was because if I saw the owner I could return it. It wasn't until a month later that I finally figured out what the Key was for."

"And . . . ?" Rose asks excitedly. Her eyes sparkle. This girl really loves a good story.

"Anyway, about a month later, I decided to grab a bite to eat at a diner—the one we ate at yesterday. I was halfway into my sandwich when this random girl sat down in my booth. She had pitch-black hair and these insanely bright green eyes. I'd never seen her before or since.

Except maybe the girl on the bus was . . . holy hell! That's why I recognized her voice! But Rose doesn't need to know any of this. Not yet, anyway.

"I, uh, I thought she'd mistaken me for someone else, so I asked her who she was looking for.

She said, 'I've already found him.' I looked around for someone else, but she was staring at me. I waited for her to say something, but she didn't, and that's when I realized she wanted to talk to *me*. But then the waitress came up and took her order, so I had to wait."

Rose is intrigued, I can tell. She's staring at me even more intently than the girl in the diner did. I take a deep breath, collecting myself for the last part of the story. "*Anyway*, she explained to me that there are other worlds besides Earth, and the Key will take me there. She told me more stuff too, like how to do it, but I wasn't paying much attention to her because I thought it was some kind of joke."

Rose smirks, probably thinking that I'm an idiot. I pretend not to notice and move on.

"She kept saying, 'Someday you'll come across a flower and your life will change.' I thought she was insane. But now I wonder if maybe she was talking about you, Rose."

That's what the whole Roses have thorns *thing meant. But how did that girl know I would meet Rose?*

I rush on with my story before Rose can asked why I paused. "So, she also explained that people would be coming for the Key, and I, under no circumstances, was to let them use, have, or know I was in possession of the Key. She was dead serious when she said

127

that. It freaked me out that she knew I had the Key, but I just thought it was coincidence and that she had escaped from the loony bin or something."

Taking a deep breath, I tell her the rest of it. "People have come after the Key. I even lost it once, but I got it back, and that's the important part. So to avoid anyone getting the Key, I learned how to fight and how to lie. I also learned how to survive on my own." I am not about to go into details about the zero help from my parents after they kicked me out for insisting the Key could take people to other worlds.

Rose is thinking hard, her fingers tapping her leg, and her eyes squinting and staring off over my shoulder. She probably has fifty questions already.

I prepare myself for the onslaught.

She sits up excitedly. "Well, if you went into that diner, that means you live around here!"

What! Out of my entire story, that's what she got?

"We could've stayed with your parents!"

Oh, no. Definitely not. "We are not, under any circumstances, going to my parents' house," I say coldly.

Rose looks taken aback at my tone. It clearly wasn't what she had been expecting. She shuts up on the subject, so I guess I got my message across.

The truth is that I don't talk to anyone about my parents. It brings up too many questions that I really don't want to answer.

Chapter 20 – Phoenix

Sitting on Sylvia's bed in the palace, I study her face as she absorbs what I have just told her about Rose and Rose's father. It's a lot of to digest, and on top of that, it's very shocking.

A look of understanding dawns on her face. "So, basically, Phoenix, what you're telling me is that Rose's disappearance and her father's death—supposed death—could be linked?"

"Yes! If you look at the connections between the two, you can see it," I say again, excited about my idea. "Rose suddenly disappeared in battle, and so did her father. Both disappeared without a trace, and there is no actual evidence that either of them are, in fact, dead."

Sylvia looks like we just found the cure for cancer. "Oh, that makes so much sense! I just had a dream about Mr. Sander's disappearance, and Rose's too!" She leaps to her feet. "Do you think they're together somewhere, Rose and her dad?"

I try to be my usual rational self and present a balanced argument. "I don't know if Rose and her father are even in the same place, let alone if she found him. I do, however, think that they are alive, wherever they happen to be at the moment. Besides, I—and I know this sounds strange—but I feel if Rose were dead, we would know."

She whirls around excitedly. "Yes, yes, I agree! We really need to test a portal to know if they're working properly."

"Yeah, and remember what Nolana Hanaway told you she did?" At the mention of Hanaway's name, Sylvia opens her mouth to say something but shuts it as I continue, "She watched for an annual portal to see if it opened in the right place and time, and it did. So, if we go to where the next annual portal is due to open, we can send someone through to actually test it."

Sylvia looks like she is going to burst with good news, so I shut up so she can talk.

"Phoenix, I need to tell you something! Frick, I can't believe I forgot!" She grabs my arm excitedly. "Hanaway told me earlier this afternoon that the flash of light that took Rose was blue and brown. So you and I need to figure out which portal is that color. And no matter which portal is due to arrive next, we'll test it to verify it's working. Then, once we have a Key, we can find Rose."

My mouth drops open as soon as I hear about the color of the flash of light. "Okay," I say, taking a deep breath, and count off on my fingers. "Here's what we'll do. Number one: We'll keep everyone researching how to make a Key. Number two: We'll find the next annual portal that's due to appear and if it looks safe enough, we'll send someone on through to test it. And number three: We'll figure out which portals have blue and brown colors so we're ready to go as soon as we have a new Key."

"Yes, you're right. That's a great plan," Sylvia quickly agrees. "So when is the next portal due to come?"

"I'm not really sure. I know Nolana checked one by her house. Isn't there some reference book that lists all the portals?"

Sylvia wrinkles her brow. "Rose has a book full of portal dates in her house. And I know there's a book somewhere in the castle, too."

"The one in the castle is closer," I say quickly, not really wanting to go to Rose's empty house; it'd be too painful.

Sylvia nods. "My mother or father will know where it is. We should go ask them," she suggests, racing towards the door. I'm right on her heels.

We pass Evelyn, who is still guarding Sylvia's door from the outside. She looks bewildered, probably because I somehow got into the room without her knowing, but she doesn't try to stop us.

I follow Sylvia through the twisty corridors in the direction of the library. When we get there, I realize just how late it is because the library is nearly empty. Almost everyone has gone home for the night.

Sylvia leads the way to Jessica, a palace maid, who is reading and has two small stacks of books in front of her.

"Excuse me, I would like to know where my mother has gone," Sylvia says in what Rose classifies as her Princess voice. It's the kind of tone expected from royalty: sort of stuck up, a little demanding. It's what her mother has taught her to do.

"The queen has retired to her chambers for the night, Princess."

"And my father?" Sylvia asks.

"He has gone up to the North Tower, I believe," the girl says.

"Thank you. That is all I need to know." Sylvia spins on her heel and heads out of the room. I smile my thanks at Jessica and then I'm right behind Sylvia.

She sets a fast pace; she is on a mission. I can barely keep up, especially on the stairs. Does she do this every day for exercise, or what? I'm panting too hard to ask her.

When we finally reach the top of the tower, we are both out of breath.

She silently motions me to follow her into the room at the top of the stairs. We pause just inside the doorway of the high-ceilinged, round room.

"Father, is it okay if I ask you a question?" Sylvia says in a soft voice that one generally uses when they are hoping for a positive answer.

The king looks up from the book he is studying at a desk in the center of the room. He makes eye contact with me, and I curtsy automatically, bowing my head.

"Yes, my daughter," he says in an even voice. "What is it you wish to ask?"

"We would like to know where the book is . . . the *Book of Portals*."

131

He leans back in his chair. "Why would you like to see it?"

Sylvia entwines her fingers in front of her. "We," she starts, then clears her throat. "We believe it will help us in our search for Rose."

"I see." The king nods. "It is in the War Room. I shall have to retrieve it for you later."

Sylvia's face falls. And I'm not too thrilled either at the wait.

Even I know that we cannot retrieve it for ourselves because the War Room is off limits to those not in Bronze Squad or higher. Because neither Sylvia nor I are even in the army, we can't go into the War Room even though Sylvia is the Princess.

The king notices that we haven't left. "Is there anything else you need from me?"

"No, Father, that is all. Thank you. We will be going now."

I curtsy as Sylvia turns to leave then pauses when her father continues speaking in a more gentle tone. "I want you to know, Sylvia, that I firmly believe your friend will find a way to return. She is a rather stubborn and persistent person."

I smile at the king's statement. He would certainly know.

When Rose was thirteen, she was invited by the General to join Gold Squad. Unfortunately, he had extended the offer before securing permission from the king, who believed at the time that women should not be allowed on Gold Squad.

So in order to convince him to change his mind, Rose sent him a letter every hour on the hour for two weeks. It was her way of showing she had the dedication needed for Gold Squad, that she could be articulate and persuasive, and that she wasn't going to give up. It worked.

Sylvia bows her head to her father. "Thank you for your faith in my friend's return. Thank you, additionally, for getting the book for us." She looks up at him with an appreciative smile.

132

I curtsy to him even though I'm wearing a pair of jeans, ones Rose had . . . *acquired* for me. What would Amara be like if Rose had not left her very distinct mark on it? It is a sad thought; I choose not to dwell on it.

Sylvia turns again to leave, and I follow her out the door.

After a few turns down the spiral stairs, I ask, "Are we going to the library?"

"Yes, we'll have to wait for a bit before my father brings us the book. We might as well do it there so we can continue to search for information about how the Key was made."

We don't have to wait long. Sylvia's father shows up shortly and sets the book on the table in front of us before heading back out of the library.

The *Book of Portals* is huge. Rose once said that there are a lot of planets to be explored, but we never grasped exactly how many. Written on the front of the brown leather book in gold lettering is simply PORTALS. I guess they weren't going for elaborate.

"Oh, there's a table of contents! Thank goodness," Sylvia breathes. I agree.

We quickly learn that the portals are organized by date, with the first month in our calendar year in the front of the book and the last month in the back. The portals are all listed in tiny rows and columns, starting with the planet name, then the date at which the portal will show up, where the portal will show up, how long the portal will last, and then how frequently the portal shows up for that particular planet. And in the very back of the book is a section with portal colors and their corresponding planets.

I quickly flip to the back of the book and look for a blue-brown portal, sliding my finger down the page to the *b* section. The blue-and-brown portal belongs to . . . Earth.

I think. Because there's also a blue, brown, and green portal. And a blue, brown, and yellow portal. And a large variety of other colors, but Earth's is only two-toned blue and brown.

"Sylvia," I whisper. "Look here." I tap the page excitedly and she smiles.

Rose has got to be on Earth! That would make sense . . . in a sort of weird way. My stomach drops. What if—

"Oh, no!" Sylvia frowns. "Crap. The portal for Earth arrived the day before Rose disappeared. And the Earth portal shows up only once a year! Which means we'll absolutely have to make a new Key unless we're willing to wait nearly a year to go get her."

I sit back and absorb that depressing information. "Well, we can still try out our other portal idea, to make sure the portals are working properly."

Without much enthusiasm, I turn back to the beginning of the book and skim the pages. It looks like portals open up around Amara several times a week, and sometimes more than one a day. I had no idea they appeared so often.

I flip through several inches of pages before we get to today's date. Sylvia quickly drags her finger down the list and stops at the next entry.

"We have three days," she announces, "until we can figure out if the portals are still working. That's when the next annual portal shows up. It's for a planet called Darnisha." She leans back in her chair and I take another look at the page, just in case. But she's correct.

"Well, so not only do we have to wait almost a year to get to Earth if we don't make another Key, but we also seem to have hit a quiet spot in portal happenings," I lament.

It's going to be a very long three days.

Sylvia's shoulders slump as she sits in her chair and stares at the library's stone ceiling. I feel the same dejection she does, but I'd rather keep busy than do nothing.

I firmly shut the book. We've gathered all the information we need from it. Sylvia calls over a maid and carefully hands it to her to return to the king.

And that's that, I sigh. I glance around the library and recall that I had asked Collin to wait here for me. That was several hours ago, but he will still be here somewhere, knowing Collin.

He waves at me from a far corner, so Sylvia and I walk over to him.

"Do you still have my books?" I ask as I plop down in the chair next to him. Phoenix dispiritedly takes a chair across the table from us.

He looks at me with a small smile. "Yes, they're in the taller stack right in front of you. I haven't been able to find anything about making the Gatekeeper Key, though. Sorry, Phoenix."

"It's okay," I reassure him. "We found out the next portal is coming in three days, so our plan is to go to it and see if it—and therefore the other portals—still work. Hopefully we will figure out about the Key before then."

"That's good. We need to reunite the Three Musketeers," Collin grins cheerfully.

"We will," Sylvia says, picking up a book. "I just really hope that it's sooner rather than later," she adds forlornly.

Collin and I nod solemnly. Sylvia's remark kills the conversation fast.

I set to work reading history books with renewed—well, not enthusiasm, but energy and hope.

Chapter 21 – Rose

"This drink is way better than coffee," I say while sipping something called hot chocolate at the 7th Avenue Diner, located a few blocks from the nice hotel.

"I still think coffee is better," Derek says, taking a sip of his coffee as if to prove his point.

Ugh. Not only is he being stubborn about the coffee, but he still didn't tell me about his parents when we were at the hotel this morning.

We've been here about fifteen minutes already, and I am on my third cup of hot chocolate. I stir the melting whipped cream and chuckle to myself. This time, in order to get a corner booth, I flat out asked for one instead of putting on the whole "Couple Show." Derek was amused by my behavior.

I flip my braid over my shoulder. "So what's your plan for IDing the man in the picture?" I ask him, curious if he has even thought about it.

"Here comes our breakfast, so I'll explain after we eat. It's fairly simple, and it has a decent chance of working."

I smile, elated. I'm one step closer to getting home.

The waitress sets down our plates of food. "Why the joyous faces?" she asks. "Anything special happening today?"

I notice a sparkle from her necklace and look at it more closely. It's a silver cross with an elegant blue stone in the middle. My eyes drift to her name tag: Sanders. That's my last name. How odd.

Derek answers her question. "Oh, we just figured out a solution to a problem we've been having." He takes a bite of his food.

The name of the waitress is bugging me for some reason. Sanders is a common enough last name, but there's a faint ringing in my head. "Is Sanders your last name?" I ask her.

"It is. My boss thinks it's more professional to go by last names."

Hmm. "That's my last name," I say. "I'm Rose Sanders."

"I'm Matilda Sanders. It's nice to meet you," she says, smiling.

My gut clenches. I don't know why. I'm not nervous, or scared, or anything else that would ignite the feeling. I hold out my hand. "Nice to meet you too, Matilda. It's weird that we have the same last name."

Matilda shakes my hand. "It is," she says and shifts her weight to her right foot. "Do I know you from somewhere?" She cocks her head, looking closely at my face. "You must be a relative of my husband's, I think. You don't look a lot like him, but I can see some resemblance. You both have the same facial structure, and he gets the same expression on his face as you have right now." She shrugs. "Well, it's probably just a coincidence."

A sweat breaks out on my face. Could she be . . . ? No. It's not possible. My gut is probably messed up because of something I ate here on Earth. That's why it's sending me a familiar message I haven't heard in a long time.

Before I can tell her my only male relative is dead, so therefore I can't be related to her husband, there's a loud bang from the front of the diner.

"Coulee, we know you're in here!" a man shouts over the scared screams of the customers.

Coulee? Wait. Where do I recognize that name from?

Matilda lets out a shriek and runs back into the kitchen.

I swing around in the booth to look at the rude jerk who yelled. *Oh, shat.* I see the source of the loud noise. The man's waving around a gun, and he looks like he knows how to use it. Add that fact to the corded muscles bulging out below the short sleeves of his dirty white T-shirt, and it looks like trouble.

Sheesh. Why can't Derek and I eat our breakfast in peace?

Two henchmen, each with his own gun, enter the diner and stand behind their leader.

"Coulee? Where are you?" the first man bellows as he brandishes his gun and looks around the diner.

A sneaking suspicion creeps up on me. I look over at Derek. "Please tell me that's not your last name," I gulp. My gut is telling me that we are about to have some trouble on our hands.

"It is." His voice is monotone and his expression resigned.

My stomach plummets. "Please tell me you don't know them," I ask, hoping for a miracle.

"I know them," he says as he watches the first man scan the room.

Wait a second . . . Coulee—Victoria Coulee! Could Derek know the woman my mother wrote about in her journal?

Before I can ask, all three men look to our corner booth and see Derek. Malicious delight crosses the first man's face and he stalks toward us, motioning for the other two to stay by the door. Escape route number one is now cut off.

My mind races into overdrive, working on other possible escape routes and wondering why these men could be after Derek. Could it have to do with his father? Could it be something about why he owed that Joey guy money? What other trouble has Derek gotten in before I met him? There's too much I don't know.

But I do know this isn't going to be pretty.

I reach for my knife in my boot, only to realize that Derek still has it. *Frick!* Why didn't I get it back from him earlier? How could I have forgotten it?

"Derek, knife, now!" I tell him hurriedly.

He looks away from the approaching man and gives me a blank stare. How in the world am I supposed to fight now? "Derek! Knife!"

"Anyone who tries to call the cops or escape," shouts the white T-shirt, who I assume is the leader, "will be shot." He swaggers over to our table.

"Derek, give me my knife," I whisper furiously. "*Now.*"

Derek finally seems to realize what I'm talking about and reaches to grab it from his backpack, but he's cut off as the leader slams his fist onto the table. Derek freezes.

"So, Coulee, we meet again," he says. He's shorter than I thought, and older. "And who's this? A girlfriend?"

And stupider, too.

Nonetheless, my stomach turns violently. He sounds much too confident for me to be able to walk all over him. Why couldn't Derek have just let me keep my knife? And why does everyone assume I'm his girlfriend?

I study my opponent, for that's what he is. The jerk looks like he knows how to fight. It's the way he holds himself loosely but ready to spring, which the extra confidence of being able to fight gives him.

Derek is still staring at the table and hasn't replied to the man's questions, so the guy whips around to me. I'm usually too fast for these humans, but this guy catches me off guard when he roughly grabs my arm and tries to yank me up from the booth.

That's so not going to happen!

I bite him. He pulls back but only to gather momentum to land a punch on me. I duck, and he's thrown off balance when his fist collides with air, and the gun in his other hand clanks against the table.

Derek, meanwhile, sits there and does nothing, his expression blank, his eyes unfocused. Gee, he's super helpful to have around in a fight.

The people in the next booth over gape at us as if they don't understand what they're seeing. At least the people in the other nearby booths have enough sense to cower under a table and not make eye contact. But, really, humans have horrible fight-flight-or-freeze responses. They tend to favor the third, and worst, option.

The gunman eyes me warily but at least he doesn't get close and try to grab me again, so I return my attention to Derek. "Derek, what does this scumbag want with you, and why in the worlds would you ever have anything to do with a guy like this?"

"I'm not a scumbag," the guy says maliciously and waves his gun in my direction, then continues, "I'll forgive you for that, though, *if* your boyfriend has the money to pay me back."

I look at Derek. So that's why this bozo has come after him.

"Everyone has connections they really shouldn't," Derek says to me weakly, not quite meeting my eyes.

"Great," I say, trying to keep calm. "You've got not only the *connection* from yesterday, but now this one." I know I'm outgunned—literally. People like this scumbag can smell fear.

Well, the best defense is a good offense.

"By the way, Derek's not my boyfriend," I say in a snarky tone to Mr. White T-shirt. "I just thought I'd point that out."

"Look," Derek interrupts. "I don't have your money now, but if you give me a week, I can have all the money I owe you."

The guy narrows his eyes and studies Derek.

"How much do you owe him?" I ask calmly and pointedly ignore the gun aimed at me. My brain zones in on one thing: survival. And that means getting this loser the money Derek owes him.

"Ten thousand dollars," Derek says quietly.

Sounds like a lot of money, but that doesn't matter at the moment. What does is getting this creep out of here.

"Yup," I say to the scumbag who's still standing way too close for my comfort. "We can get your money to you in a week."

He laughs harshly and I can smell his pungent breath. "How do you expect to do that when all he's gotten me is seven hundred dollars in a year?"

"You are horrible at getting money," I tell Derek, which makes the man laugh again.

"Give me a break! I'm a homeless teenager who's in debt to more than one person," Derek sputters. He really is panicking. Now fear rises in my throat, but I swallow it.

"Why can't you just ask your parents for the money?" I ask.

"Didn't he tell you? Little Derek's been shunned by the family," the man cackles cruelly as he blocks my way out of the booth.

This is news to me. Why was Derek shunned?

Derek finally stares at the man directly. "How did you find me?" Now he's getting into the swing of things, if only he could give me my knife—

"Let's just say a little birdie told me." The man's gaze shifts to me. "He said he ran into you and some little girl who was quite vicious. He tracked you down after he ran into you, and he's been following you ever since. The rest was quite easy."

Frick! He knows the man I beat up, the guy who followed us in the burned-out part of town. Well, that's not good. Derek was right about that coming back to haunt me.

Derek thrusts out his chin and says in a determined voice, "I'll get you the money back."

"I don't believe you," the man says, "so I'll be taking the girl." He quickly shifts his weight toward me. "For insurance purposes, I'm sure you understand."

What?

141

I launch myself onto the table to evade his grasp, but my feet slip on the booth's seat and I can't get traction. *Stupid human contraption.*

The beefy creep grabs my arm and jerks me out of the booth, then painfully twists my arm up behind my back. My attempts to grab the table are less than successful, and the kicks I aim at him don't do any good either.

My breath hitches in my throat as I feel the cool barrel of a gun press against my head. I squirm and try to twist out of his grasp and away from the gun. I rarely deal with guns, and I'm not quite sure how to get it from him without shooting myself. I can't get the leverage I need to take him down, not with one of my arms pinned and a gun in play.

"You've got one week, lover boy. If not, she'll be dead in a ditch."

I can't help it, I snort. The more scared I get, the more ridiculous this entire situation seems. If only I had my knife, then there wouldn't *be* a situation.

"Do you think it's funny?" he asks, brutally twisting my arm up higher on my back.

Ouch!

"I do think it's funny, actually," I say, forcing a laugh for good measure. If all else fails, I know not to show my fear. A basic lesson Bronze Squad learns on day one.

Sirens screech in the distance. I assume someone in the kitchen called the cops. Maybe I can stall until they get here.

"Sirens!" one of the men guarding the door shouts.

Darn. Why did they have to hear them too?

The man gripping me with his huge paw turns his head to look at his buddies by the door. I stomp on his foot, hard. As I anticipated, he lifts his sore foot, so I elbow him in the gut with my free arm, knocking him over and breaking his hold on me.

Unluckily for me, the two other guys must have seen my stomp because they're rushing toward us.

Derek grabs his backpack and we bolt towards the side door. It's nice to know that now that the situation has escalated, Derek is thinking clearly.

I'm right on his heels when someone grabs my braid and brings me up short.

"AARRGH!" I scream at what feels like my hair being pulled out. "Let go of me, you scumbag of a mundane!" I scream as I struggle desperately to get loose.

I manage to land a few blows, but something heavy—I assume it's the gun—slams against my head. Pain explodes throughout my skull and I crumple to the ground.

"One week!" is the last thing I hear before everything goes dark.

Chapter 22 – Rose

I wake up in a small, dark, musty room that smells like armpit. Loud, raucous music plays somewhere. At first I can't remember what happened, so I panic. What had I gotten myself into this time? It feels really, really serious.

Then it all comes rushing back—the battle on Amara, being stuck on Earth, meeting Derek, getting kidnapped because he owes money to some creeps.

My panic increases. Are they going to kill me? No, they need me as bait for Derek. Are they going to do something worse? Starve me to death? Beat me? I mean, they only have to keep me alive for a week. Not necessarily in good condition, just alive. How can I possibly survive? Even if they don't kill me directly. Why did my family have to be the Gatekeepers? Why not someone else? I can't die yet.

Stop. No more panicking. You're not going to escape when you're thinking this unclearly. I inhale slowly, then exhale and try to relax.

This is not good, not good at all. If only I had beaten them up back in the diner.

I silently fume. Why didn't Derek give me my knife back? Then I would've had a fighting chance. Now, I'm much farther from getting to Oregon—and home. *Frick!* My people need me, and I'm stuck in . . . in some closet that smells worse than a dead glowing-stone fish that's been sitting in the sun for three days.

My head throbs and the music doesn't help, but I ignore both annoyances. Sitting up slowly, black spots dance across my vision and I pause for a minute. Several deep breaths help to block out the pain in my head and the fury coursing through my veins. I need to think clearly.

My eyes eventually adjust to the light. The smelly room I'm in is big enough for me to lie flat on the floor and to maybe stand up in, but that's about it. The roof slopes steeply downwards; it's a normal height at the doorframe and gets progressively smaller towards the back of the room—if you can call it that. And because that wretched, pounding music is coming through the door, I'm assuming there's a bigger room on the other side. Which means I really am stuck in a closet.

I swallow the claustrophobia that rises like a tidal wave in my stomach, trying to trick myself into thinking that the room is bigger than it actually is. Trying not to focus on the fact that the darkness feels like it's wrapping around my lungs, constricting my air supply. My gut twists painfully as panic replaces anger. I'm not afraid of many things, but small spaces freak me out.

I try not to scream, so I punch the wall instead. The skin on one of my knuckles breaks open.

"Damn it all!"

I take a deep breath, close my eyes, and picture myself in a much larger room. It takes a few minutes, but the mind-over-matter thing works well enough for me not to think straight.

The music volume is suddenly lowered, and heavy footsteps approach. I breathe deeply again to lower my heart rate and sit with my legs crossed, attempting to appear calm.

The door swings open, hitting me, but I refuse to move or speak. A red-haired man I've never seen before pokes his head in and glances at me.

"She's awake," he says over his shoulder before exiting and slamming the door behind him. A key turns in the lock.

"Didn't your mother ever tell you that slamming doors is rude?" I yell so whoever is on the other side can hear me.

No response. They're obviously ignoring me, which pisses me off to no end. I don't take well to being ignored, so now is the perfect time for them to learn that.

145

Besides, the best way to ignore fear is to distract yourself. (Day two in Bronze Squad.)

"Ninety-nine bottles of beer on the wall, ninety-nine bottles of beer!" I sing—shout, actually—the annoying song I heard kids chanting one time I visited Earth.

I'm not a good singer, so I plug my own ears so I don't have to hear my wailing. The men continue to ignore me, or at least I assume so—no one's opened my door yet. How many verses will they last? I make sure to move back from the door so I don't get hit with it again.

Twenty verses later I finally get my reaction.

Someone pounds on the door. "Shut up in there!"

I sing at the top of my lungs for one more verse, but then the door bangs open and a man appears in the doorframe. A different guy this time, with a huge, angry scar marring half his face.

I instantly quiet down and feign innocence.

"No more singing," he says, scowling. He towers over me.

I look up at him with an I-wasn't-doing-anything expression, and when I remain silent, he stalks out and slams the door.

Again the lock clicks. *Dang it.*

I stare at the wall, plotting how to escape. I could kick the door down, but no, I can tell by looking at it that it's too thick. Or, the next time the door opens, I could barge out and run for it. No, I don't know what's on the other side. Besides, once I get past the first person, there's undoubtedly more of them out there.

Deciding my time would be better spent doing something other than coming up with ridiculous schemes, I stand up and run my hands over the walls. Maybe I'll find a loose board or a trap door or some other sneaky way to escape.

At least the music in the other room is loud enough that the men don't hear me shuffling around but not so loud that my headache returns.

Twenty minutes later, I'm more than a little desperate. This is what happens when imaginations wander: false hope. I've found nothing. No hidden doors or loose boards. For good measure, I check the floor again and get the same result.

Nothing to do but sit, wait, try to remain calm, and hope inspiration strikes. What was the saying? Oh ya: patience is a virtue. Ha! That's one virtue I don't have.

My thoughts turn to Amara. Will I ever see it again? I might never know what happened during the battle. What fate came to my friends, my village, my people? I might never know what happened to Lexi— if she's on some other planet as I am, or if she's still on Amara, or even if she's dead or alive.

Helplessness washes over me. I can't go back home to help my people fight. For once, I desperately wish I had listened to orders. If only I was up on the cliffs with the archers, instead of trying to get my revenge on Lexi, I could still be on Amara. I could be helping my people. Why couldn't I have just listened for once?

***

Some indeterminate amount of time later, the door suddenly opens. The ruddy-faced, red-haired man—I decide to call him Butch—looms over me and drops something in my lap, then shuts the door. The lock clicks, painfully reminding me of what a small space I'm in.

The walls and ceiling close in on me. Fear rises in my throat. I take four deep breaths to calm myself. It doesn't work very well. In fact, it doesn't work at all.

I scream a choice word as loud as I can, but I feel only slightly better, and then guilt fills me that I swore. My mother always told me it was very illiterate to swear, but I'm in a closet and might die in a week. I think she would understand, wherever she is right now.

Suddenly bitterness eats away at me. Why did my mother leave me? I was only a child. What drove her to think it was

147

acceptable to leave me and my sister all alone, unsure of what to do, where to go? Who in the worlds does that to a child? What was her selfish motivation behind that? Was I not good enough?

I shake my head to try to clear it of all these negative thoughts. They're not going to help me formulate an escape plan.

I finally remember the bag the man dropped in my lap, and pull out what vaguely looks like food—although it smells disgusting. It's some greasy blob that I believe Derek calls a burger. I gag and nearly throw up. I reluctantly choke it down. Who knows if I'll get more food anytime soon.

I hope Derek will somehow find me and help me escape . . . or that at least some magic fairy will bring me better food.

Chapter 23 – Sylvia

Two more days until the portal shows up; two miserably long days. Phoenix and Collin intently read their books across the library table from me, but I focus on the door instead. I'm waiting for my mother so we can discuss forming a group to check out the annual portal to Darnisha.

That particular portal will stay open for a day on both Amara and Darnisha, but Phoenix and I thought it would be best to go through right as it opens. That way, whoever goes through will have ample time to get back to Amara. Better safe than sorry, as they say. But, of course, I have to propose the plan to my mother and get the royal okay.

Seconds later my mother appears. I get up and briskly walk to her, resisting the urge to dash over. Curtsying, I ask in my politest tone, "Mother, I was wondering if I could speak with you?"

"Of course, my dear. What is it you would like to discuss?" My mother sits down at the table that has been reserved for her and my father.

"Last night we discovered that an annual portal to the planet of Darnisha will open in two days. It is the soonest annual portal to open and, obviously, one we do not need a Key for. Phoenix and I have been brainstorming a plan. We would like to test the portal to see if they are still working properly."

My mother nods, listening intently. So far, so good.

"Yesterday, with the help of Nolana Hanaway, we came to the conclusion that the portal that took Rose away was the portal to Earth. If the portal to Darnisha works, we will wait for the next annual portal to Earth to go look for Rose there. But first we need to know if the annual portals work."

My mother nearly—but not quite—interrupts me. "Will we continue our search for the Key and its origins in the meantime?"

"Of course, Mother, because if we find it, we can open a portal to Earth immediately. And we fully intend to just that. But, as I was saying," I continue trying not to get irritated at the near-interruption. I just want to get my plan approved and ready for action. "Our plan for the Darnisha portal is to take a small group to the ridge where it appears, and to send one volunteer through to the other side. The group that Phoenix and I propose is myself, Phoenix, Collin, and Nolana. I kn-"

"Absolutely not!" My mother's quiet voice takes a dangerous tone, and she stands up so we're at eye level. "You are all much too young to be risking going through the portal. We will send adults on the Gold Squad instead."

I take a deep breath, "Mother, please. Gold and Silver Squad are still combing Amara. We are all close to Rose, and we all want to find her. We are the best volunteers for the job."

Before my mother can respond, my father arrives. "And what might you two be discussing?" he asks. He must've seen the sour looks on our faces. He is frequently the mediator between our fights.

"Let me discuss this with your father," my mother says, stalking off, my father's hand discreetly patting her on the arm.

A couple minutes later, they return—my mother with a terse look on her face. "Your father has agreed to your group, as long as he accompanies you."

I quell the urge to jump with joy. "Thank you so much!" I squeal quietly, and go back to my table to report to my group.

***

Phoenix, Collin, and I haven't left the library for two days straight, and tonight's the night—finally—that the portal for Darnisha is supposed to show up.

But right now, we're running on empty.

Phoenix has her head propped up on her elbow as she reads, and Collin has fallen asleep. Only Hanaway is avidly reading and taking notes. Hopelessness hangs heavy in the air. We found several small references about the first Key and that a king called Ulysses was ruling then. But every time we find a part in a book where there might be more information, the pages have been torn out. Someone—at some point in time—didn't want us to know about the original Key, how it was made, or where it came from.

I glance down at the thick volume I'm currently reading. It's an old one titled, *"Great Discoveries and Creations of Our Time,"* and it was written by Joelle Herbertson, an Amarian, about three centuries ago. I am halfway through it when something piques my interest.

Quite possibly the greatest Amarian discovery was the day we found what is referred to as "The Key." It is made of brass and has the power to take us to other worlds that were never known to previously exist. The Key was discovered recently by Erin Macilnely, who wrote in her journal that she dreamt of its location.

I was granted access to the journal in which she wrote, "I received a vision that led me to the Key. It was a very perilous journey."

Anything else that may have been written in the journal I cannot say, as King Ulysses will not let me look at it for reasons unknown to me.

However, as official historian, I continued my research and learned that Macilnely found the Key inside a notebook containing secret information on the subject. The Key is thought to have previously belonged to one of Macilnely's ancestors.

I was able to convince King Ulysses to share with me that Macilnely's dream also told her how she would be able to make more Keys— but he would not tell me how this could be accomplished. 'Even if you knew how,' she told me, 'you would not be able to make a Key.' However, I am aware that the notebook Macilnely found with the *information is hidden somewhere in the great castle. I was able to glean that much from the king before he had me escorted from the palace grounds.*

That's the end of the chapter and there doesn't appear to be anything else in the book about the Key. I stop reading and look up, staring off into the distance. My mind races.

This book was quite dusty when I opened it, and extremely fragile, so maybe no one has read it in a long time. And that's why these pages are still here and not torn out. People would tend to read newer, updated editions, and not some old relic stuffed behind other ancient books on a dusty shelf.

The content of author Joelle Herbertson's words finally push past my racing thoughts. This is it! This is what we've been looking for. We have answers!

I jump up from the table, and Phoenix immediately straightens as she looks inquiringly at me.

Collin wakes up with a start. "I wasn't . . . it was only for . . . what day is it?" His voice is groggy.

With a big grin, I place the book in front of Phoenix and point to the text, ignoring Collin's confusion for the moment. Her eyes light up as she scans the page. I hurry over to one of the servants, Jessica. "Fetch my mother and father. It is urgent," I order her quietly.

"Right away, Princess," she says and curtsies before hurrying off.

The few remaining townspeople in the library look up at the sudden commotion of Jessica exiting the room in a hurry. I smile broadly at them and hold up my index finger to tell them to wait a few minutes.

Phoenix has just finished reading and her head snaps up as I approach. "This means all we have to do to help Rose," she says enthusiastically in a hushed tone, "is find a hidden notebook somewhere in the castle. It will tell us how to make another Key!"

I nod. "Yes, so now we're back to having two plans for bringing Rose home." I'm elated but also somewhat daunted. "But, Phoenix, you know how big the castle is."

Rose and I played hide-and-seek here in the castle when we were little, and Phoenix did too after she moved to Alethia. So we know how big the castle is and we know tons of hiding places—hiding places large enough for small children. There has to be thousands more secret places for small objects. And on top of that, we don't know what this old notebook looks like.

"What is so important, dear?" my mother asks when she and my father arrive a few minutes later.

"Read this section of the book," I say while carefully turning the book to face them, and pointing to the paragraphs Joelle wrote. "Please," I add, remembering my manners despite my excitement.

I wait impatiently, and I bite my lip to control myself. I can't stand still; they're taking forever to read it!

When they're done, they look at me with blank faces.

I wait in suspense.

One . . . I count silently to myself as they glance at each other.

Two . . . Their lips turn down, and my father looks thoughtful.

Three—

My mother turns to me and says sadly, "I have not the slightest clue as to where that notebook may be. I am so sorry. I will have people look for it right away, though."

I frown at the news. Wouldn't they, of all people, know? Surely they inherited some list or instructions saying where a top secret notebook is hidden?

My mother shakes her head again and my father looks at me regretfully.

Crap! Well, at least that only eliminates one plan for the moment. We can still accomplish the portal plan—I think. "But we are still sending people out to investigate the portal that is showing up tonight, right?"

"Of course, dear," my mother says sweetly.

My father looks at the large clock on the wall and doesn't say a word as he strides purposefully out of the library. What is he doing? We still have plenty of time before we need to leave for the portal. It'll only take about fifteen minutes on horseback.

My mother re-reads the relevant section of the book, then clears her throat. Uh oh. Here comes a speech. "Can I have everyone's attention, please?"

The handful of patrons in the library listen intently; the queen is speaking, after all.

"I would like to begin with thanking you all for your hard work and dedication. It is deeply appreciated. The reason I am interrupting your search is that Princess Sylvia has discovered important information surrounding the origin of the Key. Let me read you the passage in this book."

As she reads in a loud, clear voice, I look around the library and notice a couple people taking notes. I cannot believe the dedication of the people of our town to find Rose. I suddenly feel an immense love for my home and its inhabitants.

With perfect diction, my mother's voice rings out. "As you can tell by this information, an old notebook that very possibly holds the answer to our current predicament exists somewhere in this castle. I believe we can find it. We will need the help of everyone in one way or another. Further instructions will be forthcoming." She sits back down and chatter erupts throughout the library.

My father returns and walks over to my table. "All right," he says. "Let's go." Everyone at my table jumps up immediately. This is the moment we've been waiting for, even if it does seem early to me.

In front of the stables, two horses are tied to the hitching post. Torchlight dances in the darkness, making it feel warmer than it already is. I hadn't realized how dark it was already, which will slow our ride.

"Father, are there no horses for the others?" We certainly have enough for Phoenix, Collin, and Hanaway to ride.

His response is blunt. "Unless they are in the army, they do not ride with royalty. Miss Hanaway is on Bronze Squad so she may ride with us if she wishes."

"No, thank you, sir," Hanaway says respectfully. "I shall walk with Phoenix and Collin. It would be unfair of me to do otherwise."

I detest that rule, but there's no point in arguing further, which would simply irritate my father. I'd rather walk with them but that would never be allowed.

My father once again commands our attention. "Once we arrive at the Ridge, we will pick someone to go through the portal. Now, let us move out."

That was brief, even for my father. A stable boy hands me a torch. With a click to my horse, I lead the way at a slower pace than I'd like but not so fast that those on foot can't keep up. Collin, Phoenix, and Hanaway also bear torches as we head out of the courtyard. Once we're past the stables, we turn right and select the trail that will take us to our destination.

Dragon's Ridge is several miles outside of Alethia. The terrain isn't too bad—fairly smooth, but steep in places—and at night, it's hard to see. The torches help a little, but we can't see more than a few feet ahead of us.

Who will volunteer to go through the portal? It is a very risky thing considering we are not sure if they are working properly or not. If we had another Key, we could send it with the volunteer, just in case, but of course there is no other Key.

I bite my lip, realizing how futile tonight's effort really might be. Because even if we find out the annual portals are working properly, we still have to find the hidden notebook and then make a new Key.

Not willing to risk my father's reprimand, I suppress the urge to swear.

Chapter 24 – Phoenix

My walk to Dragon's Ridge is not exactly enjoyable. Hanaway and Collin, like me, are huffing and puffing after just a couple of miles.

Sylvia stops her horse every few minutes and waits for us to catch up. I know if she had the choice, she would walk right along with us, or she would insist we have horses. I sigh. I would probably refuse a horse if I were offered one, or I would insist Sylvia ride even if she could walk. Those are the manners my mother taught me. Treat royalty like royalty. Say please and thank you, and so on and so forth.

Rose, now, she's another story. She probably does not have the best manners because her mother left her when she was so young. One of Rose's mother's good friends raised her after that. I assume Rose did not listen to the woman like she would have listened to her own mother . . . although maybe that's assuming too much. I don't really know because I didn't live in Alethia when we were all young.

Instead of dwelling on Rose's lack of manners, I focus on not tripping and falling. It's very hard to see the ground with only the moon and the torches to light the path. On top of that, the torch is made of heavy wood, and occasionally bits of hot ash drop on my skin. But at least it's a warm summer night and we are not freezing. It always does a person good to focus on the good things instead of the bad; it makes the job easier, as my mother used to say.

After an unbearably long time, and when I'm quite out of breath, we finally arrive at the top of the ridge. Collin, Hanaway, and I are silent for a few minutes as we cool down and catch our breath. The king and Sylvia patiently watch us, their horses standing completely still. They are the best horses one can find in the kingdom, after all.

Collin looks at me and Hanaway to see if we're ready for whatever is next. I'm the last one to recover from the hike, and I finally give him the thumbs-up sign. He nods at the king.

King Stephan clears his throat. "Who will go into the portal?" His solemn gaze shifts between the three of us.

Whoops. Collin and I should have talked about this on the way up here. Sylvia sits uncomfortably on her horse and stares at the ground. I know she would prefer to go than to stay behind and—

"I volunteer," Hanaway says and steps forward.

But she's just a child! "You're too young to go through!" I exclaim as I walk over to her and put my arm around her narrow shoulders.

"I am nearly twelve!" she argues, and politely steps out from under my embrace. "I'm plenty old enough. Besides, I want to help."

"Miss Hanaway," the king says. "Phoenix is right. Now is not your time, but I appreciate your willingness to go." He looks at Collin and me. "So, which of you two will volunteer?"

Collin takes a deep breath and opens his mouth—to accept, I'm sure.

But in a rare moment of courage, I step forward and raise my hand.

"I will."

I'm not really thinking as I do it. Or at least not about what it will *mean* to do it. Because just before I stepped forward, Rose's voice popped into my head. *"Screw 'can't' and just do it, Phoenix!"*

That's what she shouted to me as the wind crazily whipped her hair around her face as we stood on top of the cliffs by the ocean.

Rose wanted us to cliff-dive. To jump off the cliffs and into the ocean far below! It was her idea of a party. No one had ever tried jumping off these cliffs before. Or if they did, they didn't live to tell about it. Rose said she heard that humans do it on Earth. And since Rose is never one to let anyone get the best of her—certainly not people from other planets—I can see why she was excited about this. She also told us that she thought the water was deep enough. Keywords: thought *and* deep enough.

I, on the other hand, was not sure she was right, but it was clear that nothing would stop her from trying something new and exciting. To be honest, though, I was the only hesitant one in the group. Even Sylvia was thrilled to sneak out of the castle and do something dangerous and unusual.

When Rose shouted at me above the wind to "screw 'can't' and just do it!" we were the only two left on the cliff. Everyone else had already jumped in. But to me, it looked like a far and treacherous drop to the boulders below from where I was standing.

A minute ago, Collin had yelled back to me, "Don't look down!" as he ran off the edge of the cliff, but at the moment I was too busy worrying to heed his advice.

Rose was losing patience with me. She would not go in until I did because she wanted to make sure everyone did it—especially me, her practical, cautious friend.

I walked closer to the edge to see where everyone was and to look again at the rocks below, when Rose suddenly ran at me with a laugh. In that instant, I knew she was going to push me off the cliff. This was her solution.

Just before she reached me, I realized I wanted to be able to say that I jumped off the cliff on my own—and not that I got pushed by Rose. That would not be a fun story to tell—or to hear her crow about.

I took a deep breath and followed her advice from earlier: screw 'can't' and just do it!

So I ran the last few feet to the edge and jumped off the cliff.

It was one of the most fun things I ever did. I felt like I was flying! I laughed with joy, and then remembered to wave my arms in crazy circles like everyone else did to make sure that I would stay upright and go in feet first. And just before I hit the water, I tucked my arms in at my sides so they would not slap the surface.

I slid into the water like a seal. Bubbles surrounded me as I sank into the ocean, slowing as I went. It was rather relaxing and quiet, actually. I could see all the way to the bottom; it was shallower than Rose had told us it would be—no surprise there. I looked around for fish or other sea life, but they had already been scared away by the others. I stayed under for a few seconds, admiring the clarity of the water before kicking up to join everyone else.

I resurfaced just as Rose splashed down within a couple of feet of me. Holy cow! Clearly she was impatient enough to jump before she made sure I was out of the way. She could have hit me! But maybe she could not stop her momentum when she was running at me up on the cliff. A moment later, her head popped up out of the water. "I told you it would be fun!" She laughed at me, kicking back to the shore. "Now hurry up so we can do it again."

I swam after her, proud and grateful at the same time. We jumped off the cliffs several more times that day, laughing and having fun. I was glad Rose so easily convinced everyone to come. Mostly I was glad that I did not get pushed off the cliff; I do not think that I would have survived the embarrassment.

I snap back to the urgent reality of Dragon Ridge as I feel the weight of everyone's stares. It's unnerving, and my gut wrenches. What am I doing?

Then I look at Hanaway and know it was the right choice. She is too young to be putting her future on the line by going through the portal. Even if she is only two years younger than me.

I glance at Sylvia, who looks shocked that I volunteered to do something dangerous. Yet here I am.

The king nods gravely at me. "Then get ready, Phoenix. The portal is due to show up any minute. And thank you." I doubt he knows how out of character it is for me to do this.

I take a deep breath to steady my nerves and try not to think about what could go wrong.

How does Rose laugh and smile while she does stupid things like this? She must be truly mental. She always told us that she should be locked up her entire life, but we just brushed it off, thinking she was joking. But maybe Rose is more than a little off her rocker, and it's rubbed off on me. Is insanity contagious?

Collin hugs me tightly. "Are you sure you want to do this, Phoenix? Because I'm fine with going. Or I could go with you."

"I want to go," I say with as much conviction as I can muster. "Besides, you need to stay here and help. Please, I need to do this for Rose."

"Okay. Good luck," he says, then whispers in my ear, "I'll see you when you get back." Holy cow. He *does* understand that I have to do this by myself.

I return the hug, glad for the reassurance. At least someone has faith that I won't be stuck on Darnisha forever. "Thanks. I'll be back as soon as I can." Even I can hear the false courage in my voice.

Just as Collin and I pull apart, the portal opens and flashes brightly in front of me, like it knows I am its victim.

This particular portal is one giant, multi-colored flat ball of fire. It changes colors rapidly, from bright pink, then to dark blue, and neon purple, and every color imaginable. And it doesn't have a white center like I thought portals usually have.

What the—?

I'm sure that Rose said a portal stays one or two colors, depending on the destination. Why didn't we look up in the book to see what color this is supposed to be? Are multiple colors bad? I should have asked Rose more about the portals when I had the chance.

I briefly lock glances with everyone. There's no time to discuss it or even to say goodbye. Sylvia looks like she is about to cry, but then again, Sylvia cries at a lot of things. I wish I had just another minute to hug her goodbye, but we agreed earlier that whoever went through would need to do it immediately. Hanaway looks disappointed. Collin's expression is distinctly worried. And the king simply nods gravely at me to enter the portal.

Praying to anyone or anything that will listen, I take a deep breath, two running steps, and throw myself through the portal. I close my eyes as I hit it, surprised that it does not burn me. I can tell that I'm inside it because the atmosphere changes drastically. It feels like the sky right before a lightning storm full of electricity and overflowing with energy.

I have the sensation of floating, but I cannot open my eyes or move at all. Panic flares, and I struggle to breathe calmly.

Rose never told me what it was like to go through a portal. I went through one when I was young, but I don't remember what it well. Besides, I wasn't alone that time. I truly do not think that other trip was like this, because I would have remembered it if it had been.

Something is most definitely not working right with this portal.

It seems like I have been immobile and stuck here for an eternity, but as soon as I register that thought, something happens.

I am thrown out of the portal. I try to land on my feet but land on the ground instead. Tall grass tickles my skin. An insect buzzes around me. My eyes are still squeezed shut; I am afraid to open them and see where I have ended up. How Rose manages to land gracefully—or at least on her feet when she does not hit the tree—is beyond me. Lots of practice I suppose.

I finally force my eyes open and look at my surroundings.

I am shocked by what I see. This is not at all what I had been expecting.

Chapter 25 – Rose

Days pass—I don't know how many. Food is regularly dumped in my lap, which is the only way I can tell time has passed. I also get let out twice in about twenty-four hours to use the restroom. Each time I'm blindfolded until we get there, and when we do, the men wait outside the door so I can't run for it. There's no window in the bathroom, nor is there a shower; it's very utilitarian. I think my captors use it too, so it's not a place I want to linger.

I feel like Derek will never come for me, and that I'll never think up an escape plan. It's hard to remain optimistic. To have hope.

***

Finally, sometime in between lunch and dinner on what I think is the fifth day, the door unexpectedly opens. I stand up and one of the men—Scarface—pulls me out. He doesn't blindfold me, so I know something is up.

The room beyond my own is about the size of my living room at home, but I don't take the time to look around because two other men—one is Butch—are both there, glowering at me. What are they planning on doing to me? Are they finally gonna off me? Did Derek not get the money in time? I could try running, but no, there's too many of them. I'll see what they have in store and, if worse comes to worst, fight my way out or die trying.

The other man in the room is the creep who kidnapped me from the diner. He seems like the leader, so I call him Fido (just because I can). No one says anything, so I let my gaze roam around the room. Empty beer bottles, poker chips, and cards litter a table that has several mismatched wooden chairs around it. The floor is covered in cigarette butts and ground-in ashes. The raucous music from earlier is now gone. The air is thick with cigarette smoke and the smell of unwashed humans. This must be where the horrible smell originates from.

Again I realize how much I *hate* silence.

Finally, Scarface points me to a chair next to the table, so I sit down. Buried under an empty bag of some greasy crispy food item is a large object like one I saw in the hotel room with Derek. He told me it was like a cell phone, but it doesn't travel anywhere or fit in pockets. Why people invented these large, clumsy things when there are cell phones, I will never know. And this one even has a cord that plugs into the wall, so it must need electricity. Lame!

The door on the opposite side of the room bursts open, and a fourth man stalks brazenly into the room and pauses when he sees me.

Frick! I recognize him right away and stumble to my feet, putting the table in between us. It's the man who was following us that first night, the one I knocked out. The one Derek took a picture of. My anger boils quickly to the surface.

The other three men jump to their feet while this dude studies me, his chest stuck out like the arrogant bastard I'm sure he is. So, this must be a bigger ring of tough guys with a different leader than I had thought. Old Fido, with the smelly white T-shirt, is just an underling and not in charge after all.

I look steadily into the familiar, beady eyes of the new arrival, trying not to panic or hit him or show any fear—or all three. My mind races. This puffed-up guy doesn't look like a "little birdie" who told Fido our whereabouts. But it must be, and to top it all off, this little birdie is the boss.

"Remember me?" he asks in a cruel, gravelly voice.

Duh. "I seem to remember beating your butt into the ground. Have you come back for more?" I taunt him cockily.

I sit back down in the chair, put my feet up on the table, and cross my arms on my chest. I can't allow myself to show any fear, even if my little inner voice is screaming, *Run! Run or die!*

Besides, if I sit down, maybe he won't see my knees are shaking.

He sneers at me with a malicious look on his face. He knows that this time, it won't be me beating him. I'm outgunned, outnumbered, and with the limited information I have right now, outsmarted.

At this point, I figure my life is officially over.

Chapter 26 – Derek

I pace in circles around the table in the police station, a half-empty cup of coffee in my hand. Rose has been gone for several days and I still can't believe she was abducted. Watching her be kidnapped by those dirtbags was awful. I felt completely helpless. I knew the main guy in the white T-shirt—Sal—who dragged her out of the diner. But not the second one guarding the side door, or the third one holding his gun to my head. I didn't even think about trying to fight my way out. Besides, I wouldn't have left without Rose.

As soon as Sal shoved Rose's unconscious body in a car, the other two men also hopped in. I ran outside just as the car took off down the street like it was in a NASCAR race. I tried to chase it and grab a door handle or something, but it was moving too fast. I continued running down the street after it, even as I watched it speed away.

But I did manage to get the license plate number and gave it to the police when they arrived a few moments later. They put out an alert for it and for the guy I know as Sal. They closed down the diner as a crime scene and tried to see if they could get anything helpful from the customers. I doubted they would; the kidnappers were much too confident to be amateurs, too much of an experienced team.

One of the worst parts of this whole ordeal has been knowing that I have Rose's knife. I've been kicking myself every hour since her abduction for having confiscated her knife . . . for what I have come to realize was a stupid reason. Dammit! She needs it now more than ever, and yet I have it. That knife could've been the difference between her getting away or being captured.

I toss out the coffee I'm no longer in the mood for; it's cold anyway.

Rose is gone, and I have little-to-no hope of finding her.

I told the police everything I knew about Sal. But it wasn't much and the police didn't seem very hopeful. Chicago is a big city.

The police also asked me a lot about Rose, and I told them all that I could, but there was still a lot I couldn't answer. Who are her parents? Where does she live? They also wondered why there was no record of her existence—no social security number, no birth certificate. I couldn't explain my way out of that one, so I just shrugged my shoulders. They wouldn't believe the truth even if I told them. They'd probably throw me in a mental asylum.

The police said they believe Rose is using some kind of alias, and I decided to play dumb and let them think that. After all, I only met her a few days ago, and I told them that. They made me describe her several different times, and I did so to the best of my ability. They sketched her, but it didn't look a whole lot like her; the face in the drawing had no animation or life in her eyes. It was a mournful picture of someone who could've been Rose's pale, quiet sister.

Sighing, I rub my unwashed face with my none-too-clean hands and wish I could take a shower, but I don't have anywhere to do so. Besides, there's no way I'm leaving.

From where I sit in the lounge in the back of the downtown precinct office, I can barely hear the murmur of people talking out front. I put my feet up on one of the utilitarian chairs around the small, round table, and stare blankly at the wall with the mini-fridge, counter and sink, and coffeemaker. As I've found out during the past two nights, the couch and recliner on the opposite wall are comfortable enough. This would be a very relaxing place to drink a cup of coffee or read a book—under other circumstances.

I toy with the photocopy of the ransom note that arrived the day after Rose was abducted. It's already dog-eared from me reading it so often, trying to gain any clues that the police might have missed from the typed demand for $10,000 to be delivered to a location to be determined. But none of us have figured out anything.

I could make amends with my parents and ask my dad for help. Of course, they would only allow me to return home if I admitted the Key thing was garbage and not real. Although, it would be worth it if I could get Rose back—

The police chief strides into the room, a hopeful expression on his face. "Derek, we've found something that might interest you," he says in his thick Chicago accent.

Oh, please, let this be good news!

There hasn't been anything new since the ransom note arrived. I quickly follow him into his office.

He shuts the door behind me. "We just had a witness step forward anonymously. This person managed to take pictures of the men who abducted Miss Sanders. We sent the pictures to our colleagues across the city in case these kidnappers are spotted.

"And we have more good news: we've been able to positively identify these thugs. We know who they are, including the one who calls himself Sal. And we've learned these men are not acting alone."

Yes! I lean forward in my seat, eager to see the pictures and learn the names of these scumbags who took Rose. The chief hands me the pictures of the men. I nod. Yup, that's the,.

The chief continues, "Do you know who their leader might be?"

I shake my head no, and the chief looks as crestfallen as I feel. I glance at the pictures again. They're grainy and a bit blurry, just like you'd expect from a picture taken from a cell phone.

Something nags at me. It takes me a painfully long minute, but I finally figure it out.

"I just remembered something!" I stand up and pace again, this time with excitement. Sal had said their informant had had a run-in with Rose and me . . . I wonder if that's him—the leader? The guy who was following Rose and I when we first met? And Rose had me take a picture of him—*two* pictures!

I'm so damn stupid! How could I have forgotten? If I hadn't been frozen in fear during Rose's abduction and not paying much attention to what was going on, I would've figured this out sooner. Then we might have found her by now.

Why did I have to freeze up like some coward?

I pull out my phone and scroll through the options to my photos. They're the last two I took, and I show the picture to the police chief.

"This guy was following Rose and me the first day I met her. And I just remembered that, in the diner, Sal said something about a guy having followed us and then told Sal where to find us when we were at the diner. "

Thank goodness Rose knew cell phones have cameras built in—even if she couldn't remember the word for *camera*.

Shit! How could I not have thought of this, not put the pieces together before this?

The police chief studies the photo on my cell for a moment, then turns to the cluttered bulletin board behind him and pulls down a piece of paper with a lot of mug shots on it. "Is this the man?" He hands me the paper and points to the photo in the upper right corner.

I stare at it. My stomach clenches. "Yes, that's the man who followed us. Who is he?"

"His name's Jace. We've had several cases point to him, some with him as the prime suspect, but we've never been able to find him to bring him in for questioning. Chances are, we never will. He knows how to avoid us. He's recently been linked to a counterfeit money scheme that's being run by loan sharks on the south side of town."

Seriously? The police already know about this creep, and they still can't bring him in? "That's *not* what I want to hear," I say angrily and toss the paper onto the desk. "I want to hear that you will find him. And if you don't, you will at least find Rose."

The chief looks at me resignedly. He's probably had people yell at him before and he knows how little it accomplishes. "I'm not making any promises I can't keep," he says bluntly.

So make me a promise and then make sure you keep it! I bite my tongue to keep from telling him my thoughts.

I need some fresh air, away from these incompetent cops. I stalk to the office door and open it.

The chief's voice calls me back. "One more thing before you go, Derek. We heard from them again just before I came and got you. The kidnappers have raised the ransom to $15,000 dollars by the end of the week. We found the new demand in the fax machine a few minutes ago, sent from a city library. I sent officers to check it out, and the sergeant here has already called to ask the library manager if he has security videos so we could see who was in there today, but, unfortunately, the place doesn't do them."

I slam my hand against the door, more frustrated than I've ever been. It bounces against the wall and nearly smacks me in the face.

He frowns. "I have even more bad news, son. I'm sorry, but we won't be able to raise that much for a person nobody but you seems to know. And if none of her family come forward to help, well, we can still try to use the fake money for the ransom drop like we talked about, but . . ." He sighs as he walks past me without a word.

I'm so frustrated that I punch a hole in the wall. It looks like someone has already done that. Several someones. The wall has four or five holes inexpertly patched with sheetrock. Well, now there will be another one.

My stupid mistakes of *first* taking out a loan with a stranger and *then* not paying it back on time—those mistakes are going to get Rose killed. How could I have let this happen?

Again, I'm tempted to ask my dad to help me get her back, but I can't speak to him now. Not after nearly a year of not talking to him, not when he doesn't love me enough to believe me about the Key.

As I storm out of the office, I kick the doorframe for good measure. It's solid steel, so now my big toe is more injured than the building is.

But I don't care. There's nothing I can do about it. Or, apparently, about getting Rose back.

***

Five days have passed. Five, miserably long days and nights spent at the police station, hoping something will break loose in the case as I watch the deadline approach.

"We have contact!" the chief yells from the conference room where we've been working. "Get in here now, Coulee!"

I jump out of my chair and run down the short hall to the large, brightly lit room. We had already decided that if phone contact was made, and the kidnappers let someone talk to Rose, it would be me. After all, I'm the only person who knows her.

I grab the phone. "Hello?" I listen intently for any sound that might help us determine where she is being held.

"Hello to you too," says that laughing, wonderfully sarcastic voice I've missed. "I'm sorry I've taken a rather unexpected vacation."

Words tumble out of me. "N-nice to know you're well, Rose. So, anything you'd like to say to me?" I ask her, bouncing on the balls of my feet in happiness. She's okay! Well, okay enough to be joking around.

"Yes, actually, I have something I want to tell you but seeing as there's a gun pointed at me, I'll leave that part out. I'd just like you to tell my mom, Matilda Sanders, that I say hi, and tell my dad, David Sanders, that his little Rosie Posie can't wait to see him."

What the—?

What is she saying? How can I possibly contact her parents? They're on another planet!

Then the first name clicks. *Matilda. Matilda Sanders.* Our waitress! Okay, that's weird. Why Rose wants me to give that message to the waitress, I don't know, but of course I'll do it. "Okay. Sure. Any other messages?"

"Ten seconds," I hear a gruff male voice say from the other end of the line.

"I need fifteen more seconds to get an exact location," one of the police techs whispers behind me.

Rose's voice comes back on the line. "I'll return from my little trip soon enough, I'm sure," she says dryly. "In the meantime, you should probably get a job and get some cash, my friend."

"Whatever you want, Princess," I say just before the line goes dead. I stare at the phone before I put it back in its stand.

It was her! She's really okay! And now we can trace where the call came from, and then rescue her!

"I didn't get an exact location," says the tech apologetically, "but I've narrowed it down to about a quarter-mile radius."

I let out a groan of frustration. That is still a lot of ground to cover, especially when I see the location—smack dab in the middle of highly populated, densely urban, downtown Chicago. The only good news is that it's close to where we are now.

"So Matilda and David Sanders are her parents? Do you know who they are?" the police chief turns and asks me, a small spark of hope in his eyes.

I frown. "I don't know her parents—I told you that already— but I do know a person we just met at the 7th Avenue Diner whose name is Matilda Sanders. She was our waitress. I can go back to the diner and talk to her, although I'm not sure she'll know what Rose was talking about. I was under the impression that Rose's parents don't live anywhere around here."

The chief looks skeptical.

I head toward the door. "I'm going to the diner and see if the waitress knows anything about what Rose was talking about."

"Hold on a minute, and I'll send a couple of my men with you."

"No, this is something I need to do by myself," I say firmly as I swing my jacket on and grab my backpack from the corner of the room.

"Suit yourself," the chief shrugs. "Tell the sergeant on your way out the name and address of the diner. And let us know immediately if this makes any sense to that waitress."

The diner is only five blocks down from the police station, and I walk so fast that I'm practically jogging. This could be the break we need! When I arrive, I take a seat at the counter and impatiently drum my fingers on the worn, red countertop.

"What can I do ya for?" a gray-haired guy behind the counter asks me.

"Is the waitress Matilda Sanders here?" I ask hopefully.

"No, but her shift is in fifteen minutes," he replies. "Why?"

"I've got a question for her," I say vaguely, trying not to look too impatient. Or like I'm a stalker or something. "Um, while I'm waiting, can you get me a coffee, please?"

The guy looks at me skeptically, probably wondering what I want with the waitress. He hands me a cup of coffee but I'm too tense to take a sip. I rest my head in my hands. This is going to be a long fifteen-minute wait.

Why would Rose want Matilda's husband, Mr. Sanders? Does she really think that he's her dad? Hadn't Rose said something about her kind being able to sense when their family members are nearby? So does she sense something, and maybe that's why she thinks this is her dad?

"Come back to give me a tip?" I hear a familiar voice, and then a laugh.

Matilda! Finally I can get some answers.

Swiveling around on the chair, I say solemnly, "More like to ask you a question, actually. It has to do with Rose's abduction."

"Oh dear, is she still missing? I'm so sorry."

I nod glumly. "Yes, but we made contact today with the men who took her. I spoke with her, and she told me the weirdest thing."

The waitress leans on the counter listening.

"She said, 'I'd just like you to tell my mom, Matilda Sanders, that I say hi, and tell my dad, David Sanders, that his little Rosie Posie can't wait to see him.' I'm hoping you might know what she was talking about."

Matilda straightens and frowns in confusion. "My husband's name *is* David," she says slowly. "Maybe he knows what she's talking about. We've only been married for five years. From what I know, he was married once before and had children, but he didn't live anywhere near Chicago. I don't know for sure, though; he doesn't like to talk about it." She shrugged one shoulder. "I've always believed that he has perfectly logical reasons for not telling me."

Her blind faith in him seems odd to me, but she must be a naturally trusting person.

She pats my shoulder. "Come on. I'll get someone to cover my shift and we'll go ask David about it. I'm sure he'll try his best to help you find your friend. He's really very kind. Just give me five minutes to find someone to take over. I don't want to anger my boss."

It takes less time than that. The cook's friend is quickly on her way to replace Matilda. We leave right away, and I let out a sigh of relief. All this waiting is going to kill me. Maybe this was Rose's great plan all along when she was proposing ways she could kill me. Death by waiting. Well, she certainly gets points for creativity.

"My house is about a five-minute walk," Mrs. Sanders says as we exit the diner. That's how I start to think of her—as Mrs. Sanders, which just seems more respectful.

I nod, then ask nervously, "So Rose's dad is your husband, but you're not her mom?"

"He might not be her dad," she cautions me. "I'd be surprised if he were."

I'm not sure if I'm hoping Mr. Sanders is her father or not, but whatever will get her freed works for me. "Rose seemed to think he's her dad. And he has the same name. Not to mention the fact that you said she looked like your husband." I look over at Mrs. Sanders' worried frown, and reality knocks me down again. "I guess she just wants someone to see if it's her dad or not. It doesn't really give us a clue to her location, but maybe he'll know if she was talking in a code or something." I'm feeling desperate.

We turn a corner and I pick up the pace. Fortunately, Mrs. Sanders complies.

She's quiet for another block, then asks, "Do you know what age Rose was when her father left?"

"Honestly, I don't know much about Rose. I didn't even know her dad had left. I only met her a few days ago under . . . interesting circumstances," I say with a laugh, trying to make light of the situation.

Mrs. Sanders shoots me a funny look. "Sounds a bit sketchy to me," she says warily.

Crap. I should have just told her that I didn't know. "I promise there was nothing illegal going on when I met Rose. If your husband really is her dad, I'll explain everything. If not, I'm afraid I won't be able to tell you. The reason why we banded together is a secret for the two of us alone," I explain, trying to set her straight without really revealing anything.

Well, nothing illegal except for the underage gambling, and the confrontation with that Jace guy that lead the kidnappers to finding Rose and me. If I just hadn't taken that wrong turn in the burned-out part of the city, I would still be with Rose, watching her get whipping cream on her lips when she guzzles hot chocolate, and helping her get home.

Why do I have to be so stupid?

Chapter 27 – Phoenix

I gasp as I raise my head and look at my surroundings. Even from where I lie in the tall grass, I can tell I am back on Dragon's Ridge. Alone. The portal sucked me up then spit me right back out in the same place! Well, not instantaneously. It's dawn now, so I guess I was in it for a few hours.

Defeat courses through me and I flop back on the hard ground and stare at the sky. We may never be able to get Rose back. She could be stuck some place all alone, or stuck in a portal, or worse, stuck somewhere with Lexi.

I'm sure it was a portal that took them, but it was obviously working differently than the one I was in last night. I snort to myself. And even that one wasn't working as it should. Who knows where that freak portal took them.

Sitting up, I brush the dirt from my hands and look around. The sunrise lights up the ridge. Not a soul is around. No Sylvia, no Collin, no Hanaway, no king. I guess they decided not to wait for me. I wonder if the portal stayed visible the entire time, or if it disappeared as soon as I got in it? Well, that's just one more question I'll ask Sylvia when I see her.

My thoughts crash down on me like a tidal wave, sucking me under. Frustrated, I break off a long clump of grass and throw it as far as I can. The fact that it only goes a few feet makes me feel even more helpless. Rose is somewhere, maybe dead, maybe alive, and there is virtually nothing I can do about it.

I sit on the ridge and bawl my eyes out. In frustration, and in sadness that I'll never see my friend again.

After blubbering for a few minutes, I realize how ridiculous I am. I need to get a grip, so I take several deep breaths. I clear my head and wipe the tears off my face with the sleeve of my shirt. Now is the time to march back to the castle, find that notebook, and bring Rose home at any and all costs.

Standing up and brushing myself off, I set out at a determined pace down the hill towards the castle.

When I get into town, no one is outside on the streets. Alethia is silent, despite the early morning sunlight. Something is wrong. People should be up and about, doing morning chores, opening their shops, or else headed to the castle library. Increasing my pace, I jog the rest of the way to the castle and arrive, out of breath and worried, a few minutes later at the front gates.

Dozens of people clog the entry into the palace and the grand foyer, too, I notice once I push my way in. No one pays any attention to me; they're too busy peering under rugs and poking around behind lamps and dumping everything out of the closets. They look like they're searching for something. It must be the notebook.

When the doors clang shut behind me, everyone looks up and gasps. I twirl around to see what they are looking at behind me.

"Phoenix!" Sylvia shouts and I whip back around to see her dashing toward me. In a second she's hugging me and sobbing.

"What is going on?" I pat her on the back comfortingly. Bad news about Rose? Oh, I hope not!

Other people in the room are sniffling too and eyeing me with relieved expressions.

"Oh, Phoenix, you are back," The queen rushes over to greet me, relief evident on her face. "I will get someone to let your brother know right away." She leaves and other people crowd around us after that, exclaiming that it's so good to see me.

What is going on? "Yes, I'm back, but I was only gone for a few hours. It really wasn't that big of a deal." Why are they all acting like this? Sylvia tends to over-react to certain things, but why is everyone else being so dramatic?

"You were gone for two months," Sylvia blubbers onto my shoulder.

"T-two months?"

I could not have possibly been gone for that long. I was only in the portal for five seconds, ten at the most. At least that's what it felt like. But certainly it's only been six or seven hours since we were all up on the ridge together and I jumped into the portal shortly after midnight.

"Yes, it really has been two months!" Sylvia insisted between sniffles. "After you jumped into the portal, you never came out. I was so worried that I had lost you, too," she rattles on. "We were all hoping you would find a way to get back here, and you did. How did you do it?" She stops suddenly, aware that everyone is listening to her fall apart.

But I'm still focused on what she said. *Two months?* It can't be. "Sylvia, that is crazy! I was sucked into the portal for only about five seconds. Then it spit me back out again. So I did not actually *escape* it," I clarify.

The entire crowd hears my explanation, and their expressions grow sad when I admit that I had not really found my own way out. They were all probably hoping I had escaped and that Rose would too, at some point.

"Maybe that is what happened to Rose," Sylvia suggests hopefully, "and it just has not brought her back yet."

"But why would she not be back by now if that were the case?" I say, and Sylvia's face falls. The queen notices and frowns at me. Uh oh. I quickly add, "Unless, of course, people can be held in limbo for different amounts of time. In that situation, Rose could still be out there."

Sylvia's face perks back up.

"So what has been going on since I left?" I ask, changing the subject. "Have you found Ulysses' notebook with information about the Key?"

Sylvia shakes her head no. And now that my story is over, everyone else—including the queen—goes back to searching.

179

"We have been looking for the notebook room by room," she says, "but so far we have had no luck. We have managed to thoroughly search half the castle by taking apart nearly everything. But we have not got the slightest clue as to where the notebook might be. Or even what floor it might be on. I assume King Ulysses did not think we would ever need a new Key. Or else he did not want people to know a new Key could be made."

Weird. Wouldn't he want some sort of insurance in case something happened? But maybe he thought nothing ever would happen . . . "So, we're looking in the main hall right now?"

"Yes. We are almost done, I think. I am not sure. My mother will not let me help look for it because it is too similar to cleaning, and as we know: Princesses must not get their hands or clothes dirty by cleaning or doing other household chores." Sylvia does quite the impression of her mother's voice—it's spot on. I stifle a laugh. Fortunately no one but me overhears her.

"I am sorry," I tell her, knowing how helpless she must be feeling. "Let's go to your room and look around there so you can do something. Besides, I doubt you want the entire village digging through your personal stuff later," I suggest.

"Oh, that is a brilliant idea. No one has searched my room yet, and I can simply tell my mother that you cleaned the entire thing for me while we talked. She will be happy that I actually listened to one of her rules."

On the way to her room in the west wing, we walk through a corridor where a painting of mine is hanging on the wall. I smile proudly when I see it. The castle has great statuary and artwork, and I'm happy mine is a part of it. My painting brings the lively colors of a castle ball into the hallway, whereas most of the other paintings have dull colors. Although I should pay more attention to them because I can always learn something from the great painters of Amara's past.

My gaze roams over every piece of artwork as we walk through the long hallways. Much of it is familiar to me—but not all. Tucked into a dimly lit bend in a hallway, I notice for the first time a slightly dusty life-sized marble statue of an old man—probably royalty—with what appears to be a benevolent-looking angel sitting on his shoulder and holding a book. Behind the statue is a floor-to-ceiling painting in muted colors, meant to look like a window with a view of one of the palace's many courtyards. It's really quite effective. Amazing what you notice when you actually look.

I catch up with Sylvia. The castle has seven different floors with hundreds of corridors and thousands of rooms. I doubt even Sylvia has been in every room. Although the three of us got to know sections of it when we used to play hide and seek here.

"So what do we do first?" I ask her once we reach her room. It's not exactly a small area, and it has several alcoves as well as places where the room juts out over the courtyard below. There's a lot more to Sylvia's bedroom than four simple walls.

I walk into the center and look around, trying to think of where a small object, such as a notebook, could be hidden. In loose floorboards under the rugs? Behind the paintings hanging on the walls? Inside Sylvia's enormous vanity? Maybe in a hidden drawer or shelf inside her various pieces of furniture?

She doesn't appear daunted by the task. "Let us search all the nooks and crannies that I do not often use, because I highly doubt it will be hidden someplace I see every day. It is probably concealed behind some sort of trap door, or a secret door, maybe," she says enthusiastically and sets off towards the right side of the room.

I go to the opposite side. Geez. This bedroom is big enough to house several people. Come to think of it, we have had some grand slumber parties here over the years. I grin at the memories, and get to work.

Chapter 28 – Sylvia

Even after two hours of pulling up all the rugs to look for trap doors or loose floorboards, and examining the wood trim along the edges of the floor, we still have not found anything. Except a few cobwebs and a spider or two. We have yet to inspect the paintings, however, and all the walls and the furniture too. There are a lot of potential hiding places.

"Now I see why it's taking so long to go through the castle." Phoenix stretches and her back cracks loudly.

I cringe, disgusted. It drives me absolutely crazy when someone cracks things like their back or their knuckles. It always reminds me of the sound of when I broke my wrist when I was little. Rose says I hate it because I think it is uncivilized and that my inner princess is coming out. I think Rose just enjoys teasing me.

"So . . . two months and nothing?" Phoenix asks, looking at me sadly.

My eyes fill with tears and I cannot hold them back. The past few months have seemed completely hopeless. After a few sniffs, I wipe my nose on the handkerchief my mother insists I always carry, but I wish I was brave enough to just use my sleeve. Rose would.

Phoenix politely ignores me, then changes the subject. "Umm . . . so have you checked for false backs in the dressers and cabinets? Those seem like great hiding spots."

I manage to pull myself together. "Good idea. We also still have to check all the bricks to see if they move. There could be a cubbyhole behind one of them that holds the notebook," I toss out, even though the idea is actually someone else's. Collin had come up with it partway through our first day of searching, probably in an attempt to keep his mind off of Phoenix's disappearance.

And speaking of Collin, he is going to be overjoyed when he hears that Phoenix is back. But I am not ready to share her yet, so I head to a wall to push on the bricks.

"This is going to take a lot of work," Phoenix says while methodically pushing on individual bricks on the wall opposite me. "Searching the castle would have taken forever without everyone's help, and as it is, you have been doing this every day? That's incredible. I cannot believe I was gone for two whole months . . ." She is quiet for a moment, then adds in a lower voice, "Oh, uh, by the way, how is Collin?"

I silently laugh at her crush; not that she would ever admit she has one. I watch her while I reply.

"He is fine. I am surprised he has not come busting in here already to see you," I say, choosing not to tease Phoenix; well, at least not that much.

She blushes and changes the subject. "How have the meetings with your mother been going?"

"I have not been to any," I tell her honestly.

"How queer. Is your mother letting you off the hook, so you can search for the notebook?" she asks, her brow furrowed, as she pauses between bricks.

"No. She has simply put this search ahead of her meetings. The other officials are meeting on their own and they keep notes on what they are talking about. That way, she can catch up when she is available to attend the meetings again." Actually, my mother really has been behaving oddly since Rose disappeared, and even more so since Phoenix left through the portal. I shrug, and offer the only explanation I have come up with. "Besides, no big decisions are being made now due to her absence."

"Interesting," is her thoughtful response to my long-winded answer.

"Some people change when bad things happen," I say, reflecting on the changes since I last saw Phoenix.

183

My father, for one, has only left a couple of times for meetings in other parts of Amara, which is a great improvement from before.

My mother has stopped her official duties all together.

The townspeople have reduced their own stores' business hours to a minimum so they can devote every spare minute to look for the notebook. Only a few people are still running things in the town, making sure the necessities get done.

This has been going on for all these weeks, which, when I think about it, is an incredibly long time. It is taking a toll. Everyone is becoming more stressed and tired, and every day they become a little less motivated. I do not know how long this many people will continue to search. If someone does not find the notebook soon, I fear it will only be me and Collin and Hanaway and now Phoenix who still search with single-minded determination towards our goal . . . although I have to be careful not to let my mother catch me searching.

I pause, a new, unwelcome thought crowding out my semi-positive attitude. What if someone found the notebook and took it, or threw it away so nobody would ever find it? Why someone would do that, I do not know, but it certainly is a possibility. Even if it is not very probable, there is still a chance it happened.

Crap. I sit back on my heels and rub my knuckles that are sore from rapping on bricks.

As if she can read my mind, Phoenix asks, "How long do you think it will take to find it?" Without missing a beat, she continues pushing at bricks.

"I have no idea." I absently watch her while I fill her in on our research efforts while she was gone. "We have found out that King Ulysses was supposed to be really smart, so it is probably in some obscure place, like in a wall or something. I have been doing research on him when my parents are around and I cannot help look

184

for the notebook. I have been hoping to come across some clue about where he hid it, but so far I have had no luck. The books all have the same boring history on his life and what he achieved, which apparently, was not much, despite him being so smart," I explain to her. "Well, he added a lot of artwork to the castle, but he didn't do much for all the other citizens of Amara. So, unfortunately, if we are being really honest with ourselves, it could be a long, long time before we finish searching."

Phoenix runs over and hugs me. "Sorry. It must have been terrible. First Rose disappears, then me—and you still haven't found the notebook. And . . . and I have to tell you, Sylvia, it is a shock, being gone for two months," she says apologetically. "I mean, it didn't feel like two months. It feels like it was just last night. I could swear on my life I saw all of you that recently." She stops hugging me and studies my face with a very worried expression on her own.

I am a little concerned about Phoenix. She is usually the optimist; I am the pessimist. And Rose is whichever one she feels like being that day.

I study Phoenix, who now looks confused and exhausted. Here I am telling her about all my issues, and she is trying to cope with the fact that two months of her life just disappeared. She sniffs, and it is my turn to pat her back. "I know it is hard, Phoenix. I cannot imagine what you have been through." I nudge her toward my bed. "You should probably get some sleep. You must be exhausted."

She agrees and, in a matter of seconds, her breathing is regular and she is asleep.

And I return to pushing on bricks.

Chapter 29 – Rose

My kidnappers hang up the phone on Derek and then eye me speculatively. I stare back at them. Aside from shifting in their chairs occasionally, none of them move or talk—they just look at me and wait.

For what?

Whatever, I mentally shrug. My message to Derek is going to get me out of here—I know it. My internal tracking system couldn't have been wrong when I met Matilda. I got that feeling of familiarity and warmth that always indicates someone is family, so she must be.

If not, I'm screwed.

The deafening silence stretches on. I'm not sure what they're doing or what they think about while they stare, but it's making me uncomfortable. I have a hard time not squirming—or stupidly leaping up and trying to make a run for it.

The same four guys are still in the room: the three henchmen—Fido, Scarface, and Butch—are seated around the poker table where I am, and the creepy man who I beat up on the first day leans against a nearby wall, his arms folded across his chest and more than a glimmer of malice in his eyes. He looks a lot angrier now than he did when he followed us through the burned-out section of town.

I finally decide to shake things up, and I go about it in the only way I know how: to be loud and annoying. Besides, it's high time I got out of here and before I can do that I have a small war to win.

"You blinked! I win," I shout to all of them, smirking and leaning back in my chair.

They continue to stare, although Mr. Follower shakes his head, as if he can't believe my behavior.

I take it to the next level by addressing him. "I'm sorry you didn't win. It truly is unfortunate. Now, if you'll excuse me, I'll be going back to my closet," I say, standing up. He motions to Butch who shoves me back down on to my seat. "Oh, rude! I know you're sad about losing, but you don't have to be a bad sport."

Why does Mr. Follower not get in my face himself? I look right at him. "Scared?"

His lip curls. "Listen here, little girl," he snarls from his safe position on the wall. "You'll do exactly what I tell you, when I tell you."

Ha! No one pushes me around like that! I keep my face impassive even though I want to hurt him.

"Got it?" he asked, narrowing his gaze menacingly. I resist the urge to beat the crap out of him.

Instead, I quirk an eyebrow. "Basically, all the words that come spewing out of your mouth, I am supposed to listen to them?" I can't help my digs sometimes; sarcasm is the natural defense against stupid. And these men are all clearly very stupid. I've never been in a room with people who have such a collectively low IQ. Because any idiot knows that hell hath no fury like a woman scorned. Especially this woman.

He straightens, still glaring at me. "You *will* follow all my demands, starting with shutting your trap."

"Well, I don't really like most of your demands. And you might get farther if you add *please* and *thank you*." I lean forward, giving him a big fake smile. "Your tone could be nicer too, and you could just let me return to my closet like I'm sure you are going to do anyway. I mean, I'm just trying to make things more convenient for you."

The man opens his mouth to speak but closes it again. Hopefully he's remembering how I kicked his butt a few days ago. He shifts his weight to his other foot, and his brow wrinkles as if he's thinking. Hmm. Now that I'm standing up for myself, he backs down. He doesn't seem too anxious to fight. Probably doesn't want to get hit in front of his little henchmen. That would be more than embarrassing for him, although it would be rather entertaining for me. That's probably why he's having Butch get in my face instead of doing it himself.

Speaking of the red-haired devil, Butch still has his hand on my chair when he looks inquiringly at Mr. Follower, who nods once. "Go back to your closet," Butch snarls and leans toward me, pointing at my door.

Sheesh. Has he ever heard of a toothbrush?

Just to mess with them a bit more, I cross my arms over my chest and lean back in the chair again, then put my feet up on the table. "You seem to be forgetting a certain magic word in that sentence."

Fido leaps out of his chair, and I yank my feet off the table. But I'm not fast enough. He grabs my arm, pulls me up, and yells, "Now!"

As rude as he is, I'm impressed. That was actually a fairly decent reaction on his part. He pulls me across the room and throws me back into my closet. I go along for the ride willingly; no need to anger him anymore. Besides, I think I just won this battle.

I listen for the lock to click, but it doesn't. *Yes!* The psychological war is won. Now it's time to launch the final attack.

"That wasn't the magic word!" I shout. No response.

I put my ear to the wooden door and listen to the shuffling and muffled words in the other room. They seem to be settling down, so I use the time to make a plan.

Since the lock didn't click, I can open the door at any time and escape. And the best time for that will be before dinner. I can't wait until everyone is asleep at night because when they bring my dinner, they'll undoubtedly re-lock the door. I won't get that lucky twice.

So my only chance is surprise. I've got to burst out at a random and unexpected time and sprint for the door on the opposite side of the room. From there, I have no clue what I'll encounter; I can only hope for the best and run fast.

My well-being always seems to rely on me running fast. It's like the universe knows I don't have my full speed right now, and it's laughing at me.

I listen through the door, waiting for them to be seated and start playing poker. That way, they'll be distracted and slower to follow me. Even a small lead can make a world of difference.

The music resumes, and the four men talk to each other. I give them a few more minutes to relax.

And then I'm ready. Now is my only chance.

I grasp the doorknob and turn it slowly. I take a deep breath, clearing my head. My reaction time will need to be faster than it's ever been. These men are stronger than me, and while I may be more nimble, that won't help me in such close quarters.

This just might be the scariest thing I've ever done. Well, okay, maybe not, but it's pretty high up there on the list.

I yank the door open and burst out like a rocket. I sprint as fast as I can through the room and grab the other door handle, praying it opens. It does. I can't believe they didn't—

Oh, but they're so stupid that I *can* believe they didn't lock the outer door. Too bad for them! They should know that nothing ever goes as planned.

By the time I'm through that doorway, the men have lumbered to their feet. Footsteps pound after me. I dash down a long hallway and reach the door at the end of it. Yanking on the handle with great force, I rattle it but it doesn't budge an inch.

Shat. It's locked. From the outside.

The men are just entering the hallway, and I do a one-eighty, trapped. My brain is whirling faster than it ever has.

Time for an impromptu Plan B. I usually don't bother with a Plan B because if a Plan B is needed, it means Plan A was never going to work. I like to think that my Plan As don't suck, but they really do sometimes. Like now.

"Stop!" Fido is a few steps ahead of the others, and there's not a moment to lose. What are my options?

To my right is a large, open window—with a ledge on the outside. I could probably just about stand on it—

I hop out of the window with Fido and his henchmen breathing down my neck. The ledge is wide enough for me to scoot along, so I do.

Before I've gone more than a couple of feet, Fido is leaning out the window and reaching after me. "Come back now and we won't hurt you," he says in what is supposed to be a persuasive voice, I'm sure.

Cautiously, and with my heart racing, I shuffle my way farther down the ledge. Ten feet away is the metal scaffolding that supports a fire escape ladder. Freedom!

"Climb out after her! Hurry up!" Fido shouts to someone inside.

Scarface tries to climb out the window, but he's awkward and slow. My quick sidestepping soon gets me closer to the fire escape . . . and to another window that opens into the same hallway the men are standing in. Fortunately, the window is closed. *Please don't let them get smart and actually go open that window to grab me as I go by.*

I need to distract them, so I resort to my usual method: my sarcastic and always lovely mouthiness. "You know, lying isn't an attractive trait," I say conversationally, but even I can hear my voice shake. My foot slips, and I squeak in terror.

So far, I've avoided looking down. But my fear gets the best of me, and I succumb to the temptation.

Two-story drops and people trying to grab me—combined with a lack of sleep, fresh air, and exercise—do not bode well for controlling my reaction. My stomach knots painfully, and sweat breaks out on my forehead.

To distract myself from the great distance down to the cement sidewalk, and to distract the bad guys from realizing there's another window they can reach me through, I resume my one-sided conversation. "People tend to not appreciate liars all that much," I tell them, trying to focus on nimbly moving my feet more than an inch or two at a time.

Scarface has given up trying to climb out on the ledge. Fido pokes his head out now, glances toward me and notices the window, then withdraws and shouts to his buddies, "Open that window farther down the hall! Quick! Before she gets to the fire escape!"

Damn it. Fido isn't as stupid as I wanted to give him credit for.

I look up and down the street but no one is around. No point in screaming for help. I try to quicken my pace without falling off. Unfortunately, I'm edging past the window when I hear it creak open.

No way in hell are they capturing me again.

To prevent that, I do the stupidest thing I have ever done in my life.

I jump.

Chapter 30 – Derek

My impatience to see if Mr. Sanders is Rose's dad or not is making the walk to the Sanders' house feels as though it takes forever, even though Mrs. Sanders and I walk at a brisk pace.

Finally, we're here. I nervously follow her up the brick steps to her tall, narrow home that looks exactly like the others crowding it on both sides.

I wet my lips and my mouth suddenly goes dry. I have no idea what's about to happen.

She opens the front door and calls, "Honey? There's someone here to see you."

"Who's here?" comes a voice from what I assume is the living room. A man rounds the corner into the main entryway.

Rose's father. This is him. Mrs. Sanders was right. There's a resemblance between him and Rose, though it's not based on looks. He has short brown hair, dull green eyes, and is thickly built—not to mention tall. How Rose ended up being so short with this man as her dad, I will never know. But instead of physical features that mark them as father and daughter, it's the resemblance in the way they hold themselves. Shoulders back, confident expressions, and an air about them that suggests you should think twice before messing with them. And when he lifts his brows inquiringly at me, it's the same expression Rose wears when she drills me for information.

Rose is right; this has to be her dad. If it isn't, and she and I are both wrong, then he at least has to be related to her in some way, shape, or form.

I step forward and extend my hand. "Hi, I'm Derek Coulee. I'm here about a recent abduction that happened in the diner where your wife works." I choose to leave out that the person who got abducted is probably his daughter.

I glance at Mrs. Sanders, but she remains quiet, studying her husband anxiously.

He nods and shakes my hand. "Oh, yes. Matilda told me about that. Come in and sit down," he says, motioning beyond him to a little living room at the end of the hallway. "And I'm David Sanders, by the way." His voice is low, and rough, though friendly enough.

I take the single brown leather chair. Mr. and Mrs. Sanders sit together on the slightly worn couch.

Taking a deep breath, I speak. "Sir, I think my friend Rose—"

"Yes, tell me first about your Rose, and then what happened to her," he says warily. He has clearly heard about Rose, and that she's the person who is missing. His wife must have told him . . . but is he also wondering if my Rose is his Rose?

He leans forward in his seat. He has to wonder; otherwise, he wouldn't be so interested. Do his Amarian mental powers help him sense a family member is nearby?

I clear my throat. "Well, first, I need to tell you the message she gave me because I assume it confirms whether or not you are actually her dad, and then I can tell you the entire story." I have to be one-hundred percent positive he's her dad before I can tell him anything about what's happened.

Mr. Sanders doesn't even flinch when I use the word *dad*, although his expression turns sad. "She probably said, 'Tell my dad, David Sanders, that his Rosie Posie says hey.'"

I freeze. *How—?*

I have to open and close my mouth a few times before I can string words together. "That's, that's almost exactly what she said!"

How did he know that? Maybe they have a secret code or something for times like this. I lean back, still astonished. "So, then I can assume you're her father?"

He looks apologetically at an astonished Matilda and reaches out to squeeze her hand. "I used to be, a long time ago," he says mournfully. His use of past tense is alarming.

"What do you mean, you *used to be*?" Rose never mentioned her dad didn't live with her. Actually, Rose never mentioned anything about her family, or even very much about her life back on Amara.

Sadness fills his green eyes. "Things happen." He clears his throat. "Tell me your and Rose's story."

I don't seem to have much choice. There's a lot I don't know, and I don't know if I should tell him what I *do* know. My mind races from one scenario to another. But I always come back to the bottom line: Rose wanted me to contact him, and this might be my only chance of finding her.

I sit up straight and let the words pour out. "Well, it started a few days ago when I first met Rose in a burned-down neighborhood here in the city. A long discussion and a few threats later,"—Mr. Sanders smiles at this—"she decided to trust me enough to let me help solve her problem. And we're, well, we're both Gatekeepers. I assume you know what those are? I'm the one from Earth and she's the one from Amara, your home planet."

Mrs. Sanders gasps and pales, but I'm the only one who notices.

Mr. Sanders is staring at me intently. "Rose . . . she's a Gatekeeper now?" His eyes mist. I'm taken aback. How long has it been since he's last been home to see his daughter?

I glance at Mrs. Sanders. She's wide-eyed, but she shakily pats her husband's hand as she nods at me to continue.

"How come she came to Earth?" her husband asks abruptly.

"Well, sir, I don't know. Your daughter has somehow ended up on Earth with no way to return home. She's not even sure how

194

she got here, although we both suspect it was a malfunctioning portal of some kind."

An odd look flashes across Mr. Sander's face—anger? Anger at what, though? At what happened to his daughter?

Then his shoulders sag and his expression grows morose. I wonder how it would feel to not hear anything about your daughter for years, and then the first thing you hear is bad news, and that she isn't safe. Judging by the look on his face, it'd be pretty painful.

"I was trying to help her get home safely. Then there was a fight, and then some old enemies of mine showed up at the diner that day she was abducted."

I feel the weight of the two Keys heavy in my pocket. They're Rose's hope for getting home. Yet I have her Key and she doesn't. Nor does she have her knife.

My thoughts return to the present. Mr. Sanders is furrowing his brow, concentrating on something. How to help Rose, maybe. I don't know.

My mood sinks further when I remember there's more I should tell him. "Her kidnappers found us because the man Rose fought at the beginning of our adventure was a friend of theirs, and he told them where we were . . . which resulted in us being held at gunpoint in the diner, as you know, and Rose being abducted."

Mr. Sanders' eyes flash with anger. I wonder if it's towards me, or the people who took his daughter.

This is hella hard. I put my head in my hands and take a deep breath before looking up and continuing, "I guess they thought this would be motivation for me to meet their demands." I decide to leave out exactly what their demands are. It's clear that all of this is my fault, so it's not like I need to share every detail with Rose's dad. He'll probably never forgive me, as it is.

Mr. Sander's face sinks further into despondency. He swallows hard and grasps his wife's hand as if for comfort.

I continue. "About an hour ago, we got a call at the police station, where I've been helping the cops with their search efforts. The caller was Rose. She didn't give us any tips or clues as to where she was being held, but she did tell me to deliver that message to you."

Sweat is running down my back as I wait for his reaction. I add, "Please say that you can help us. Please." I need to get Rose back, and right now this man is my biggest hope.

He doesn't say a word—just stares blankly at the wall behind me.

My stomach twists painfully. The suspense is making me sick. What if he doesn't help? And why do I have the feeling he hasn't been home in a long time? Why does his wife not know about him being from Amara? Why isn't he answering me? Mr. Sanders shifts his now-guarded gaze back to me. "I'm sorry, but I can't help you."

What? All that emotion and concern he showed for his daughter, and he says no? *What the hell?*

I must look stunned, because he adds, "I left that life a long time ago."

Am I really hearing this? Frustration rises in me like a tidal wave. Why, why won't he help us? I can tell he knows how to find Rose. He has to, because Rose wouldn't have sent me on a wild goose chase to find him if he didn't. Besides, he was laughing a minute ago about Rose's behavior, and then he was furious at her kidnappers, so how could he not help her now? He's her father, for god's sake.

"So you're going to let your wonderful, crazy daughter, who is my friend, get killed by some lunatics—when you can help her?" I say, my voice rising, as I try to fathom the man's decision.

He shakes his head but still manages to look me in the eye.

196

My temper is rapidly running away from me. I jump to my feet. "And why not? Because you can't face whatever happened in the past, so you've been hiding out here on Earth? Is that it?"

Mrs. Sanders squeaks, and Mr. Sanders' face turns sour very, very quickly. That last line struck home.

His face reddens and now he, too, is on his feet. "What I do or don't do is of no concern to you!"

It crosses my mind that this is the source of Rose's temper: her father. But I stand my ground and glare at him. If he's going to be a coward and not help my Rose, then I'm not going to back down from him.

He takes a step toward me. "You don't understand! My life was torn away from me, and I'm choosing not to re-open the wound. The longer Rose stays away from the portals and all of that nonsense, the better, as far as I'm concerned. I have my reasons, young man, for not wanting to help you find Rose and bring her back into that mess. My reasons are my own. You don't know what's going on here, and I'm not about to tell you. So get out of my house and get out of my life," he roars, pointing at the door.

"David!" Mrs. Sanders puts her arm around him. She murmurs something to him, but I can't hear it.

Besides, I'm too angry to care.

"Your daughter will most likely die, do you hear me? *Die*, if you do not help me. I don't have the money for the ransom, and it will take weeks to search all the places she could be. By then, my time will be up, and she'll be six feet under. How can you not care about Rose?"

I stalk around the room and try a new approach. "Surely you remember your own daughter? You remember the way she gets distracted at the smallest things, the way she loves to win at everything, then gloat about it? Her ability to keep calm under pressure and to joke around when most people would be too scared? Hopefully you remember her contagious laughter. How can you just ignore all of that? How can you just ignore her existence? *You* are going to be the person that gets her killed!" I'm in his face, yelling, but I take a step back, away from this cruel man who doesn't deserve to be Rose's father.

"You are despicable," I spit the words out like venom.

Mr. Sanders is fuming with anger and his fists are clenched at his sides. "You've only known my daughter for a few days while I've known her for years. Besides, I know she won't die," he grinds out.

"You left her a long time ago! How long have you really known her for?" My anger towards him is consuming me.

"You have no clue what our life was like," he growls. "You can't even imagine the pain she's been through. I will not be the person to inflict more."

I can't believe this guy! "I'd rather inflict pain and help her get better than have her dead in a ditch somewhere." I resume pacing in the small room. "You don't know for sure that these men won't kill her. I may not have known her for very long, but I know that if she dies, she'll die as my friend. I will never forgive myself for getting her into this mess, and I most certainly will not stand by to see someone flat-out refuse to help me get her back!"

Mr. Sander's face loses some of its anger, which is replaced by surprise. "You care about her that much, despite having only known her for a few days?" he asks quietly, a curious expression on his face.

But I'm not about to be placated or distracted. "People bond through shared experiences. Rose and I both know what it's like to be singled out as a Gatekeeper, and I guess both of us also know the feeling of a father's abandonment. I hope you never forgive yourself for this," I say spitefully, turn on my heel, and walk out.

Slamming the door behind me, I stomp down the street. I am through listening to that man's sorry excuses. He can't know she won't die.

And what was he even talking about, with that whole she-needs-to-stay-away-from-the-portals thing? She can't stay away from the portals or she'll never get back home. She's the Gatekeeper, for crying out loud! Going through portals is literally in her job description. She can't just stay away—that's impossible.

He's going to be the reason she dies, I fume. And his mind is firmly made up.

Yelling in frustration, I kick over a garbage can unlucky enough to be in my way.

Chapter 31 – Rose

I hit the pavement hard, landing on my left ankle. It pops and cracks nastily, and pain shoots through my foot and up my leg. Out of habit, I immediately tuck and roll; my momentum tumbles me a few feet more. My shoulder aches from rolling on it to avoid a face plant.

But I have to ignore the pain for now. Rising unsteadily to my feet, I take off down the street, limping. Not twenty seconds later, footsteps pound behind me.

Frick!

I look around for help and see an approaching cab, so I hail it. Inside, I quickly slam the door shut.

"Drive, because your life depends on it!" I scream in the driver's ear.

He apparently gets the message and slams down on the gas.

"Drive so they can't follow you," I command, trying to catch my breath and look over my shoulder at the same time. And try to ignore the worsening pain in my ankle.

The taxi swerves to the left. I'm thrown to the right. Grabbing the edge of the seat, I alternate between watching for the bad guys behind us and attempting to figure out the wild maneuverings of the cab driver so I'm not flung about.

There's no sign of my pursuers, so I tell the cabbie he can ease off the sharp turns. Letting out a shuddering deep breath, I settle back in the seat. Good thing there actually was a taxi to pick me up. I could never out-run Fido and his crew on foot, not with my ankle.

"Why are you running away?" the driver asks as he swerves around the slower-moving traffic. He's still setting a good pace, for which I'm grateful.

"More like escaping abduction than running away," I respond casually, trying to get my wits about me. "I didn't exactly want to be back there, you know, and I didn't have a choice."

The driver looks at me in surprise in his rearview mirror.

"Eyes on the road!" I yell, whacking the plastic barrier between the front and back seat for emphasis. Pain shoots up my arm.

"Hey, calm down, young lady!" He scowls at me. "So should I take you to a police station?" He sounds like he just wants to dump me on the side of the road.

"Yes! The police station closest to the 7th Avenue Diner," I tell him.

I glance out the back window again. A caravan of black cars is snaking behind us, probably loaded with Fido, his troops, and who knows who else. How the heck did they already catch up?

I call to the cabdriver, "But first you'd better lose those guys behind us in the black cars!"

The cabbie gives me a grudging glance and swerves the cab around a corner. Unfortunately, the ominous-looking black cars all make the same turn.

"Drive faster! They're right behind us!"

"My foot is all the way to the floor, lady. What more do you want?" He jerks the wheel around another sharp turn.

"For the rear window to show me that there aren't people following us!" I'm trying not to panic.

"Hey, do you even have money to pay me?"

"I was just abducted!" I scream. "Do you think they'd let me keep my money?" Was this guy's brain turned on when he asked me that? "Of course I don't have any money!"

The driver slams on the breaks and the car jolts to a stop. I brace myself as my knees crash into the seat in front of me.

"What are you doing?" I protest, my voice going up a painful octave. A stubborn taxi driver was not part of my improvised Plan B.

"I am not risking my life for you, lady. You're on your own," he says coldly. "Get out."

"No! You've gotta drive me!" I yell, wishing I could smack him through the plastic barrier. Now I know why they put these stupid things up.

"Get out!" he demands again as a black car slides to a stop on my right.

Time for me to move on to Plan C.

I jerk open the door on my left, weave through oncoming traffic, and try to sprint down a litter-strewn alleyway. But with the messed-up ankle that the universe just *had* to add to my dilemma, well, anyone can tell I'm done for.

Car doors open and slam shut, and horns honk behind me. The men's footsteps pound on the pavement. It sounds like all four of them are chasing me.

I risk a quick look over my shoulder. Fido is in the lead, followed by Scarface, and then Butch. The ringleader lazily jogs along . . . Typical! He *is* a follower, after all.

Stretching my legs out in front of me as far as I can, I also try to pick up the pace. Is it working? A glance over my shoulder shows it's not. They're nearly upon me!

I swerve toward a dumpster so I can climb on top of it and swing up onto a fire escape, but—

"Gotcha!" Fido yells. He grabs me and yanks me loose from my tentative grip on the dumpster lid. The other three jerks are just a few feet away.

Beyond them, at the end of the dirty, narrow alley, I glimpse a sign for a diner, and an arrow pointing down the block. I recognize that sign! It's for the 7th Avenue Diner.

Suddenly, a feeling of familiarity and comfort pours through me. Could it be Matilda?

I briefly close my eyes, because I can also feel a growing sense of warmth and home, the same way I felt as a child when my father was nearby.

But I will have to wonder about that later. There is a more important issue at hand right now; the fact that I'm about to meet my maker.

My eyes pop open and I try to assess the situation, but Fido wrenches my arm up behind my back to keep me from running, and I gasp in frustration and pain. I'll have to talk to my maker about my sprinting abilities on Earth because he really sold me short on that useful tool.

So if I can't run, what else is there for me to do?

Time for plan D. I suck in a deep breath of air and scream for my life.

Chapter 32 – Derek

I leave the Sanders' home and storm back to the diner. What felt like a long walk earlier takes me only a minute or two now.

Plunking down into a booth, I rest my chin in my hand. I need to think of a new way to find Rose.

I could go to my dad for help, but he wouldn't be at all happy to see me. When I last spoke to him, all we had were slamming doors, angry voices, and him telling me to never come back.

A waiter with long dreads approaches me. I must look fairly awful. I haven't showered, eaten, or slept much in days.

Jacobson, according to his name tag, asks sympathetically, "Girl problems?"

"Girl problems . . . Yeah, you could say that," I reply vaguely.

"I feel for you, man. Girls are complicated. Whatever it is, I hope you fix it soon."

I hope so too.

"What do you want?" He poises a pen over his order pad.

My brain screams, *I want Rose to be okay!* But instead I just order a coffee like any normal person. He nods and strolls off to fill my order.

A few days ago, the police chief gave me a twenty to buy donuts and chips from the vending machine at the station. I pull the last two dollars out of my pocket. Rose had all of my money, although her kidnappers probably have it now.

Maybe I should just go ask my dad for money, but then again . . . I rub my forehead, my frustration evolving into a massive headache. No, the only thing my dad is good for is when I use him as a threat towards other people. They tend to not want to mess with the mayor and his son; bad things happen to people who threaten a political figure's family.

That's the only reason the men didn't come to collect earlier, I'm sure. Now I wish they had because then they wouldn't have taken Rose. Just thinking of her causes my gut to twist painfully, and a giant lump forms in my throat.

Not a minute later, the waiter returns and sets a mug down in front of me, pours steaming hot coffee into it, and leaves without saying a word.

I slowly nurse my drink. Where could they have taken her? What did they do to her? Is she locked up somewhere? Dead? Beaten? Could she have fought them? If she tried, would she fail? Succeed? I just don't know.

After a second refill of my coffee cup, someone slides into my booth. I look up—and glower when I see who it is.

"I'm going to help you find her," Rose's dad says gruffly, "but that doesn't mean I'm going to talk to her. She sent you to me because Amarians have internal tracking systems for each other. We know when a family member is around. So if you can get me close to her, I'll be able to pinpoint her location."

A smile breaks across my face. Yes! We're going to get her back!

Suddenly something Rose had told me comes to mind. "Wait, I thought your powers didn't work once you went through the portals and left Amara?"

"Our physical powers don't work, but our mental powers do. I don't know why, but that's what happens," he shrugs.

"Okay, well, to get her back we need money—fifteen thousand dollars," I tell him. I doubt he has that much, and certainly not on him.

"Don't worry about that. I figured we'd need to pay the ransom money. I just did some business with a loan shark, so I have money. I'll pay to get Rose back to you, but as I said, I won't talk to her."

That was good enough for me. "Come on, then. Let's go!" I say excitedly and stand up. "The police have a quarter-mile radius on her location, and we're in it right now." The waiter will have to be satisfied with the measly two dollars I leave on the table.

"We won't need the police's help," he says firmly, "because I can—"

His head suddenly whips in the direction of the door. "Rose?" He dashes out of the diner. I follow him down the street. Man, he can run fast for an old guy.

I'm a few paces behind him when, in the block ahead of us, I see a black car screech to a stop beside a yellow cab. A young woman jumps out of the cab and runs awkwardly into what's probably an alley, but I'm too far away to see. Three other black cars pull up behind the cab. Three men leap out and join the guy who's exited the first black car, and they all dash into the alley after the girl.

My jaw drops as what I just saw sinks in. All four men look disturbingly familiar. And so does the girl.

Mr. Sanders picks up speed and I'm right on his heels.

Then I hear a short, blood-curdling scream.

Rose!

Chapter 33 – Rose

My scream cuts through the stale summer air as I continue to struggle. Butch or Scarface—I can't tell which—claps his hand over my mouth, effectively cutting off my yell for help.

But too bad for them, because my scream has apparently already done its job. Out of the corner of my eye, I see someone at the diner-end of the alley run toward us. Help is on the way!

I struggle to break loose from Fido's grip but his muscles work well for him. I kick one of the other guys who's trying to help Fido hold me, and I bite the hand over my mouth that's all but suffocating me.

"What the hell?" The owner of the hand—Butch—bellows and lurches away to examine it. Good. I hope it's bleeding.

"Help!" I yell again. My shoulder is screaming in pain, and I can't feel my ankle anymore.

But all my struggling does nothing. Fido has too much weight and height on me, and they drag me toward their cars . . . which means we'll run smack dab into the guy who's coming to help me. Haha, thank you, universe!

I continue to struggle to distract Fido's group from my approaching savior. I glance in that direction and see a second guy right behind him. My knees nearly collapse with relief.

"Let go of her," the first man yells.

At the sound of his voice, memories from my childhood flood through me.

. . . A youthful-looking man teaching me how to shoot a bow and arrow . . . then the same man teaching me how to swim, how to whittle with a knife . . . Telling me that I should never join in a fight I can't win, and that words work better than fists.

They've seen the two men running toward us and obviously can't agree on what to do with me. The ringleader shouts an order but I don't really hear it.

While Fido and his group continue to pull on me, and my vision blurs with tears, I stare at my father. It really is him. He's not dead! Eight years and he's still alive. And he's just feet away, his chest heaving with exertion from sprinting.

All my cares and pains fall away.

All I can think of is *him*. My dad. How did he find me? I mean, I thought Matilda's husband *might* be him, but it was just a long shot. Like some random hope I was reaching for and trying to grasp, but I didn't actually believe it.

The ringleader's voice barking at my father draws my attention. "Don't come any closer unless you have our money."

My father—sweating and looking angrier than I've ever seen him—pulls a big wad of cash out of his pocket. And just how did my dad get rich enough to do that?

But instead of approaching Mr. Follower with the money, like I expect him to do, my father hands the cash to the second man who ran up the alley and is now standing at his side.

Derek.

I can feel Fido straining toward that huge bundle of cash. He draws me tightly to his side although his eyes never leave the cash. The roll has to be bigger around than my fist.

Around the edges of my confusion, anger seeps in and takes hold. Who the hell is my father, to have me thinking he's been dead all these years?

Derek steps forward. "Here's all your dammed money." He shoves it into Mr. Follower's chest. "Now give her back to me." He takes a menacing step toward Fido and me.

Fido looks back and forth between the bundle of bills, and Derek. The ringleader nods once as he stuffs the roll of bills in a pocket.

Fido pushes me away from him, and they all four dash back to their cars. My father and Derek don't try to stop them, just let

208

them pass. And almost before I can take another breath, it seems, they're in their cars and gunning the engines as they take off.

Well, shoot, I'm free. My father is still standing a few feet away from me. It isn't a hallucination. And when I realize Derek's wrapping his arms around me, I sob.

"You f-found my f-father," I say, turning into his embrace.

Sirens scream in the distance. The police are late to everything. Typical humans.

Derek strokes my hair. "I did find him. But you led me to him, Rose. It was you who found him. You're okay now. I promise nothing like this will happen again," he adds.

I want to fling myself at my father, but something holds me back in Derek's arms. Besides, I'm too angry at my dad, and I'm too overwhelmed with emotions to deal with anything, let alone confronting the father I loved about why he abandoned us and let us think he was dead.

Realizing that Derek is still holding me, and what we must look like, I attempt to cover my embarrassment. "I feel like I've been shot," I joke weakly and try to step back, but the adrenaline has already left my body. Pain shoots up my leg and I nearly fall.

Derek shakes his head and picks me up, bridal-style. "You can tell me later the story of how you got hurt, and I'm sure it'll be an interesting one."

He is careful of my shoulder, and I don't complain about being carried. I am too tired. I put my head against his chest and close my eyes to drift into the welcoming arms of unconsciousness.

I ignore my father.

Chapter 34 – Rose

I wake up, and for a second I think I'm still a captive in that horrible, smelly closet. Naturally, I panic.

"When do you think she'll wake up?" Derek's worried voice reaches me from a distance, and I open my eyes. I am definitely not in that closet anymore. More like a bedroom. A guest bedroom, I'd say. Derek must be out in the hallway.

"She'll wake up soon enough. She needs lots of rest though, so let her be," Matilda replies to him.

That old warm feeling floods me, telling me I am near a family member. So this must be my father's house. Derek must have brought me here.

I'm safe. And I'm starving.

I gingerly get up and throw on some clothes. My ankle throbs, but I put my boots on for the extra support. It works enough that I can hobble through the open door and down a staircase, even though I wince with every step.

Following my nose to the kitchen, I almost trip in my rush to get to the cinnamony-smelling rolls on the counter across the room. Just as I'm about to grab one, the plate is snatched away.

Derek holds it above his head and grins like a crazy man. Matilda chuckles and quietly leaves the room.

"Give it back!" I yell, trying to jump on one foot and grab the plate. "If I wasn't crippled . . . " I threaten half-heartedly.

"How long can one person sleep? I thought you were dead," he says with a wicked gleam in his eye, watching me jump.

"Please, I'm starving, and I'm not against hurting you for cinnamon rolls," I laughingly warn him, and he finally sets the plate down. I happily stuff my face with the sweet pastry that's almost as good as what Neva makes in Alethia.

"By the way, I have something of yours," he says sheepishly and sets a familiar object on the counter. "Here's your knife. I'm really sorry I took it."

I quickly lick my fingers and pick up my knife. "Oh, how I missed you," I smile and hug it to my chest tightly. "I am never letting you out of my sight again." Derek watches me as I tuck it back in my boot where it belongs.

I straighten and put my hands on my hips. "So, Derek, why in the worlds did you not give it back to me at the diner when I asked for it? And, actually, why didn't you help me at all during that whole fiasco?"

Derek looks at the ground. "I, I wasn't thinking. I froze. I'm sorry. It'll never happen again, I swear." His face turns red, and he shoves his hands deep in his pockets.

"Oh." My anger dissipates. "It's okay." I wave it off with my hand, and smile to lighten the mood. "It all turned out fine in the end, right?"

"Ya . . . but I'm sorry."

He's still not meeting my eye so I put my hand under his chin and lift it so he's forced to look at me. "I lived. End of story," I say in a reassuring tone. "Time to move on." I take my hand away from his face, and he smiles sheepishly at me.

"Oh, and your Key." He pulls it out of his pocket.

I grab it. It's bent and broken, but at least I have it.

Now it's time to deal with a bigger problem—my father.

I walk into the hallway to peek into the living room. Matilda isn't here. Did she leave the house? Because aside from me and Derek, it feels empty here—and very quiet.

There's no sign of my father anywhere.

***

I've been at my father and Matilda's house for twenty-four hours, but I still haven't seen my father. The only people I talk to are Matilda, and Derek, who never leaves my side. We haven't

211

managed to come up with anything to help me get home. So our plan now is to catch up to my father and see if he knows anything about the portals breaking down.

I'm getting even more attached to Derek than I know I should. I've filled him in on everything, like how my father supposedly died and how my mother ran away. I've told him all about life on Amara, about my cottage in the woods, and about my two best friends, Sylvia and Phoenix.

My ankle and shoulder are healing quickly. Matilda checked out my foot shortly after I woke up on the first day. She was training to be a nurse years ago, but she had to drop out of college because she didn't have enough money to continue. Fortunately, my ankle wasn't broken, but badly sprained. She wrapped it in something and told me to use it as a little as possible and to keep ice on it for fifteen minutes every hour. As for my shoulder, that was just badly bruised and also needed to be iced and rested. On Amara we would've done pretty much the same thing: ice and rest.

I worry that I should be working on a plan to get home, but I secretly allow myself to think that staying here forever wouldn't be too bad either. I mean, there's Derek, of course, and I could get used to Matilda doting on me. And I know I'll eventually talk to my father. At least, I think I will. Staying on Earth with my family for a little while longer couldn't be considered selfish, could it?

But then I remember the battle with Lexi on Amara. My resolve stiffens. The next time I see my father, I'll ask him if he knows anything about the battle. I have a lot to ask him. *A lot.*

***

When I wake up the next morning, I hear his voice downstairs. It's time for our little father-daughter chat, especially about his so-called death.

I limp down the stairs. He must hear me coming, and I'm relieved he doesn't leave the house. When I reach the living room, I lean against the wall—arms crossed—and let all my anger surface.

"What, exactly, were you thinking?" I demand spitefully.

My father sighs. "What are you talking about?"

I straighten. "What the hell do you think I'm talking about? Don't you remember the day you left me? My sister? My mother? You left us all to think you were dead. No letter, no contact, and you never came home. Or did you forget? Do you know how much hurt you caused? Mom left after that, then Elizabeth left. All because your quote-on-quote *death* caused mom to go insane and leave, because she couldn't deal with it."

His face hardens, and he, too, crosses his arms. "I did what I had to in order to protect you."

"Protect me from what?" I demand. I do not need protecting as if I'm some precious doll.

"I can't tell you." Remorse replaces the hard look on his face, and his fists clench tightly. He stares at me, and the expression in his eyes is softer. But I'm not falling for that.

"That's a load of bull," I shriek in frustration. Who cares if the rest of the family is still asleep upstairs. "You can't tell me why you left and stayed away? Oh, that's rich. I can assure you, there's nothing you protected me from by leading me to believe you were dead."

Now I clench my fists. "You're simply a coward, running from something. You are spineless, and weak, and have the whitest heart of anyone I've ever met."

My father's eyes flash angrily and he takes a step toward me. "You couldn't even begin to imagine the evil I'm trying to protect you from. It would serve you best not to disrespect me like you are right now. I am still your father!"

I force my voice to go flat. "My father is dead. *You* have no power over me."

He stops short. A hundred emotions cross his face—hurt, anger, grief, regret.

But I toughen my heart against him. "I don't owe you anything. You lost all my respect the moment you 'came back to life,'" I tell him as I stalk toward him. "You have no place, not a single centimeter of space, to be telling me how to act."

He takes a step back, putting more space between us. "You have to believe me. I did what I had to do to protect you, Rose," he says firmly and without much anger. "There is more going on than you know. I couldn't come home because that would bring your fate closer, and you weren't ready yet. You're still not."

I fume. How dare he presume to know anything about me! "Ready for what? I am one of the best warriors Amara has ever seen. I'm a member of Gold Squad, and I can beat any enemy. I. Am. Untouchable." I pause between each word for emphasis. "I own a Key to all the worlds. No normal bounds hold me back. I am ready for anything. Unlike you, I am not afraid."

His face becomes grave. "If I tell you, *you will die,* Rose."

He's not lying. The wind goes out of my sails, and I lose my aggressive stance. If he were lying, an alarm would go off in my head. That's how it is between family members. And there's no alarm.

But I'm not letting him off that easily. "How can you know that?"

His brow furrows. "I wish I could somehow tell you without speeding up the process, but I can't. You have to trust me."

"How am I supposed to trust a man who let me think he was dead?" Surely he can't expect me to do that.

Yet even as I speak against him, I wonder, *should I trust him?*

He reaches out to me but I ignore it. "Your mother disappeared one month after I left, did she not?"

214

I take a step back. "How do you know that?" And what does her disappearance have to do with me trusting him?

"Like me, she did that to protect you. I made her another Key, should she ever need a spare. So there should actually be two Keys right now: one you have, as the Gatekeeper, and one she has."

My mother has a Key? And not only did she run away from Alethia, but she left Amara all together? Why?

My father responds, answering my unasked question. "She needed to go fight off your fate."

What in the worlds is he talking about now? I stamp my foot. "What are you going on about? My mother went insane and left! She *abandoned* me."

"Rose, when you get home, and I know you will soon, go to our old house. Retrieve the trunk from the back of the closet, but promise me you'll only open it when you have the dreams. Everything you will need to know is in the trunk. That's all I can tell you right now. Anything more would be too much of a risk."

He isn't lying, because, again, there's no alarm in my head. Nothing. But how can he not be lying? He *can't* be telling the truth.

But he is.

"Rose?" he asks gently.

"Okay." My shoulders sag in defeat. "I'll do it. And I even know what trunk you're talking about. But I wish you could tell me about these dreams I'm going to have, though."

He shakes his head and I know he won't change his mind. He approaches me slowly and lightly touches my shoulder. "Do you forgive me?" His face is sincere and concerned. "I did what I had to do."

I stare into his eyes. He still isn't lying.

What should I do? I thought he was dead for so long, then he wasn't dead, and now apparently he was fake-dead in order to protect me from . . . something. All the answers I need are in the trunk in my old house, but I can't look at them now because I can't

215

get home. And I have to wait for some dreams to come? *Frick!* What a mess.

But he's right. I need to forgive him and to trust him. And I need to get the heck back to Amara and figure out what he's talking about. And in order to return home, I need his help.

I nod and give him a brief hug. "I forgive you, but you have to tell me what's going on."

He frowns as he releases me. "I can't tell you anymore than I already have. Wait for the dreams to start, then open the trunk. That's all I can let you know."

I narrow my gaze and try to put myself in his position. He must have faked his death for a really good reason. He wouldn't have simply run away because if that were the case, he wouldn't have helped me escape from Jace and his gang. And besides, I would know if he were lying.

So what is he so scared of? What lies in my future that drove both my parents away, and why can't he tell me? I've already forgiven him, so now it all boils down to whether or not I can trust him.

I study his face. It's the same face—although older—that I loved so fiercely when I was young. And he loved me back. Maybe that hasn't changed.

"Okay, Dad, I'll trust you," I say while taking a mock-threatening step closer to him. "But if it turns out I shouldn't have, you bet I will be back, and it won't be pretty."

He closes his eyes briefly, then opens them. "I understand and I expect no less from you," he says soberly. Without another word, he leaves the room and walks out of the house.

Suddenly exhausted, I collapse on the couch. There's a lot I need to think about.

Chapter 35 – Phoenix

In the past four days since the broken portal dumped me out on Dragon's Ridge—after holding onto me for two months—I've discovered how much I missed when I was gone.

On the other hand, it also seems like little actually happened during that time. Certainly nothing has happened here in the castle during the past four days, either. No one has found the notebook, and there are still vast portions of the castle that need to be searched.

Unfortunately, everyone's dedication is wearing thin. Fewer townspeople hike up to the castle each day to help search; more and more of them are resuming their old lives. Even the search efforts of the palace servants are lackluster and dispirited.

I kick at the elegant little trash bin in the corner of Sylvia's room and groan in frustration. "I can't believe Rose hasn't found a way to contact us yet. Even if she is on another world, I would think she'd have figured out how to send some sort of message."

"I know. Do . . . do you think that means that she—?"

"It does *not* mean that!"

"Phoenix, I think it's something we have to consider." Sylvia picks worriedly at her bedspread and avoids my gaze. "It's been a long time. She might not ever come home."

No. I can't even think of that. I *have* to find that notebook. It's too bad there are so many books in the castle. A lot of them are in the library, but we have already looked at all of those. Then there's the ones in the War Room—those have been carefully searched. And the notebook in . . . wait a second!

I've figured it all out. I know where the old notebook is. The one that Erin Macilnely wrote about in her journal. The one we've been searching for.

I sprint out of Sylvia's room. She calls to me, but I don't answer.

The alcove I want is in a main hallway between the front entry of the castle and Sylvia's room in the west wing. And what I really want is the marble statue of the old guy with an angel on his shoulder, and in the angel's hand—is a book. A very old book, I bet.

It's got to be the notebook.

Why didn't I realize this sooner? A king, a book—it all makes sense. The statue is made of marble, *but the book isn't*. It's a real book.

It is the perfect hiding place. King Ulysses was indeed clever. Hide something important in an obvious place, and no one will ever bother to look closely at it. Everything with top secret information is assumed to be locked up somewhere, not hidden in the upraised, dusty hands of a marble statue where just anyone could stumble upon it. Plenty of people see that statue every day. Hiding it in plain sight was genius. I stand on tiptoes and snatch the book out of the angel's secure grasp . . . which looks like it was carved just for this journal. It figures, I snort. It undoubtedly was.

Sylvia catches up to me as I blow the dust off the cover. "What is going on?" she asks me, bewildered.

"This is it," I say excitedly while holding it up. "This is the notebook Erin Macilnely wrote about in her journal. I'm sure of it."

Sylvia's eyes widen, and I quickly open the old book, trying not to harm it. I hold my breath as we gently flip through the pages.

Sylvia presses against me and looks over my shoulder. Together we discover pages and pages of handwritten words. We avidly read sections of the faded black ink, everything a Gatekeeper could possibly want to know.

Well, almost everything.

Sylvia and I catch each other's eye. Nervously, I turn to the last pages in the book.

And there I find what we've really been looking for:

REPLICATING THE KEY, the page heading says.

"In order to replicate the Key—a device that can open portals to thousands of worlds—you must first . . ."

A list of directions follows.

"Sylvia, we did it!" I squeak, pointing at the page.

"Yes!" Sylvia shouts, jumping up and down. "We found the instructions. I cannot believe it."

We smile hugely and hug again, then all but float back to her room. With plump pillows at our back, we sit side by side on her bed and reread the all-important section of the notebook.

Five minutes later, I leap off the bed because I want to scream the exciting news from the rooftops of the castle.

Sylvia's voice stops me. "Let us go tell my mother and father first."

She's right. We need to do this properly, and that means letting the king and queen know immediately. Especially since we'll need their help.

She motions for me to follow her. "Come on. We are wasting daylight!"

The king and queen are nearly as excited as we are, although they exercise more restraint. They help us gather the few items we need: a key mold, a fire, a few other special ingredients, and, of course, Sylvia and myself. It is so simple.

The queen also has one of the servants go spread the good news: the notebook has been found, the process of making a new Key is underway, and we will use the Key tomorrow morning to bring Rose home.

The new Key is completed by sundown. We're flushed with success, grinning, and patting each other on the back.

Chapter 36 – Rose

The doorbell peals, startling me. Derek laughs at me as I nearly jump through the ceiling.

"Jerk," I call to him as I get up to answer the door, knowing he's following me.

Before I unlock and open the front door, I instinctively reach for my boot to grab my knife. Then I recall that I am not, in fact, wearing shoes. Besides, Matilda took away my knife. She got upset when I stuck it in the wall next to Derek's head after I got mad at him. Apparently it's expensive to fix walls on Earth.

But all thoughts of my knife flee when I open the door. My shocked mind takes a moment to register what I'm seeing, and then I glower at the person on the doorstep. My body tenses. I can only hope my face portrays the get-off-my-front-steps look I feel and try to communicate—my eyes shoot daggers, my lip curls in disgust, and hatred radiates from every square inch of me.

Who is *she* to show up here? She has no right! Besides, what in the worlds is she even doing on this planet?

Derek must have seen my reaction because he immediately stiffens beside me.

"What are you doing here?" I growl at her.

"What a nice way to greet me," says the girl with dark-brown hair and green eyes that match my father's. "I came here because I sensed you were here. Besides, I figured our father is probably lurking about somewhere. I thought, since he is my dad too, he should at least give me a room to stay in until I can figure out how to get back home." She uses that snotty tone she knows I hate.

She brushes past me into the house. I quickly decide to jump her from behind and damage her face, but Derek grabs my arm.

"Who is that?" he asks. He pulls me along the hallway as we watch her enter the living room, look around, and make herself comfortable on the couch. She's taller than I am and moves gracefully.

Her gaze is riveted on Derek and she checks him out. She shouldn't be looking at him. I must have made a noise because her eyes dart between the two of us.

"Derek, that is Elizabeth Delilah Sanders, my enemy, aka Lexi, and my not-so-lovely older sister, who I had sincerely hoped was dead," I say loud enough for her to hear.

"Temper, temper, dear sister. You always had an issue with yours," she says cattily.

I try my hardest not to beat the snot out of her. "Attitude, attitude, dear sister. Yours is extremely unattractive."

"Explanation, please?" Derek looks back and forth between the two of us. He's probably only standing close to me because he knows he might need to restrain me.

I have to get away from this vile girl before I kill her, so I drag him up to the room I've been staying in and shut the door. I flop down on the bed and stare at the ceiling. Derek lies down next to me. I hope Lexi stays on the couch where I left her, but frankly, I wish she'd just get bored and leave.

I groan in frustration. Now I'm going to have to tell Derek about her. It was easy to ignore her existence when she wasn't here, but now I have no choice.

"Elizabeth—or Lexi—is my sister." I blow out a frustrated sigh. "After my father supposedly died in battle, my mother had a mental breakdown and abandoned me and my sister. Well, except now I know she didn't have a breakdown—she *had* to leave—but she still abandoned me and my sister."

Derek rolls on his side and props his head on his hand. His eyes are wide, and he looks shocked. I guess my family history isn't exactly the prettiest.

"No one in our village even remembers Elizabeth."

Or maybe they just never talk about her in front of me, since the rest of my family is a taboo topic in my presence—I've made that clear enough to everyone.

"I mean, they didn't even go look for my sister after she disappeared, so clearly there's no need to remember her."

"Wow," he says. "That's . . . that's really weird."

"Yup. And since then, no one has made the connection between Lexi, our enemy who is apparently mad at the world, and my sister, Elizabeth, who mysteriously disappeared."

He sits up to study my face. "Why did your sister run away?"

"I was getting to that. Be patient." I try not to snap or take my anger out on him. "We fought a lot after we were abandoned. We only had each other to blame and scream at."

Derek's eyebrows shoot up.

"Anyway, Elizabeth ran away, and I didn't see her again for years. Not until after I joined the army. Then I met her because she'd formed her own army—later I figured out she was trying to take down the public servants and other people who hadn't wanted to look for our mother. She got me off by myself on the battlefield the first time we met, and she yelled at me that she despised every single person in our village who had simply accepted our mother's disappearance and had moved on with their lives." I swallow hard as I remember the hatred and resentment in her eyes that day. I was shocked, but even then, I didn't realize how messed up she'd become.

"Basically, she just couldn't cope. She was a monster, leading an army of wicked beings, trying to burn our homes and kill those she felt were responsible for mom still being lost. She was cruel and evil. My hatred for her increased when I saw what she had become. I felt repulsed that I was related to her. No one but me knew her real identity. She did a lot to cover it up, plus about three years had passed, so she looked different and no one really saw her up close."

"How do you know no one knew her real identity?"

"No one ever talks about Elizabeth; they just talk about Lexi." I sit up as well. "If they knew our enemy was my sister, they would handle the battles between us differently, I'm sure. Although that would piss me off if they did."

"So you never told them?"

What a stupid question. "Of course not. She isn't my sister anymore. The day she left, she failed to be family to me. From then on out, she was Lexi, my enemy, the person trying to attack my village."

"Okay . . ." Derek says warily, glancing at me out of the corner of his eye.

"My sister and I were very close when we were young. We were practically the same person back then, but now we couldn't be any more different."

Derek nods slowly and watches me closely as I continue.

"She fights against our kind. She lives only to destroy those who have hurt her in the past, and she doesn't know right from wrong. She can't get it through her thick skull that the past is the past, and we can't change it."

I'm getting so worked up that I have to stand and pace the floor. "Even though we'll likely never see our mom again, Lexi still feels the need to come after everyone, to destroy everything she once loved. Elizabeth has always been a whiney brat and had to always have mom's attention. So with mom gone and no one seeming to care, well . . ." I shrug. "And now she's sitting here, in our father's living room." I throw my hands in the air.

A sensation fills my gut, and warmth and comfort flow within me.

Frick! Why does he choose to show up now of all times, with *her* here? I feel like throwing something, I'm so angry.

But what's the point?

Resignedly, I tell Derek, "My father's home. I guess it's time for some family counseling," I snort.

Derek looks thoughtful as he nods absently and stares at the wall. "Good luck," he calls, his mind clearly elsewhere.

Fine. I leave him, stomping down the stairs and into the living room. Derek doesn't follow. Smart guy. Family fights are for family only.

Lexi is sitting on one end of the couch and my father is in the single chair. Matilda is clanking around in the kitchen, probably baking something, which she does a lot. I stand in the doorway to the living room, my arms crossed, not moving into the room.

My father turns in my direction and I notice he's holding Lexi's knife. Hmm. Interesting. When Dad sees me, his look of pleasure turns even brighter. "Rose! Your sister is here." He sees the glare I shoot her, so he frowns and gestures towards the couch. "Although I gather you're not happy to see her. Please come in and sit down."

"No," I refuse, not moving a muscle. "I am *not* sitting next to her."

My father speaks in a commanding tone I haven't heard in years. "Now."

I roll my eyes and saunter over to the couch, sit down and cross my legs at the knee. And refuse to look at my *dearest* sister.

"Girls, I think you two have some explaining to do," he says calmly.

Lexi and I turn and point to each other. "She drove mother away," we say at the same time.

"Did not!" we reply in unison.

Okay, that was freaky—how quickly we fell back into old patterns of arguing but also of thinking the same thing.

"Girls, your mother's leaving was not your fault. She had her reasons for going away, and with time, you will discover them for yourselves," Dad says gently but firmly.

This is the same thing that came up the other day—mother apparently went to fight off my fate. But why?

"You two need to understand that there is more going on here than meets the eye." He sighs, his shoulders sagging as if the weight of the worlds is on them. "The two of you need to team up and get along because soon, Rose is going to need all the help she can get." He looks at me painfully, like I'm going to die.

But I'm not going to, am I? I square my shoulders. Of course I'm not going to die.

"Well, I certainly don't need *her* help!" I protest. If anyone is going to kill me, it would be Lexi. His ambiguity is annoying me, but I have to keep trusting him. He has yet to lie. "Dad, what are you even talking about?"

"I cannot tell you. You will find out in due time," he repeats impassively, looking at each of us in turn.

"Wow, you're helpful," I sass back. I can't help it. His reticence is grinding down my patience.

His eyes narrow at me and anger passes over his face before he takes a deep breath and noticeably relaxes. With a serious look, he explains, "Just know you will soon be facing something on a very large scale, Rose, and you will need all the help you can get. You two used to get along splendidly as children, and there's no reason you can't go back to that."

He leans forward and catches our eye. "Rose, don't you remember when you wanted to be just like Elizabeth? You thought she was the coolest big sister ever. And Elizabeth, don't you remember when you would do anything for Rose? When you made sure she was always taken care of?"

Lexi and I avoid looking at each other and neither of us answers him.

He continues, "Sure, you two had your fights, mostly over pets, but you always forgave each other and went back to being best friends. You guys used to be attached at the hip, the unbeatable duo."

I know he is telling the truth. Darn it! This conversation is not going well, because he can make Elizabeth and I agree to anything. When we were little and she traumatized my pets, I was ready to go to war with her, but in minutes he always calmed me down and magically turned us back into best friends again.

"She created an army to attack our city," I say childishly.

He doesn't look very surprised as he glances between the two of us. How can my father not be mad at her? She made an *army*. I mean, there's teenage rebellion, and then there's teenage anarchy. I get the whole "I'll always love my child" thing he's got going on, but seriously—anarchy! He can't just brush over that, and skip to the "oh, she never meant it" stage. You can't just *accidently* gather a group of giants to pillage Alethia. It's impossible.

"Elizabeth, do you regret leading that army?" he says sternly to her.

Lexi sighs and finally answers him. "Yes, Dad, I do regret it. And I did every time I had to lead it, too." She looks at the floor. "I created the army out of my hatred for those villagers who didn't help us look for mother, but that was only in the beginning. After that, it wasn't my choice anymore." Her voice lowers until I can barely hear it. "It was never my choice."

Oh, baloney! "How was it not your choice?" I scream at her. "You caused wars against our hometown!"

"You don't understand, Rose. You will never understand what I went through," she says miserably.

Really? Is she that ignorant? "I went through the exact same thing as you when mother left. You're not some special little flower who gets excused for her wrong actions."

226

"I had no choice." Tears come to her eyes. "Please understand. I wish it had never happened."

She really does look like she regrets it, and I'm surprised. But years of bitterness toward her refuse to be quelled. "Right, because it was an accident that—"

"Girls!" My father interjects loudly.

I close my mouth and we both turn to him.

"The point is, she regrets it. See? You heard for yourself. And now that you know that, do you still hate her?" he asks me.

"With every fiber of my being," I say snottily.

"Liar!" Lexi shouts and points at me.

How dare she accuse me of lying. She should be able to tell I'm not lying. She's Amarian, after all, and on top of that, she's my sister.

Um . . . okay, well, it sure *feels* like I'm telling the truth. I mean, after all she's done to our village, how can I not detest even the thought of her?

I look over at the tears threatening to roll down her cheeks, and I open my mind to the possibility that she's telling the truth—that she really, truly regrets what she's done.

Once I do that, waves of her honesty and sincerity wash over me.

Leaning back against the cushion, I feel deflated, like something hard and ugly has disappeared from inside me. Well, so maybe I don't hate her as much now that I know she regrets the army and attacks, but that doesn't mean I still don't dislike her.

My father looks at me pointedly as he waits for my reply. "Answer truthfully," he says. "Do you still hate your sister?"

I squirm and admit sullenly, "Not as much as before," and shoot Lexi a glare. It feels like she's winning this battle.

My father leans forward and clasps his hands together. Now he's going to take his final step in getting us to forgive each other.

He always does the same thing after one of us admits she regrets what she did, and the other one (usually reluctantly) forgives her.

He's gonna tell us stories of when we got along.

"Come on, girls, don't you remember the time your mother brought back firecrackers from Earth for you? And you two decided to set them off in the middle of class?"

I resist the urge to smile because I remember that day very well.

"And we all got let out of school early because our teacher thought the world was ending?" Elizabeth says, faintly smiling.

I laugh to myself. Our teacher had run out of the room screaming that we were all going to die, and that we all needed to go home to our families. I was only six and Elizabeth was nine, and it was our first prank on the people of our village.

I smile warily at Elizabeth, who returns the look.

Sharing a smile over an old memory feels good. Really good. An overwhelming emotion swallows me. I just want to be a family again. I want to be that happy family who always helps each other, and not what I am: a single person who lives in a lonely, one-person cabin in the middle of nowhere.

Then I remember the reason I live in a cabin all by myself. And that reason is currently in the room. The past can't be undone.

I frown at Lexi and turn away to stare at the ceiling, attempting to stop the tears that gather in my eyes. I refuse to be the first one to completely lose it!

I can feel Dad's scolding eyes on me. "Girls, you have to understand that the things that happened in the past happened for a reason. Now if you just—"

I jump to my feet, both angry and worried. "And what, exactly, is that reason? Since you seem to like to bring it up, why don't you just tell me?"

"Rosalyn!" He frowns and nods at the couch to indicate I should sit back down. No one has called me Rosalyn in a long time. "We talked about this, and I was dead serious. I *cannot* tell you. Trust me."

And I do. I trust him . . . but I'm just not used to being left in the dark. I hate not knowing something that other people do.

But I guess that's the way it's going to be. I blow out a deep breath of air and sit back down again.

His eyes plead. "Please, girls, forgive each other, and forgive me. I'm sorry for what I did. The grief of leaving my girls almost killed me, but it was something I had to do. The fighting between the two of you is senseless. You need to understand that none of what happened—my 'death', your mother's disappearance—they weren't the fault of either of you. We all need to forgive and forget and to move on together as a family."

My father says this in such an earnest tone, and with so much regret, that tears form in my eyes once again.

They threaten to spill over but I hold them back. "I, I want to forgive her," I say brokenly as I stare at the floor, "b-but I don't know if I can." All the pain of my wretched childhood after my parents were gone comes rushing back to me: The pain of living as someone's pseudo-child until I was twelve and put my foot down. I got a job and built my own little house, far away from everyone.

I look at my father and my sister through watery eyes and realize that that little girl, now grown up, just wants a family again.

Elizabeth returns my gaze and her voice wavers, "I m-missed you."

My heart soars. "I missed you, too," I say, standing up and hesitantly opening my arms towards her.

She wavers for a second before rising to hug me. We hold onto each other tightly for a second before awkwardly pulling apart.

"So you girls have forgiven each other?" Dad asks. We both nod. "Then can you forgive me as well?" My father stands up, his eyes earnest.

Elizabeth and I hug him in answer to his question. I look up and see he's smiling. We all are.

I have a family again, a real, actual family. We can do family things now, and live the happy ending I never thought I would be able to have.

All of that calls for one thing. "How about we go to the 7th Avenue Diner to celebrate?" I suggest. Before they have a chance to reply, I shout through the house, "Derek! Matilda! We're going out. Come on!"

Derek gallops down the stairs, and Matilda rushes out of the kitchen, a wooden spoon in her hand and flour on her apron.

"Did I hear we are going out to eat?" Derek asks, excitedly rubbing his hands together.

Matilda's face lights up as she catches my father's nod. "Yes, we are, so hurry and put on your shoes, dears," Matilda says, ushering us to the entryway and removing her apron all at the same time.

I grab Elizabeth's shoulder, and we stay behind for a second, "How did you know Dad lived here?"

"I, look, I'll tell you later, okay?" she says, and walks into the entryway.

I nod and quickly follow.

We slip on our shoes without saying much because we're in too much of a hurry to get out of the house and to get to food as fast as possible. And we've just talked about some really emotional stuff, so it's a lot to process.

Dogs start barking outside. I don't understand why humans keep them as pets. They're loud and annoying. At home the only pets we have are horses, and, out in the country, some animals that resemble Earth's cows, but ours are light pink.

But who cares about barking dogs? I finally have a family again. Smiling, I swing open the door.

And come face to face with the one person I'd hoped to never see again.

Fido.

Chapter 37 – Phoenix

The next morning, Sylvia and I set out bright and early from the castle and head into the village. It's a beautiful day for Rose's return: early fall, the leaves are changing colors, and it's warm out.

"The portal we are going to open *is* for Earth, right?" Sylvia asks as we walk through the square and admire the festivities already underway. "I mean, that is what we agreed was the most likely choice based on the color. Are you still okay with that?"

"Yes, I really believe that's the planet with the portal that took Rose away," I confirm. "Come on. Let's go to where that portal usually shows up." Sylvia immediately agrees.

As we hike through the woods and discuss the specifics of our plan, I realize Sylvia knows more about how to use the Key to open portals than I do. Much more. As a Princess, it's one of the many things she has to know how to do even though *theoretically* she should never actually have to use the Key to open one.

When we arrive at the place where Rose always crashes into the tree, I hand our creation to Sylvia. "You know how to open the portals. I don't." She looks surprised and gently wraps her fingers around the Key, as if it were delicate.

She says timidly, "I just close my eyes and imagine Earth, right?" Her hand shakes a little as she holds the Key. Sylvia is clearly nervous.

"I believe so." A memory pops into my head. "Do you remember what it looks like from when you sneaked there with Rose that one time?"

"Yes, I remember. But why did you not come with us then? It was only for a few hours," Sylvia asks, frowning.

"I did not have a traveling permit at the time and I, unlike you and Rose, do not break the rules."

"Fair enough," she laughs.

Whew. She bought it. I smile. "Let's do this."

She nods. "I am glad my parents let us do this alone," she says, closing her eyes. A look of concentration wrinkles her brow. I can see her eyes moving back and forth beneath her lids, and her hand clenches the Key as if it were going to disappear any second.

This is a big moment for Sylvia. Her parents had originally insisted they should be present when we tried this. Sylvia, however, stood up for herself and told them no. She said this was something for just her and me to do, to welcome our sister home. And so they agreed, trusting her to use the Key to open a portal.

That is one thing that changed while I was gone: Sylvia has taken a strong leadership role in the search for Rose—and for me, too, when I was gone—and she gained the trust of her parents. Quite an accomplishment and I'm proud of her.

A bright light suddenly appears—a portal! The whirling circle of vivid colors throws light into the clearing around us. Blue and brown hues mix in a circular pattern and pulsate around a white center. Like a beacon for the lost.

I stare in awe. A thrill runs through me and a familiar sensation tugs in my gut. Home.

I ignore it and turn to Sylvia. "Are—?"

She jumps at my disturbance of the silence, opens her eyes, and swiftly draws in her breath at the sight of the portal.

I shift nervously from foot to foot. "So you're going through it to look for her? Because I don't think the portal will go off by itself to Earth and seek her out," I say. The feeling in my gut keeps growing stronger the longer the portal is here.

Sylvia frowns in concentration as she stares at the spinning colors. "I was thinking of Rose when I opened the portal . . . do you think it will have shown up on Earth near her because I did that?"

I search my limited knowledge of how Earth portals work, and come up empty. "I have no idea. I know only the basics."

Sylvia faces me, concern marching across her face. "Um, Phoenix? What if she isn't on Earth after all?"

The thought had already crossed my mind too many times to count, to be honest. Since this is the only portal we can open up by ourselves, if she doesn't come through it soon, we'll have to go back home and arrange for someone who's familiar with other planets to help us, which could take days.

"I mean, there are thousands of planets, and quite a few with portals of blue and brown shades," Sylvia continues, panic seeping into her voice. "What if we have to—"

Sylvia and I both gasp at what we see come through the portal.

Chapter 38 – Rose

I freeze. What the heck? Why is Fido here? He is *not* allowed to waltz in and ruin my life just as I'm rebuilding it.

The smile quickly drains from my face and I scowl at the smug-looking man on the top step of the stairs leading up to the porch. And where are the rest of his goons? I don't see them, but that doesn't mean they aren't nearby. *Dammit all!* Why is Fido here?

Derek wraps an arm around my waist and pulls me behind him; I only protest slightly. I'd rather stay back and scope out the situation than face it head on. Maybe I'm learning not to be so impulsive.

Besides, I don't know what to do. My world was absolutely wonderful for a few brief minutes, and then everything fell to pieces: Fido is *still* hounding us, I *still* don't know how to get back to Amara, and my mother is *still* missing. So much for happy endings.

My father pushes his way past me and Derek, and steps out onto the small porch. Fido and Dad stand nearly nose to nose, and the rest of us are in the doorway.

"What do you want?" Dad says menacingly.

"Counterfeit bills don't go over well with me, old man." He whips a gun out of his jacket pocket and levels it at my father. Matilda shrieks but Dad stands firm.

I stare at the familiar gun. *Hell no!*

How dare Fido have the audacity to point that thing at my father. I try to push past Derek but he blocks me and grabs hold of my arms.

Fido continues, "Did you think we weren't going to find out that the money was counterfeit?"

Counterfeit bills? Where did my father get those? Why did he have them? What is going on?

I eye the gun again, then stare at Fido's squinty, pissed-off expression. Is he gonna shoot my dad? No, I reason, not if he still wants the money.

My father straightens his shoulders and snarls, "This is a matter between you and me. Leave my family out of this."

"Oh, but where's the fun in that?" The sadistic smile on the man's face makes my stomach churn.

He aims the gun now at Derek, who raises his chin defiantly at Fido. Well, I was right about him not shooting my father, but, but . . . *Derek?* This time when I lunge in front of Derek, I'm beyond his grasp before he can grab me.

"Rose!" Derek tries to squeeze onto the front porch with my dad and me, but there's no room. Even Fido is forced to take a step back down toward the sidewalk. He's having trouble keeping his gun aimed at Derek, which was exactly my plan.

I glare down at Fido. He and I have some unfinished business. Fido grins but doesn't pull the trigger. *Keep him talking until one of us thinks of something!* "How did you find us?" I manage to ask him.

Fido shrugs a shoulder and his lip curls on one side. "I don't answer questions from silly little girls." His gaze shoots back to Derek and Elizabeth, who somehow manage to squeeze themselves out onto the porch behind me. Matilda must have remained just inside the door, but I can hear her quietly begging my father to be careful.

"You shoot, and you'll wish you had never been born," I say in my most threatening growl.

Fido's menacing stare is riveted on me once again. "And what exactly is a little girl like you going to do to stop me?"

My first instinct is to throw myself at him and beat the guy to death, but I resist the urge. Words in this situation are going to work a whole lot better than my fists. I'm finally remembering the lessons my dad tried to teach me all those years ago.

He looks me up and down. "You have thirty seconds to make your case before I shoot." He aims the gun at me, but I try to focus on my words and not the weapon.

"Okay, um, well, you see—"

Fido's hand tightens around the gun, and his finger clenches the trigger. Uh oh. I am rapidly running out of time. Even I know a smart shooter doesn't put a finger on the trigger unless he plans to fire. And I would never give Fido credit for being smart.

I hold up my hands to stop him. "Okay, no, wait," I falter as I realize I'm about to get shot. "Then, umm, I-"

I break off. *I'm going to die.*

A sense of true fear runs through me. Never before have I thought I was going to die, not even when I've battled Lexi. No witty comeback is rolling off my tongue, and I can't— . . . I'm gonna die. Just when things were finally going well, I'm going to ruin them all by dying.

Fido sees my panic and smiles. Apparently there is no lost love between us, or else my time has just run out.

His finger twitches and he pulls the trigger.

I shut my eyes, expecting to feel a hole blasted in me. There's nothing I can do to block a bullet. My entire body tenses, and I instinctively turn away from the noise of the gunshot. Fear and adrenaline rush white-hot through me in a split second.

Fido screams.

My eyes fly open. Why aren't I dead?

But then I wish I am. Because surely death is better than the devastating agony taking over the place where my heart once was.

On the porch steps lies my father, face up, staring at the sky, and completely still. Blood is rapidly pooling around him, and his shirt and jacket are already saturated. Could he have survived such a direct hit?

I hear a choked cry. It's me, but my entire body is frozen in shock. I can't feel anything except pain. More blood—from a different direction—runs into the pool forming around my father's feet on the lowest step, and my gaze numbly follows its source.

A yard from my father lies Fido, dead but from a different weapon. A very familiar-looking knife I have personally battled against is sticking out of his chest.

Elizabeth stands over the man, her face a pale mask of disbelief. As far as I know, she's never actually killed anybody.

My mind spins in a million directions. How did she get her knife back? I don't have mine and I didn't see her retrieve hers.

"David!" Matilda screams in anguish as she hurls herself across the porch and down the steps to her husband's body. I'm not the only one who has just lost a loved one.

My thoughts stop running in circles and instead focus on the tragedy that's just sinking in. My father has been shot—killed. But that bullet had been coming for me . . . which means that he must've jumped in front of it.

No, he couldn't have. But he did. No . . . no . . . no.

"Daddy!" I scream, and lunge toward him to check his pulse to see if, by some miracle, he's still alive.

Derek grabs me. I struggle desperately to get out of his grip.

"Let me go." Tears are streaming down my face. My whole body shakes as I sob. I can't believe what I'm seeing. All that blood, all that blood on the steps is my father's.

"It's over. I'm so sorry, Rose," Derek says, holding me tightly around the waist. "There's nothing you can do. He's gone. Mrs. Sanders has confirmed it."

"No. I just got him back," I shout, my voice cracking. "He can't leave me now. That isn't fair. This isn't right! Why? Why did he have to do that? That's supposed to be me on the ground, not him." The words tumble out of me.

A sharp pain is nearly crushing me. I have just met my father for the first time since childhood, and now he's gone. The unfairness overwhelms me, and I feel so alone. I've lost him a second time. I feel like a little girl again, waking up to an empty house, abandoned.

But I wasn't completely abandoned back then, and I'm not now. Elizabeth is here, and she must be as horrified as I am. Probably even more so, since she's always been more emotional and sensitive about things than I have. And on top of that, she just killed a man.

Her face is blank, unreadable. She's staring, her eyes empty and her jaw slack, at the bodies.

A lone tear rolls slowly down her cheek, and a broken noise comes out of her mouth. "I- no-"

A bright blue light suddenly illuminates the street, forcing my attention away from the tragedy surrounding us. Elizabeth whirls to look at it too.

And despite Derek's strong grip on me, I gasp and nearly collapse.

Because there, in the middle of the street, is a portal. A beautiful, familiar bluish-green-colored portal. Its sapphire hue is shot through with emerald green, and the entire thing—bigger than my arms spread wide—seems alive as it rapidly spins clockwise. Even better, the center of the circle is the usual white color that all portals have.

Home. That portal will take me home. Tears stream down my face again as I look at it. I can finally go home.

But...but what about my father? H-his body? And what about Derek? I can't leave him. What about Elizabeth? Matilda? I stare at each of them in turn. My gut twists painfully. What am I supposed to do?

"That's, that's the p-portal to home," I say and point at it but look at Derek. For some reason, he's frowning at the portal. Elizabeth is staring at it.

Suddenly all I can think of is home. My home. Amara. My beautiful woods, my picturesque village, and my friends.

I can *finally* go home. All the time I've spent trapped on Earth has come to an end.

My tears slow down as my brain whirls with thoughts of what I need to do now.

I need to make a decision. A really, really difficult one.

I throw up my protective emotional walls, and I block out my sadness and grief, just like I have been doing for years. There's no room for those emotions, because I need to focus on the decision at hand. It's a simple choice, but it's the hardest I've ever had to make.

How can I be expected to choose?

But I have to.

Derek looks at me and different emotions cascade across his face—confusion, fear, grief, worry, regret, longing. I wonder if he knows how life-changing this moment is.

Urgency fills me. I need to decide what my life will be like—and where. Do I return home and wait for the fate my father hinted at? Is it ridiculous to go back home, when my own father said I might die if I do? Or should I stay on Earth—with Derek? Is that too much like hiding from my responsibilities, my fate?

Elizabeth catches my eye, a question written all over her face. But in her eyes, I see my answer. I've known it all along but I was unwilling to face it.

I answer her with a reluctant nod. Compassion sweeps across her face, along with relief. The decision was easy for her.

So now we both know what we have to do, but can *I* do it? I know Elizabeth can.

And so she does. After a quick look of farewell to each of us, and a lingering look of grief at our father's body, she strides over to the portal and jumps inside. She did it with such determination that it's as if she hasn't a single regret about leaving Earth.

I look at my father, who is a pale, unnaturally blue color in the light from the portal. He is dead, and there's nothing either Elizabeth or I can do about it.

Perhaps in a fit of envy at the ease with which Elizabeth left, my thoughts—not surprisingly—turn cynical as I stare at the blazing portal she just jumped through.

She's good at running away.

That's all she's ever done when faced with difficulty. She ran away from her problems. She ran away from me. And now she's done it again, and left me to deal with everything.

Anger towards Elizabeth builds quickly in my chest. But as soon as it does, I hear my father's voice encouraging me to forgive her.

He's right. After all, I've done my own version of running away: all these years I've blocked off my feelings and never allowed anyone—except Sylvia and Phoenix—to get close to me.

Matilda's sobs grow louder as she cradles my father in her arms. He's gone. I'll never see him again. I've lost him—again. My heart has been ripped out of my chest, and I can't just leave it behind. I can't just walk away. My opportunity to get to know him again, to have a parent again, has been stolen from me.

I glance at Fido's body with the knife sticking up from his chest. Even though he's dead, he got the best of me. Rage consumes me.

"Dammit, *damn it all.* It's not fair," I collapse to the ground, crawling toward my father. "It's not fair . . ."

"Rose, Rose, calm down. You'll get through this. It's gonna be okay." Derek kneels next to me, placing his hand on my chin to make me turn and look at him.

I shake him off, whipping my head back towards my father. "No, it's not. Don't you see? Nothing is ever okay. You think it is

241

and then it isn't. It's all one cruel ride you can never get off of."
Tears run down my face and splatter on the ground beneath me as I
rock back and forth.

"Rose, stand up, please," Derek pleads with me and I let him
pull me to my feet.

It doesn't matter. Nothing matters anymore. I stand limply
in his arms, looking over at the portal glowing at the end of the
walkway. It's my ticket home—the one thing I have been dying to
see since I woke up on this forsaken planet. But right now, I hate the
sight of it. Its appearance demands a choice—one I don't want to
make and resent being forced on me. But, of course I've already
made it, and Elizabeth saw it on my face as clearly as I saw it on
hers.

I study the portal for a few seconds. Is it spinning faster than
it was a moment ago? What does that mean? Is it going to close
soon?

So now it's my turn.

I look up at Derek. I want so badly to tell him that he can
come with me, that he *should* come with me. But the rule about
humans not being allowed on Amara is a strict one.

My heart screams that we could surely make an exception
for Derek; he's a Gatekeeper, after all. But my head replies with the
answer I know the king and queen would give me:

No.

I swallow hard and whisper to him, "I'll miss you."

He frowns and looks confused. Then his eyes widen and he
glances at the portal. He tightens his grip on me and a look of
desperation splashes across his face.

He knows.

Before he can say anything, I break free of his grip and kneel
next to my father. Matilda is still sobbing quietly.

Something glimmers in my father's hand from the bright light of the portal. It's my knife. I uncurl his fingers gently and take it out of his hand. When Fido turned up, my dad must have slipped Elizabeth's knife back to her, and he probably planned to use mine on Fido himself.

My father always told me that a good knife can solve many problems. He was the reason I bought this knife. Another tear slides down my face. I silently vow to always keep this knife with me and never let it out of my possession again.

I gently shut his eyes and kiss his cold cheek, then cross his hands over his chest and say an old blessing of death in a language foreign to Earth. It's the native language to Amara, an old dialect that I force to break through the language translation portal travel forces. Peace flows through me as I speak, and the wise old words and sounds comfort me.

Matilda sits back on her heels, giving me space. This blessing is the most I can do for him. And the last thing.

After I finish, she struggles to speak through her tears. "I-I'll take care of him, Rose. I promise."

"I know you will. Thank you so much, for everything you've done for me, and for my father. I think he was happy here with you."

I stand up, and she does too. I hug her and she strokes my back comfortingly, reminding me of my own mother.

I pull back. "I have to go now." I glance at Derek out of the corner of my eye. "Alone." We've grown too close, and I can't let him come with me. I should've stuck with my old ways—not letting anyone get too close to me. My father's death proves it. It's far too painful to be worth it.

I have a job to do on Amara, and I can't let any emotions get in the way—especially emotions for a boy.

"What?" Derek says, shock widening his eyes as he takes a step toward me. "Why can't you stay? Why can't I come with you? You'll be back, right?"

I look one last time at the man lying on the steps in the pool of blood, now nightmarishly blue and purple in the reflected light of the portal. Blood he willingly shed to save me, I realize. Now I am convinced beyond a doubt that he truly wanted only to protect me all these years and that's why he never came home.

Derek's pleas echo in my head, and I know I need to answer him. Even if it is something neither of us want to hear.

I face him and look him straight in the eye. "I have people back home who need me. I'm sorry, Derek."

As soon as the words are out of my mouth, I take a few firm steps away from him and the bodies before I give in and pause. Everything in me is screaming to stay with him, but I know I can't do that. My heart is yelling at me, protesting against yet more hurt in such a short amount of time, but I can't listen to it.

With my back still to Derek, I lean forward to take another step, but I can't move. My feet are stuck in place, refusing to listen to my brain's command.

I close my eyes and shake my head in frustration. This is just another example that proves that letting emotions become invested in anything—or anyone—is a very bad idea.

Derek suddenly grabs my arm. I should have known he would not let me leave. I pull out of his grasp, but I finally have the courage to look at him again.

Deeply etched into his face are lines of sorrow and resignation. "Remember me," he says before he tugs me to him and kisses my lips.

It is a short but sweet kiss goodbye. My heart plummets and soars all at the same time. I never imagined my first kiss would be in goodbye.

I drag myself out of his reach. The shimmering portal beckons, and time is running out. Elizabeth went through the portal several minutes ago.

Without another glance back, I run the best I can on my injured ankle down the walkway and toward the portal, tears streaming down my face harder than ever.

The universe truly is cruel.

Derek doesn't follow me. I'm glad he doesn't. After all that's happened, I don't know if I have the willpower to send him away or to block him from entering the portal with me.

Go forward, with no emotional investment in anything or anyone, I remind myself again.

Without slowing down, I run into the portal, and it shuts after me.

Chapter 39 – Phoenix

Sylvia and I both gasp as someone suddenly tumbles out of the portal and quickly springs to her feet a few yards from us. I do not know the tall woman whose entire body is tense, ready for . . . something. She's looking around, soaking everything in, when her eyes settle on Sylvia and me, and a look of surprise crosses her face.

"E-Elizabeth?" Sylvia gasps.

Elizabeth? This is Rose's sister? The one we never talk about?

"The one and only," she says, flipping her long black hair over her shoulder. "Hi, Sylvia."

Beside me, Sylvia's mouth hangs open and she's silent, so I follow her cue and don't say anything.

So where did Elizabeth come from? Earth? No one seems to have had any idea where she's been all these years. I know, because we occasionally talk about Elizabeth when Rose isn't around. How would she have gotten there, though? And why? And when?

Sylvia is still staring at her.

Elizabeth looks inquiringly back and forth between the two of us, then shrugs and points over her shoulder at the portal. "Rose should be coming through fairly soon. She just has to say goodbye to someone," she casually adds.

Or maybe not so casually. Worry clouds Elizabeth's green eyes, and it almost looks like she's blinking back tears. Why? Is Rose okay? Is something the matter with her? I try not to panic, but I need information.

"What happened? Is Rose okay?" The questions spill out before I can stop them. I'm still not sure what to make of her, and Sylvia is being no help.

Perhaps hearing my voice releases Sylvia from her fog, because she puts her hand on her hip and demands, quite venomously, of Elizabeth, "Where have you been all these years?"

Elizabeth looks uncomfortably at the ground, and I realize how rude we're being to her. I shoot a warning glare at Sylvia and add a friendly note to my voice as I say reassuringly to Elizabeth, "You don't have to tell us if you don't want to, Elizabeth. I'm just a stranger to you, although I've been told I'm a good listener. And I'm Rose's and Sylvia's best friend. How . . . how is she, by the way?"

By now I've left Sylvia's side and approached Elizabeth. She sniffs as she tries to hold back the silent tears rolling down her cheeks. "There was some trouble when we were on Earth." As she speaks, she looks worse and worse. "Our f-father is d-dead," she gasps, wiping away her tears. "And Rose . . . Rose has to leave someone else behind, someone whom she cares for."

Sylvia draws next to me, her face registering the shock we both feel. "But Rose's father died years ago. I was at the funeral."

Elizabeth shakes her head and her voice quavers. "Turns out our father has been on Earth the entire time, to protect Rose, but h-he was k-killed a few minutes ago."

What is going on? I look back and forth between the other two. I am so lost that I can't even begin to try to put together what is going on. I moved to Alethia so late that I missed all the important things. None of this makes any sense.

Sylvia seems as overwhelmed and confused as I am. "I didn't . . . how did he die?" Her voice is barely audible.

Elizabeth shakes her head no, as if she doesn't want to talk about it. Instead, she squares her shoulders and changes the subject. "It's good to see you again, Sylvia," Elizabeth smiles sadly and embraces her. "So you are still best friends with my sister?" She glances at me and adds, "The two of you are?"

"Of course Phoenix and I are her best friends," Sylvia gestures toward me. "We always will be. And I haven't introduced you to Phoenix yet. I'm sorry. She moved here after you, uh, you left."

"No wonder I don't recognize you," she says to me. "Phoenix, nice to meet you. What town are you from?"

My mind races. "I'm from no-man's-land between towns. I moved here with my brother once my mother let me," I tell her, hoping she doesn't see through my half-truth.

"Wait a second—sorry, Phoenix, I just thought of something totally off subject," Elizabeth says, stepping out of Sylvia's hug and looking at both of us. "How did Rose manage to get my mother's Key? It's supposed to be passed down from mother to *oldest* daughter."

Sylvia shakes her head and looks uncomfortable.

Embarrassment floods Elizabeth's tear-stained face. "Oh, but I wasn't around, was I, as the eldest daughter. So I guess Rose ended up with it. Although I've always assumed my mother took it with her when she left."

Sylvia put her hand on Elizabeth's arm and said sympathetically, "Your mother gave the Key to a friend of hers to keep until Rose was old enough. I, I don't know why she didn't have the friend keep it for you. But you were gone and, well, Rose only acquired it a couple of years ago."

While we've been talking, the portal has dimmed, but now it flares brightly again, almost as if it's sending out sparks to get our attention.

We all turn to stare at it just in time to see Rose stumble through, barely keeping her feet beneath her. At least she doesn't crash into the tree.

Thank goodness, she's home. But she's crying. Something is seriously wrong.

Chapter 40 – Sylvia

I race towards Rose and envelope her in a huge hug, fighting back tears of happiness. "I am so glad you are home. Oh, Rose, we were so worried about you."

Phoenix joins in, and the Three Musketeers are reunited at last. "I missed you, my dear Rose."

Another set of arms joins our group hug. Elizabeth's.

Happiness and worry battle within me. Rose looks—and sounds—miserable. She is home, but at what cost did it take her to get here?

She returns the hugs. "I missed you guys, too. Humans aren't good company," she sniffles on our shoulders.

My head hurts from all the questions piling up and I am dying to find out why Rose is crying, but she looks like she is about ready to drop. "Should we go home?" I ask. "Get some food, and rest a bit? I am sure you are tired, Rose. You too, Elizabeth."

Phoenix nods. "We can go to your house, Rose. It's closest."

"Ya, please. . . . Is there still cake at my house?" Rose asks with a weak smile, doing what she does best—making sure the conversation is not too heavy.

"I don't think it's good anymore, Rose," Phoenix laughs. Then her smile drops. "You do know you've been missing for more than two months, don't you?"

She stops in her tracks. "Excuse me—I've been gone *how* long?"

"Let us go to your house and talk," I say, taking a few steps in the right direction to urge us all along. My brain is overwhelmed with thoughts, emotions, and questions; I am sure Rose's is too. "We will have plenty of time to answer all your questions then."

Everyone follows quietly. Phoenix and I walk on either side of Rose, and Elizabeth trails slightly behind us. Thank goodness Rose's house is only minutes away.

As soon as we arrive, Rose disappears into her room without saying a word. What is she doing?

Elizabeth sits in one of the chairs, and Phoenix sits on the couch. I guess we are all assuming Rose will emerge from her room soon. And if not, well, we will all be here when she does.

A moment later, Rose returns. At least she is no longer crying.

She has something in her hand—a book. Why would she bring out a book?

"The day before I disappeared, I went to Earth to get this book. Here's why: About a week prior to that, I found a journal of my mom's in a box I had taken out of her old room. I started going through all her things in an attempt to organize them, maybe find more pictures of my family. Instead, I found her journal and, and," Rose clutches the book tightly, her voice shaking. "Well, my mom knew other Gatekeepers. There's a Gatekeeper on every planet! I'm not the only one. My mom knew the one from Earth, Victoria Coulee, and Mom wrote about how Victoria had a book with the names of the other Gatekeeping families in it. So I went to Earth, and I found it. It's this book." Rose holds it up so we can all see it, as if she doubts we believe her.

Elizabeth squirms and draws my attention. Hmm. Rose's words about the book remind me that Elizabeth, as the eldest daughter, was supposed to have the Key and be the Gatekeeper. Too bad she disappeared, but to where? And how did she and Rose find each other on Earth?

Rose continues talking and I give her my full attention. This is obviously important to her. "The book has some sort of, of—I don't know what to call it—magical property, maybe? The contents automatically update as the Keys on various planets change hands. Do you know what this means?" Excitement rises in Rose's voice. "It means I can find the other Gatekeepers—all the current ones. I can connect everyone. My mom wrote about how Gatekeepers used to all know each other, how they used to work together. But something bad happened to separate everyone and keep them that way; she didn't know what. So she and Victoria were trying to reunite the Gatekeepers, and get them working together again.

"But she never said what the goal was they were all working toward . . ." Rose trails off, biting her bottom lip in thought.

Whoa—time out. Rose's behavior right now doesn't make any sense. When she first arrived, she seemed almost traumatized. Which is understandable, given what Elizabeth said about their father dying, and that Rose had to say goodbye to someone else she cared about too.

But now Rose is acting as if nothing bad happened on Earth at all—as if her tears and heartache a little while ago were just whisked away. As if nothing else matters except for the exciting news about this book. But how could she so quickly forget about all of the terrible things that happened on Earth?

That is crazy. I mean, I can imagine that finding out about other Gatekeepers and maybe someday meeting them is super exciting to Rose, and I know she is an incredibly strong person who can set aside her emotions and focus on what needs to be done, but...? *Really?*

It is as if the contents of that book are more important than anything that might have happened on Earth. More important than anything in all the worlds.

Epilogue

I can never go back to the place my father died. Even though it's been nearly seven months, it would be too much. Most of the time I spent at his house in Chicago, I was mad at him for having pretended to be dead.

Now he really is dead. That bullet was supposed to be for me—not him. He's gone, and I had only just forgiven him and let him become my parent again. How unfair is that?

Just as he predicted, the dreams have come to torture me when I sleep and worry me during the day.

They appeared only six short months after I returned from Earth, and for the past week, I've been constantly plagued by them. But you won't read this anytime soon, I don't think, so how long it's been doesn't really matter, does it?

Anyway, I'm fifteen now. My new age means I'm a legal adult on seven planets that I know of, which means more adventures await me! None of which will take place on Earth, if I have my way.

I told Phoenix and Sylvia everything—almost everything—that happened during my time on Earth. They were shocked, and then let me cry on their shoulders and offered me condolences and words of comfort. Even more than that, though, they really wanted to know about you—but I shut down that conversation *very* quickly.

Life moved on, and so did we.

I threw myself back into daily living and tried to get through my grieving for my father. No offense, but it was—and is—too painful to think about you. Besides, I can't spare you any extra thoughts these days.

Except for this letter. This is my indulgence.

I want you to know that I can't let myself go back to Earth. If I did give in to temptation and visit you, it would drag you into things.

Remember that mysterious fate my father spoke of and warned me about? Ya, it's coming, quickly.

Lots of things are different here now. It seems like everyone changed while I was gone, which I suppose makes sense given everything that happened. But still, I feel as though I was away from Amara for years.

You're probably wondering about Elizabeth. She is now a regular part of Alethia's activities. She has a job at the seamstress's shop, and she lives with me. There's still plenty of tension in the house, but it's something we're working on together. She needs to parent me less, and stop telling me what to do. I lived on my own for a long time, and I don't need her unsolicited advice every three seconds. We both try, though. We know we need each other after all that's happened.

She and I haven't told anybody who she really is— not even Sylvia and Phoenix. Fortunately, no one here's done more than ask cursory questions about where she was all those years. We're just going to let them think what they already think— that she was on Earth— and move on.

Sylvia has become a picture-perfect princess. Which is exceptionally weird; Sylvia always said that she would never fit the Princess mold that her mom set for her. She even sat all the way through a long meeting of the councilors not too long ago. At least now her mother lets her talk during the meetings— not a lot, but she still gets to have input. And she says the old councilors actually listen to her, too. It's weird . . . she even said she kind of enjoys the meetings now that she can speak. I know you don't know exactly how odd that is, but trust me, it is. She also has a regaler air about her, and she seems more like her mother— more proper, more formal, and all together very odd compared to how she used to be. I guess it's a good thing. She's still the same old Sylvia when it's just she and I and Phoenix, but I miss her having free time for adventures— and being willing to do them.

Speaking of free time, Phoenix invited us all to go camping and cliff-diving with her a few weeks ago. Can you imagine! She has become a whole lot more courageous. Which is very good news for my plans. I mean, adventures are so much more enjoyable and fulfilling when people I care about are around to participate in them. Not that she takes part in any of the really big stuff, but I'm working on that. Soon enough, I'll need her help to cause general chaos and mayhem on a more serious level. Lives will depend on it. Or at least that's what the dreams are telling me, and I believe them.

Collin joins us more often than not these days. Phoenix isn't so nervous about showing that she cares for him in a way that is more than friends. Nothing has happened yet, but between you and me, Collin plans on asking Phoenix's brother if he can ask her out on an official date.

And myself? Well, I've only made the most important discovery in the history of the worlds! I still haven't figured out why I appeared in the burned-out section of Chicago that day, or why the Earth portal was acting so weird. But I think I'll have an answer to that soon. Do you remember when my father told me to go back to our old house and look in the closet for a trunk? I did and—well, that's a story for another time; one I'll tell you after it's over.

Because once I remove any threat of danger to you and certain other people, I'm coming back to slap you in the face for that kiss you gave me! It was not warranted, I'll have you know.

In the meantime, duty—and adventure—awaits!